SUSAN MALLERY

Delicious

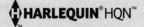

HARLEQUIN® HQN™

Recycling programs
for this product may
not exist in your area.

ISBN-13: 978-0-373-77940-6

DELICIOUS

Printed in U.S.A.

www.Harlequin.com

Dear Reader,

Thanks for picking up *Delicious,* book one of my Buchanan Family romances. The Buchanans laughed and loved and fought their way into the world in 2006, and these books remain reader favorites. I'm thrilled that readers can rediscover them today. I was an only child, so writing about the boisterous Buchanans was a bit of fantasy fulfillment for me, as I imagined what it would be like to grow up with such a strong (albeit sometimes strained) support network.

One of the great joys for me as a writer is the chance to try on a hundred different careers through my characters. I get all of the glamour and none of the tedium. Have you ever thought it would be fun to own a restaurant? I have, in a dreamy "I could go there any time and they would feed me, but I wouldn't have to work" kind of way. That's the experience I lived while writing *Delicious* and the other Buchanan Family romances, because I went to lots (and lots and lots) of restaurants in the name of research. They did feed me, and they didn't make me work.

I loved writing *Delicious,* a story of first love reunited. Cal and Penny were married once upon a time, but they let circumstances—and unspoken feelings—tear them apart. Now Cal has hired Penny, the best chef in Seattle, to get the family's waterfront restaurant back on its feet. Working together brings all those lingering emotions to the surface. But this time around, Penny has a secret that just might end things once and for all.

Visit my website, www.susanmallery.com, to see a full list of all of my books in order of publication, including the Buchanan Family romances.

Happy reading!

Susan Mallery

Delicious

CHAPTER ONE

PENNY JACKSON KNEW THAT it was probably wrong to be so excited to see her ex-husband come crawling back, but she was willing to live with the character flaw.

"You know he's going to want to hire you," her friend Naomi said.

"Oh, yeah. The sweet smell of validation." Penny leaned back in her chair and considered the possibilities. "I want him to beg. Not in a vicious, I hate your guts way, but more as a…"

"Show of support for divorced women everywhere?" Naomi asked.

Penny laughed. "Exactly. I suppose that makes me petty and small."

"Maybe, but you're looking especially fabulous today, if that helps."

"A little." Penny smoothed the front of her loose sweater and glanced at the clock. "We're meeting for lunch downtown. A neutral location—no memories, good or bad."

"Stay away from the good ones," Naomi warned her. "You always were a sucker where Cal was concerned."

"That was so three years ago. I'm completely over him. I've moved on."

"Right." Naomi didn't look convinced. "Don't think about how great he looks in his clothes, or out of them. Instead remember how he broke your heart, lied about wanting children and trampled your fragile dreams."

Easy enough, Penny thought, a flicker of annoyance muscling in on her good mood.

Nearly as bad, four years ago she'd applied for a job as a cook in Buchanan's, one of Cal's family's restaurants. The job had been strictly entry-level—she would have been in charge of salads. There had been ten other applicants. Worried she wouldn't make the cut, Penny had asked her then-husband to put in a good word for her with his grandmother. He'd refused and she hadn't gotten the job.

"This time the job is coming to me," Penny said. "I intend to take advantage of that. And him. In a strictly business way, of course."

"Of course," Naomi echoed, not sounding the least bit convinced. "He's trouble for you. Always has been. Be careful."

Penny stood and reached for her purse. "When am I not?"

"Ask for lots of money."

"I promise."

"Don't think about having sex with him."

Penny laughed. "Oh, please. That isn't an issue. You'll see."

Penny arrived early, then stayed in her car until five minutes after the appointed time. A small, possibly insignificant power play on her part, but she figured she'd earned it.

She walked into the quiet leather-and-linen bistro. Before she could approach the hostess, she saw Cal standing by a booth in the back. They might have friends in common, and live in the same city, but since she'd done her darnedest to avoid close proximity to him they never ran into each other. This lunch was going to change that.

"Hi," she said with a breezy smile.

"Penny." He looked her over, then motioned to the other side of the booth. "Thanks for joining me."

"How could I refuse? You wouldn't say much over the phone, which made me curious." She slid onto the seat.

Cal looked good. Tall, muscled, the same soulful eyes she remembered. Just sitting across from him caused her body to remember what it had been like back when things had been good and they'd been unable to keep their hands off each other. Not that she was interested in him in that way. She'd learned her lesson.

Plus, she couldn't forgive the fact that in the three years they'd been apart, he hadn't had the common courtesy to get fat or wrinkled. Nope, he was gorgeous—which was just like a man.

Still, he needed her help. Oh, yeah, that part was very cool. While they'd been married the message had been she wasn't good enough. Now he wanted her to save the day…or the restaurant, in this case. While she planned to say yes, eventually, she was going to enjoy every second of making him beg.

"The Waterfront is in trouble," he said, then paused as the waitress came by to take their order.

When the woman left, Penny leaned back in the tufted seat of the booth and smiled. "I'd heard it was more than in trouble. I'd heard the place was done for. Hemorrhaging customers and money."

She blinked, going for an innocent expression. No doubt Cal would see through her attempt and want to strangle her. But he couldn't. Because he *needed* her. Was, in fact, desperate for her help. How she loved that in a man. Especially in Cal.

"Things have been better," he admitted, looking as if he hated every second of the conversation.

"The Waterfront is the oldest restaurant in the infamous Buchanan dynasty," she said cheerfully. "The flagship. Or it used to be. Now you have a reputation for bad food and worse service." She sipped her water. "At least that's the word on the street."

"Thanks for the update."

His jaw tightened as he spoke. She could tell he was furious about this meeting. She had an idea of what he was thinking—of all the chefs in all of Seattle, why did it have to be her?

She didn't know either, but sometimes a girl couldn't help catching a break.

"Your contract is up," he said.

She smiled. "Yes, it is."

"You're looking for a new position."

"Yes, I am."

"I'd like to hire you."

Five little words. Words that weren't significant on their own, but when joined together, could mean the world to someone. In this case, her.

"I've had other offers," Penny said calmly.

"Have you accepted any of them?"

"Not yet."

Cal was tall, about six-three, with dark hair. His face was all sculpted cheekbones and stubborn jaw, and his mouth frequently betrayed his mood. Right now it was thin and straight. He was so angry, he practically spouted steam. She'd never felt better.

"I'm here to offer you a five-year contract. You get complete control of the kitchen, the standard agreement." He named a salary that made her blink.

Penny took another sip of her water. In truth she didn't want just another job. She wanted her own place. But opening a restaurant took serious money, which she didn't have. Her choices were to take on more partners than she wanted or wait. She'd decided to wait.

Her plan was to spend the next three years putting away money, then open the restaurant of her dreams. So while a big salary was nice, it wasn't enough.

"Not interested," she said, with a slight smile.

Cal's gaze narrowed. "What do you want? Aside from my head on a stick."

Her smile turned genuine. "I've never wanted that," she told him. "Well, not after the divorce was final. It's been three years, Cal. I've long since moved on. Haven't you?"

"Of course. Then why aren't you interested? It's a good job."

"I'm not looking for a job. I want an opportunity."

"Meaning?"

"More than the standard agreement. I want my name out front and complete creative control in back." She reached into the pocket of her jacket and pulled out a folded piece of paper. "I have a list."

DOING THE RIGHT THING had always been a pain in the ass, Cal thought as he took the sheet and unfolded it. This time was no different.

He scanned the list, then tossed it back to her. Penny didn't want an opportunity, she wanted his balls sautéed with garlic and a nice cream sauce.

"No," he said flatly, ignoring the way the afternoon sunlight brought out the different colors of red and brown in her auburn hair.

"Fine by me." She picked up the sheet and started to slide out of the booth. "Nice to see you, Cal. Good luck with the restaurant."

He reached across the table and grabbed her wrist. "Wait."

"But if we have nothing to talk about…"

She looked innocent enough, he thought as he gazed into her big blue eyes, but he knew better than to believe the wide-eyed stare.

Penny could be convinced to take the job; otherwise she wouldn't have bothered with a meeting. Playing him for a fool wasn't her style. But that didn't mean she wouldn't enjoy making him beg.

Given their past, he supposed he'd earned it. So he would bargain with her, giving in where he had to.

He would even have enjoyed the negotiation if only she didn't look so damn smug.

He rubbed his thumb across her wrist bone, knowing she would hate that. She'd always lamented her large forearms, wrists and hands, claiming they were out of proportion with the rest of her body. He'd thought she was crazy to obsess about a flaw that didn't exist. Besides, she had chef's hands— scarred, nimble and strong. He'd always liked her hands, whether they were working on food in the kitchen or working on him in the bedroom.

"Not going to happen," he said, nodding his head at the paper and releasing his hold on her. "You know that, too. So where's the real list?"

She grinned and eased back into the booth. "I heard you were desperate. I had to try."

"Not that desperate. What do you want?"

"Creative freedom on the menus, complete control over the back half of the store, my name on the menu, ownership of any specialty items I create, the right to refuse any general manager you try to stuff down my throat, four weeks vacation a year and ten percent of the profits."

The waitress appeared with their lunches. He'd ordered a burger, Penny a salad. But not just any salad. Their server laid out eight plates with various ingredients in front of Penny's bowl of four kinds of lettuce.

As he watched, she put olive oil, balsamic vinaigrette and ground pepper into a coffee cup, then squeezed in half a lemon. After whisking them with her fork, she dumped the diced, smoked chicken and feta onto her salad, then sniffed the candied pecans before adding them. She passed over walnuts, took only half of the tomato, added red onions instead of green and then put on her dressing. After tossing everything, she stacked the plates and took her first bite of lunch.

"How is it?" he asked.

"Good."

"Why do you bother eating out?"

"I don't usually."

She hadn't before, either. She'd been content to whip up something incredible in their kitchen and he'd been happy to let her.

He returned his attention to her demands. He wouldn't give her everything she wanted on general principle. Plus it was just plain bad business.

"You can have creative control over the menus and the back half of the store," he said. "Specialty items stay with the house."

Anything a chef created while in the employ of a restaurant was owned by that restaurant.

"I want to be able to take them with me when I go." She forked a piece of lettuce. "It's a deal-breaker, Cal."

"You'll come up with something new there."

"The point is I don't want to create something wonderful and leave it in your family's less than capable hands." She glanced at him. "Before you get all defensive, let me point out that five years ago, The Waterfront had a waiting list every single weekend."

"You can have your name on the menu," he said. "As executive chef."

He saw her stiffen. She'd never had that title before. It would mean something now.

"And three percent of the profits," he added.

"Eight."

"Four."

"Six."

"Five," he said. "But you don't get a say in the general manager."

"I have to work with him or her."

"And he or she has to work with you."

She grinned. "But I have a reputation of being nothing but sunshine and light in the workplace. You know that."

He'd heard she was a perfectionist and relentless in her quest for quality. She had also been called difficult, annoying and just plain brilliant.

"You can't dictate the GM," he said. "He's already been hired. At least in the short term."

She wrinkled her nose. "Who is it?"

"You'll find out later. Besides, the first guy's just coming in to do cleanup. Someone else will be hired in a few months. You can have a say on him or her."

Her eyebrows rose. "Interesting. A gunslinger coming in to clean up the town. I think I like that." She drew in a breath. "How about five percent of the profits, a three-year deal, I get some say in the next GM and I take my specialty items with me." She held up her hand. "But only to my own place and you can keep them on The Waterfront menu as well."

He wasn't surprised she wanted to branch out on her own. Most good chefs did. Few had the capital or the management skills.

"Oh, and that salary you offered me before was fine," she said.

"Of course it was," he told her. "That assumed you didn't get this other stuff. How many are you bringing with you?"

"Two. My sous-chef and my assistant."

Chefs usually came with a small staff. As long as they worked well with the others in the kitchen, Cal didn't care.

"You'll never take the vacation," he said. At least she never had before.

"I want it," she said. "Just so we're clear, I *will* be using it."

He shrugged. "Not until we're up and running."

"I was thinking late summer. I'll have everything together by then."

Maybe. She hadn't seen the mess yet.

"Is that it?" he asked.

She considered for a second, then shrugged. "Get me the offer in writing. I'll look it over and then let you know if we have a deal."

"You'd never get this much anywhere else. Don't pretend you'll back out."

The smugness returned. "You never know, Cal. I want to hear what your competition puts on the table."

"I know who's interested. They'll never cut you in for that much of the profit."

"True enough, but their restaurants are successful. A smaller percentage of something is better than a big chunk of nothing."

"This could make you a star," he said. "People would notice."

"People already notice."

He wanted to tell her she wasn't all that special. That he could name five chefs who would do as good a job. The problem was he couldn't. In the past three years, Penny had made a name for herself. He needed that to dig The Waterfront out of its hole.

"I'll have the agreement couriered over to your place tomorrow afternoon," he said.

She practically purred her contentment. "Good."

"You're enjoying this, aren't you?"

"Oh, yeah. I won't even mind working for you because every time you piss me off, I'm going to remind you that you came looking for me. That you *needed* me."

Revenge. He respected that. It annoyed him, but he respected it.

"Why are you doing this?" she asked as she picked up a pecan. "You got out of the family business years ago."

Back when they'd been married, he thought. He'd escaped, only to be dragged in again.

"Someone had to save the sinking ship," he said.

"Yes, but why you? You don't care about the family empire."

He threw twenty dollars on the table and slid out of the booth. "I'll need your answer within twenty-four hours of you getting the contract."

"You'll have it the following morning."

"Fair enough." He dropped a business card next to the money. "In case you need to get in touch with me."

He walked out of the restaurant and headed for his car. Penny was going to say yes. She would screw with him a little, but the deal was too good for her to pass up. If she pulled it off, if she made The Waterfront what it had once been, then in three years she would have more than enough capital to start her own place.

He would be gone long before that. He'd agreed to come in temporarily to get things up and running, but he had no desire to stay to the bitter end. His only concern was saving the sinking ship. Let someone else shine it up and take all the glory. He was only interested in getting out.

PENNY WALKED into the Downtown Sports Bar and Grill a little after two in the afternoon. The lunch crowd had pretty much cleared out, although a few diehards sat watching the array of sports offered on various televisions around the place.

She headed directly for the bar and leaned against the polished wood. "Hi, Mandy. Is he in?" she asked the very large-breasted blonde polishing glasses.

Mandy smiled. "Hi, Penny. Yeah. He's in his office. Want me to bring you anything?"

Caffeine, Penny thought, then shook her head. "I'm good."

She walked to the right of the bar, where a small alcove offered restroom choices, a pay phone and a door marked Employees. From there it was a short trip to Reid Buchanan's cluttered office.

He sat behind a desk as big as a full-size mattress, his feet up on the corner, the telephone cradled between his ear and his shoulder. When he saw her, he rolled his eyes, pointed at the phone, then waved her in.

"I know," he said as she wove her way around boxes he had yet to unpack. "It is an important event and I'd like to be there, but I have a prior engagement. Maybe next time. Uh-huh. Sure. You, too."

He hung up the phone and groaned. "Some foreign government trade show crap," he said.

"What did they want you to do?" she asked as she swept several folders off the only other chair in the office and sank onto the hard wood seat. She dumped the folders onto his already piled desk.

"Not a clue. Show up. Smile for pictures. Maybe give a speech." He shrugged.

"How much were they willing to pay you?"

He dropped his feet to the floor and turned to face her. "Ten grand. It's not like I need the money. I hate all that. It's bogus. I used to play baseball and now I'm here. I've retired."

Just last year, Penny thought. With the start of the regular season just weeks away, Reid had to be missing his former life.

She poked at one of the piles on the desk, then glanced at him. "I distinctly remember you saying you wanted a desk big enough to have sex on. It was a very specific requirement when we went shopping for one. But if you keep it this messy, no one will be interested in getting naked on its very impressive surface."

He leaned back in his chair and grinned at her. "I don't need the desk to get 'em naked."

"So I've heard."

Reid Buchanan was legendary. Not just for his incredible career as a major league pitcher, but for the way women adored him. Part of it was the Buchanan good looks and charm that all the brothers had. Part of it was that Reid just plain loved women. All women. Former girlfriends ranged from the traditional models and actresses to mother-earth tree-huggers nearly a decade older than him. Smart, dumb, short, tall, skinny, curvy, he liked them all. And they liked him.

Penny had known Reid for years. She'd met him two days after meeting Cal. She liked to joke that it had been love at first sight with the latter and best friends at first sight with the former.

"You'll never guess what I did today," she said.

Reid raised his dark eyebrows. "Darlin', the way you've been surprising me lately, I wouldn't even try."

"I had lunch with your brother."

Reid leaned back in his chair. "I know you mean Cal because Walker is still stationed overseas. Okay, I'll bite. Why?"

"He offered me a job. He wants me to be the executive chef at The Waterfront."

"Huh?"

Reid might be a part of the family but until he'd blown out his shoulder in the bottom of the third late last June, he'd never been involved in the business.

"That's the fish place, right?" he asked.

She laughed. "Yeah. And Buchanan's is the steak house and you're running the sports bar and Dani takes care of Burger Heaven. Jeez, Reid, this is your heritage. You have a family empire going here."

"No. What I have is a two-for-one appetizer special during happy hour. You gonna take the job?"

"I think so." She leaned forward. "He's paying me an outrageous salary and I get a percentage of the profits. It's what I've been waiting for. In three years I'll have enough money to open my own place."

He looked at her. "I told you I'd give you that money. Just tell me how much and I'll write you a check."

She knew he could. Reid had millions invested in all kinds of businesses. But she wouldn't take a loan from a friend. It was too much like being bailed out by her parents.

"I need to do this on my own," she said. "You know that."

"Yeah, yeah. You might want to think about getting that chip off your shoulder, Penny. It's making you walk funny."

She ignored that. "I like the idea of bringing back The Waterfront from the dead. I'll become even more of a star, which will make my restaurant even more successful."

"Not that you're letting all this go to your head."

She laughed. "Look who's talking. Your ego barely fits inside an airplane hangar."

Reid walked around the desk and crouched next to her. He cupped her face in his hands and kissed her cheek. "If this is what you want, you know I'm there for you."

"Thanks." She brushed his dark hair off his forehead and knew that in many ways life would have been a lot simpler if she just could have fallen in love with Reid instead of Cal.

He stood and leaned against the desk. "When do you start?"

"As soon as the paperwork is signed. I've heard the old place needs a total renovation, but we don't have time for that. We're going to have to make do. I need to put together menus, hire a kitchen staff."

Reid folded his arms over his chest. "You didn't tell him, did you?"

She squirmed in her seat. "It's not important information."

"Sure it is. Let me guess. You figured he wouldn't hire you if he knew, but once you're in place, he can't fire you for it."

"Pretty much."

"Slick, Penny. But it's not like you to play games."

"I wanted the job. It was the only way to get it."

"He's not going to like it."

She rose. "I don't see why it matters one way or the other. Cal and I have been divorced nearly three years. Now we're going to work together. It's a very new-millennium relationship."

Reid looked at her. "Trust me, when my brother finds out you're pregnant, there's going to be hell to pay and for more reasons than you know."

CHAPTER TWO

FOUR DAYS LATER PENNY drove to The Waterfront and pulled into the empty parking lot. The day was typical for March, cool, cloudy with a promise of rain later. As she stepped out onto the cracked pavement, she inhaled the smell of wet wood, salt water and fish. There were seagulls crying loudly and an air of desolation to the old building. Several remodels and patch jobs couldn't disguise that the structure had been through tough times.

There was nothing sadder than a deserted restaurant, she thought. It was midmorning. There should be activity as the prep cooks arrived to start their day. The chef should have already planned the specials and checked on deliveries. There should be the scent of lingering wood smoke from the grill and a savory hint of spices. Instead a page from the *Seattle Times* blew past her car.

This was her place now. She'd signed the papers and delivered them back to Cal's office. For the next three years, this was her world and she was master of its fate.

Excitement and anticipation knotted in her stomach. Under normal circumstances she would celebrate with friends, food and wine. For now the wine would have to wait.

"For a good cause," she whispered as she put a hand on her stomach.

A car pulled into the parking lot. She turned to watch a dark blue BMW Z4 pull up next to her. She eyed the expensive convertible and thought of at least a half-dozen comments she could make when Cal climbed out. Had he been paying attention to the weather for the past thirty-one years? Was a convertible in winter really a smart idea?

But when he opened the door and stepped out, she found herself unable to do much more than smile and wave. As he straightened to his full six-plus feet and adjusted his leather jacket, she felt like a bit player in a men's cologne commercial. Her job was to watch the male model in question while staring with slack-jawed adoration. Any speaking parts would have to be played by someone with a functioning brain.

Not good, she thought as her throat got tight, her thighs trembled and her already sensitive breasts seemed to strain toward him. Under the circumstances, a visceral reaction to her ex-husband seemed like a very bad idea.

She wasn't worried about them actually meaning anything. She was pregnant, which meant spending her days in a hormone bath. She teared up at Hallmark commercials, sobbed when little kids clutched puppies and generally wanted to send the world a candygram.

Nope, whatever she felt this moment about Cal had

nothing to do with him and everything to do with the pencil eraser-sized zygote in her tummy.

But that didn't mean she wasn't fully capable of making a fool out of herself.

She had to remind herself she was a big, bad chef with a reputation for being tough and difficult and something of a perfectionist. She worked with very sharp knives for a living. She could snap chicken bones with her bare hands.

"Ready to take on the world?" Cal asked as he approached.

"Sure. At least my little part of it." She followed him toward the front door. "I'm going to need a key."

He reached in his pocket and pulled out a ring. "They're marked. Front and back doors. All the storerooms. The wine cellar and liquor storage."

He unlocked the right side of the wood-and-glass double door, then stepped aside to let her enter. She pushed into the dim, open space, then wished she hadn't when the smell hit her.

"What is that?" she asked, waving her hand in front of her nose. The odor was an unfortunate combination of singed fur, decaying fish and meat and rotting wood.

"It's a little strong," Cal admitted. "The storerooms weren't cleaned out before the place was shut down. When I came by last week, the smell was worse."

She couldn't imagine worse. As it was, she had to fight to keep from throwing up. In the nearly four months she'd been pregnant, she'd never had a moment of nausea until now.

Cal propped open the front doors and turned on the fans. "It'll get better in a moment."

She rubbed her shoe against the carpet. "The stink isn't going to come out with just a cleaning."

"I know. There's hardwood everywhere in the dining room but here. We'll refinish the floors, then replace this carpeting."

She hoped that would be enough.

At least the space was good. High ceiling and big windows. People dining on the water generally wanted to look at the view. She saw large easels with renderings of the dining room. Cal stepped toward them.

"As you can see, we're making cosmetic changes. We don't have time for a total remodel."

"Uh-huh."

Penny walked past him. The front of the store wasn't her concern, nor did it interest her all that much. She had other places she would rather be—namely the kitchen.

She walked to the back of the dining room and through the large, single swinging door. The smell was worse here, but she ignored it as she took in what would be her domain.

At least it was clean, she thought as she looked at the large wood grill, the steamer, the eight burners, the ovens. There was the prep area, a long, stainless counter with a sink for salad, stacks of pots, sauté pans and bowls. She didn't even have to close her eyes to know what it would be like. The blinding heat from the grill and the burners. The hiss of the steam, the yells of "order up" or "ready to fire."

Because of the age of the restaurant, the kitchen was large and well ventilated. The mats looked new and when she picked up one of the pots, it was heavy and of good quality. Now for the storeroom.

"You could pretend to be interested," Cal said from just inside the kitchen.

She turned to him. "In what?"

"The front of the store. The color scheme and how the tables will be set up."

"Oh, sure." She thought for a second, not sure what to say. "It was great. Impressive."

"Do you think I'm fooled?"

"No, but you shouldn't be surprised, either. The only thing I care about is how big the dining room is and the table configuration."

It was important to know how many tables of six and eight and the policy on large parties. There were few things a kitchen staff hated more than a surprise order for twelve.

"I'll get you that information," he said. "So what do you think?"

She grinned. "Not bad. I'll need to take a complete inventory. How much is my budget for new equipment?"

"Get me a list of what you need and I'll get back to you."

She wrinkled her nose. "I'm the executive chef. I should have final say on what I buy."

"You forget that I know you. You'll be online picking up God knows what from Germany and France and sucking down twenty grand before I blink."

She turned away so he wouldn't see her smile. "I'd never do that."

"Oh, right. This from a woman who asked for a set of knives for her wedding present."

She spun back to face him, more than ready to take him on. "Cal—"

He cut her off with a quick shake of his head. "Sorry. I won't bring up our marriage again."

"Good."

News of her relationship, or former relationship, with Cal Buchanan would be common knowledge to the kitchen staff within fifteen minutes of opening. Kitchens didn't have secrets. But that didn't mean she wanted it shoved in their faces. Or hers.

Seeing Cal, talking to him, was strange. She wasn't sure what she felt. Not angry. Awkward maybe. Sad. Things had been good once. But he hadn't cared. He'd...

Okay, maybe she was a little angry. It had been three years. Who would have guessed there would be so much unfinished emotion?

At least she wasn't going to have to deal with him on a regular basis.

"I'll get you a list," she said. "I'll take an inventory after we're done."

"Okay." He looked at her. "Try not to scream."

"About what?"

"There are contracts in place."

She knew he didn't mean with employees, which only left food and services.

"Not my problem," she told him.

"It is, because you have to deal with them."

So typical, she thought. Cal was management. He might intellectually understand what it took to get dinner out for two or three hundred, but he didn't feel it in his soul.

"I'm not working with crap," she said.

"Can they screw up before you assume it's crap?"

"If the food had been good quality, the restaurant wouldn't be shut down," she told him. "So there was something wrong, and I'm guessing it was the food. I have my own people I like to deal with."

"We have contracts."

"No, *you* have contracts."

"You're getting a cut now, Penny. You're part of us."

As there weren't any profits from which to get a cut, it wasn't a happy thought. "I want to bring in my own suppliers."

"We honor these first."

She recognized the stubborn set of his mouth. She could fight and scream and possibly threaten physical violence, but he wouldn't back down. Her only option was logic.

"Fine. I'll use them for now, but if they screw up even once, it's over. I'll go to someone else."

"Fair enough."

"You better have a talk with them. I'll put money on the fact that they haven't been delivering their best here. That had better change."

"I'll get on it." He pulled a PalmPilot out of his jacket pocket and wrote on the small screen. Cal was such a guy—always in love with his toys.

"Shouldn't the new general manager be handling

that?" she asked. "Don't you have coffee you should be selling?"

"Funny you should mention that," he said.

She leaned against the counter and looked at him. All the warning signs were there—the brightness in his eyes, the slight smile, his sense of being totally in charge of the situation. Not that he was. This was her dream they were talking about and she wasn't going to let anyone mess with it.

"Let me guess," she said dryly. "I'm not going to like who you've hired."

"I don't know." He shrugged, then smiled. "It's me."

She'd been expecting either a name she didn't recognize or someone she'd worked with in the past and hadn't liked. But Cal? Her stomach heaved once as emotion flooded her.

No. Not Cal. *So* not a good idea.

"You won't have time," she said quickly. Oh, sure, he was good—she remembered that much. He'd walked away from the family steak house to start his own thing, but it hadn't been because he was failing. On the contrary, profits had been up substantially. But here? Now?

"I'm taking a leave for four months," he said. "I'll still go in to The Daily Grind office, but just for a few hours a week. My focus is The Waterfront."

"Why didn't you tell me when I asked the first time?"

"I thought you'd turn down the job."

Would she have? She wasn't sure. Not that she would let him know she wasn't sure.

She laughed. "Gee, Cal, I thought your brother was the one with the big ego. Now I see it runs in the family."

He didn't even look uncomfortable, which was just like him. Instead he stared at her.

"Given our past, it was a reasonable assumption. Working together under any circumstances could be challenging, but in a restaurant…" His voice trailed off.

She turned away. Her point exactly. "I don't care who I work with as long as he or she is good at the job. So show up, give a hundred and fifty percent, and we'll be fine."

"Penny?"

She breathed deeply, not wanting to give in to the anger inside of her. Deep, buried anger that made her want to lash out. It was the past, she told herself. It was long over. She had to remember that.

But her list of grievances—his wrongs—wouldn't go away. She wanted to scream them all and demand explanations. Talk about unreasonable.

Still, she couldn't help venting about at least one of them. An easy one that didn't really matter anymore.

She turned back to him and put her hands on her hips. "What the hell was wrong with you?" she demanded. "I was your *wife*. It was a dumb entry-level job. Salads, Cal. Just salads. Why couldn't you pick up the phone and put in a good word for me? Was it because you thought I couldn't handle it?"

That's what she'd always wondered, but hadn't been able to ask. That he hadn't believed in her. Because what else could it be? But she hadn't been sure, and now she wanted to know.

He took a step toward her, then stopped and shook his head. "You make me crazy. It's been what, four years since that job interview? Does it really matter?"

"Yes. It does."

He shifted. "You won't believe me."

"Try me."

"It wasn't that I didn't believe in you. Never that. You were great. The best. It was about my family."

She frowned. "What? That your grandmother would see your wife working? She already knew I had a job, Cal. It wouldn't have been a surprise."

"No. I didn't want you involved with her. Exposed to her."

Penny knew he and Gloria had never been close, but she had a hard time believing that was the reason.

"I grew up with two sisters, and the three of us had to share a bathroom," she said. "I know how to play well with others."

"I didn't want to risk it. I didn't want to risk you. It was never about you doing the job."

She didn't actually believe him, but as he'd mentioned, what was the point in fighting about it now? He'd come back, begging her to work for him and she'd agreed.

"Whatever," she said with a shrug. "I'll accept you as the temporary GM. Just don't get in my way."

"Not my style."

"It is interesting," she told him. "I distinctly remember you once telling me hell would freeze over before we would ever work together."

"You're taking that out of context. We were married at the time. A restaurant is too small for a married couple to coexist in."

"You sure made a lot of pronouncements back then. How many of them were accurate?"

She expected him to be annoyed that she'd dared to question him. Instead he grinned. "I figure about sixty percent."

"You're being generous."

"That's because of the subject matter."

"Yourself?"

The grin broadened. "Who else?"

"Men," she grumbled, shrugging out of her coat and dropping it onto the counter. She was careful to keep her back to him so he wouldn't see her smile.

She could see that Cal still had the ability to make her want to chop him up into matchstick-size pieces, but he'd never been boring.

"We're not married now," she said. "I'm sure we'll do fine together, as long as you remember where your authority ends." She turned to him and pointed at the entrance to the kitchen. "This is my world. Don't even think about stepping into it and taking charge."

"Fair enough. And Gloria has promised to stay out of the restaurant, except as a customer. It was part of the deal to get me back. She won't be bothering you, either."

"Good to know." While she didn't think his grandmother was the demon he did, she and the older woman had never been exactly close. Whenever Penny was around, Gloria had a way of sniffing the air as if the odor was unpleasant.

She pulled a notepad out of her pocket. "Okay, let's talk specifics. I need about a week to get the kitchen up and running. I already have a lot of ideas about staffing, so there's only cleaning and stocking both equipment and food. Before I can stock, we need to talk menus."

"When will you have them finished? I get final approval."

She raised her eyebrows. "Are you going to tell me what to cook?"

"In this matter, yes."

She didn't think so, but she would pick that battle when the menus were done. "I'll let you know how it's going in a couple of days. How much time do you need for the front of the store?"

"Two weeks."

He used a slender stylus to access information on his Palm Pilot. She moved closer to look over his shoulder.

Big mistake. Suddenly she was aware of him. Heat from his body seemed to warm her from the inside out. She breathed in the scent of him. Unfortunately, he still smelled the same. Just clean male skin and something that was uniquely his own.

Scent memories were powerful. She'd learned that in culinary school and often used the fact to her advantage when cooking. Now she was trapped in a swirl of memories that included lying naked next to him, listening to his breathing after he'd just left her trembling and exhausted from sexual satisfaction.

She took a big step away.

"I assume there's a plan for the opening," she

said, happy that her voice sounded normal. Sexual thoughts were so inappropriate where Cal was concerned. Not only were they divorced, she was pregnant. She doubted he would find that a turn-on.

"I want a big splashy party on the first night. No dinner service, just a crowd and samples. You'll be able to show off what's to come. We'll invite local press and the beautiful people."

She smiled. "The beautiful people?"

He shook his head. "Business leaders, celebrities, whatever."

"They'll be so happy to hear how enthused you sound."

"I want the restaurant up and running. The party is a necessary evil."

"Don't put that on the invitation," she suggested. "I'll work up a menu for that as soon as I finalize the menu for the restaurant. And just so you know, I'll use your contracted people for regular deliveries, until they screw up, but for the party, I'm getting my own stuff in here. I have some fish people I use."

"Actual fish people?" he asked. "Gills? Fins?"

She rolled her eyes. "You know what I mean. I'll be using them for special orders."

"Fair enough."

She studied the notes on her pad. What else was there to discuss? She looked at him. "Did you have…" She frowned, catching his puzzled stare. "What?"

He took a step back. "Nothing."

"You have the weirdest look on your face. What are you thinking about?"

"I said nothing."

"It has to be something."

"No, it doesn't."

Cal swore silently. He couldn't remember the last time he'd gotten caught staring at a woman's chest. What did he care about Penny's parts?

He didn't. He hadn't in years. It was just…she looked different. There was an air of confidence he didn't remember. That could have come from her recent success. But there was also the issue of her breasts.

They were bigger. He was sure of it. He dropped his gaze to her chest, then looked away. Yup, bigger. Her sweater hugged her curves before falling to just below her waist. He'd been married to her, had seen her naked countless times. While he'd always liked her body, she'd complained about being too boyish. All angles and lines. Her breasts had been small. But now…

They were bigger. How could that happen? Oh, sure, he knew about implants, but Penny wasn't the type, was she? And if she was willing to have surgery to increase her cleavage, wouldn't she have gone for more than a cup size?

He shook his head and told himself to think of something else. He was the cofounder of a multimillion-dollar corporation and in charge of a good-sized restaurant. He was also over thirty. Surely he could get through the rest of the meeting without obsessing over his ex-wife's breasts.

"Who are you bringing with you?" he asked to change the subject. "You said two people."

"Edouard, my sous-chef, and Naomi."

He swore. "No."

She raised her eyebrows. "Excuse me, but you don't get a vote. She helps me. Naomi handles things for me and she's the best expediter in the business. We'll need that when we get busy."

He knew that a good expediter was worth any price when the restaurant was swamped. Someone had to get plates out to tables, making sure the various parties were all served the right food at the right time. The expediter was usually loyal to the back of the store, while helping out in the front. The expediter knew everything that was going on in both places and could keep the chef in the loop.

"How do you know we're going to be that busy?" he asked. "It takes time to build up a clientele."

She smiled. "Hey, it's me. They'll come."

"Talk about *my* ego," he grumbled.

"No, thanks."

She went down her list and brought up several more items. "I'll be paying my cooks really well, so brace yourself."

"I have a budget."

"And a restaurant with a reputation for serving horrible food. You're only here for four months, Cal. I know what that means. You want to dazzle, then get out. I'm fine with that, but dazzle don't come cheap."

"Keep it reasonable."

"I'll do what it takes."

He liked that she pushed back. She'd come into her own.

"Let's meet on Monday and see where we are," he said. "Say noon?"

"I'll be here, holding interviews. Come by when it's convenient." She put down her pad. "I'm going to stay and look over the kitchen."

"You have the keys. Just lock up when you're ready to go."

"Sure." She smiled and turned away, which put her in profile. His gaze dropped to her breasts. What the hell was up with that?

AFTER HIS MEETING with Penny, Cal returned to his office at the headquarters of The Daily Grind. He'd nearly cleared up everything for his four-month absence, but there were a few final details.

He made his way to his office and checked his messages. His assistant would contact him directly at The Waterfront if anything came up while he was gone and he would have biweekly meetings with his partners during that period.

The corporate headquarters were on the top floor of an old manufacturing building by the 5 freeway. He could see across much of downtown, toward Lake Union and the Space Needle. On a clear day, he could see farther, but this was Seattle and there weren't that many clear days. Even now a light rain fell against his floor-to-ceiling windows and the skylights overhead.

He settled into work, only to have his assistant buzz him twenty minutes later.

"Your grandmother is here," she murmured.

Cal wished briefly for an excuse not to see her. Unfortunately the downside of saving The Waterfront was closer contact with the old woman.

"Send her in."

He rose and walked around the desk to greet her. Gloria Buchanan swept into the office with the grace and style of someone born in a much more elegant age.

She was slender and of medium height. She stood straight, despite her seventy-plus years, wearing a tailored suit and dangerously high heels. Her hair was white and always perfect, her face relatively unlined. Dani, his sister, swore Gloria had had cosmetic surgery. That, or she really was a witch and could summon supernatural forces to keep her looking good.

"Gloria," he said as he pulled out a chair.

She nodded and took the seat. As he sat across from her, he thought about the fact that he had never called her Grandmother. Not even when he'd been young. She'd discouraged it from the start.

She shrugged out of her white fur-trimmed coat and set her pale-blue purse on the carpet next to her feet.

"I assume you're ready to make the transition," she said.

He nodded. "I'll be at my office at The Waterfront starting tomorrow."

She glanced around the spacious office and sniffed. "It's not as if you'll miss this place."

"Of course I will. We started with nothing and built an empire worth millions." Something a normal person would respect, he thought grimly.

"Oh, yes. Beverages and cookies. Quite the empire," Gloria said.

Cal had learned there was no point in arguing with

her. She saw the world as she wanted to, and from what he could tell, her view was cold and depressing.

"You're not here to talk about The Daily Grind," he said. "So why don't you get to the point?"

"I want to talk about the restaurant," she said.

"No, you don't."

Her dark blue eyes widened slightly. "Excuse me?"

"Tread carefully," he told her. "There are specific rules in play. If you get in my face about any detail of the restaurant, I quit. I promised you a turnaround in four months, on the condition that you stay away. I meant it. One word of advice, one suggestion and it's all over."

"You'd really walk away from your legacy?" she asked, her expression both annoyed and imperious.

"I already have. It's easier than you'd think."

"I have bled for this family and our company," she told him, her voice icy. "I have given up a life of my own."

He'd heard it all before. "You've done exactly what you wanted," he reminded her. "Anyone who stood in your way got taken down and thrown to the side of the road."

She'd lived and breathed the family business for as long as he had been alive and he suspected the obsession had started long before then. Gloria would do anything to promote the Buchanan name. The irony was she wasn't even a blood Buchanan. She'd married into the family.

"Let's be clear," he said. "I'm not doing this for you. I'm only coming in to help because of my brothers and Dani. Hell, Dani should be the one saving The

Waterfront. She cares about it more than the rest of us combined."

Gloria's eyes narrowed. "Dani isn't—"

He cut her off with a shake of his head. "Spare me the lecture. It's boring. Like I said, I'm not doing this for you. I'm doing it in case one of us has kids who care. I'm putting in my four months and then I'm walking away without looking back."

"You make it sound like a prison sentence."

"In some ways it is."

"Callister."

He looked at her and for the first time she actually seemed old. Frail, even. But he knew better than to be sucked in by her tricks. She was a wily old bird and he'd been pecked more than once.

"Fine. Four months," she said. "I heard who you hired as the chef."

Her tone indicated he might have made a deal with the devil.

"She does great work and her name will bring in customers," he said. "She drove a hard bargain, but I got her and that's what matters."

"I see." Gloria didn't sound as if she could see at all. She sounded annoyed.

Cal wondered what the old bat had against Penny, aside from the fact that she, Gloria, hadn't handpicked her.

He knew Penny hadn't believed that he'd done his damnedest to keep her off his grandmother's radar when they'd been married. Back then he'd been afraid of what the old woman could do.

Now, everything was different. Penny had a reputation for being tough. He was willing to bet she could hold her own against Gloria. They would butt heads eventually; he only hoped he was around to see the show.

"If Penny cooks, they will come," he said.

Gloria shifted in her seat. "I hope there won't be any unfortunate incidents in our establishment."

Cal knew he was being set up, but his curiosity was too strong for him to ignore the lure. The only thing he knew about Penny's life since the divorce were the odd bits Reid dropped in casual conversation.

"What incidents?" he asked.

"She once stabbed a member of her staff. Apparently the man wouldn't do what she said, so she took a kitchen knife to him."

Cal started to laugh. Gloria glared at him.

"It's not funny. She's practically a murderer."

He continued to chuckle. "Was she charged with anything?"

"I'm sure I don't know."

Which meant she hadn't been. "I hope the story's true," he said, still amused. "I can't wait to ask her for all the details."

CHAPTER THREE

"IT'S ALL FINE AND good to look at qualifications," Naomi said. "But I want someone I can have sex with."

Penny ignored her friend and glanced at the application in front of her. "I hear good things about him," she said, making notes on a pad. "Put him on the list."

"But he's married and he doesn't cheat." There was a definite whine in Naomi's voice. "I can accept one, but not the other."

"We are talking about raising a restaurant from the dead. Not your sex life."

"Why do they have to be mutually exclusive? I can be a good employee and have a great sex life. In fact, getting laid on a regular basis keeps me cheerful."

Penny looked at her papers so Naomi wouldn't see her smile. "Focus," she said.

Naomi sighed. "You're less fun now that you're in charge."

"And likely to stay that way. Who's next?"

While Naomi shuffled through papers, Penny glanced around the transformed dining room. The place had been painted and there were new window coverings. The old carpet was up and the floors had been refinished. The scent of varnish competed with the smell of cleanser and bleach coming from the kitchen. The horrible odor of rotting food had been driven from the place, which made Penny grateful. She was well into her fourth month and she didn't want to experience morning sickness at this late date.

"Asshole alert at ten o'clock," Naomi muttered.

Penny turned and saw Cal walking toward them. He looked good—tall and handsome, wearing a black leather bomber jacket and jeans. He walked with an easy, loose-hipped grace that all the Buchanan men had. Good genes, she thought, which, unfortunately, came from Gloria. Penny might not like the old woman but she knew her stubbornness and determination had been passed on to her grandchildren.

"He's not an asshole anymore," Penny said, ignoring the sudden quivering in her belly. "He's our boss."

"To me, he'll always be the jerk who made you cry for two weeks straight when he walked out on you."

Technically Penny had been the one to move out of the apartment, but she knew what Naomi meant. Cal had done nothing to keep her and certainly hadn't come after her.

"That was a long time ago," Penny reminded her. "I've let it go. You should work on that, too."

"Maybe."

Cal approached the table. "Ladies." He held out a cardboard container with three cups of coffee. "A little something to help with the hiring process."

Naomi grabbed a cup and looked at The Daily Grind logo. "I'm more a Starbucks person, but any port in a storm."

"Nice," Cal said, looking at her. "Hello, Naomi. It's been a long time."

"It has." She stood. In her black leather boots, she was nearly eye-to-eye with Cal. "How's it going?"

"Great."

"I hear you're in charge."

"That's right."

She took a sip of the coffee. "Every time I go into one of your stores, I remember the time I saw you naked. It always gives me a little giggle."

With that, she strolled away.

Penny closed her eyes and winced. Unfortunately Naomi *had* seen Cal naked. She'd walked in on them making love, once. After retreating, she'd stood behind the closed door and complained bitterly about people who didn't have the common courtesy to at least make some noise while doing it so the world could know what they were up to and not accidentally walk in.

Cal took the seat she'd vacated and picked up one of the remaining coffees. "Do you really need her?" he asked.

"Sorry, yes. She's great at her job and she watches my back." Naomi would also take some of the heat off Penny as her pregnancy progressed. "We've become something of a team."

"Great."

"You're only here for four months," Penny reminded him. "How bad could it be?"

"We're talking about Naomi. It could be a disaster."

"Not for our big, bad general manager."

He looked at her. "I don't think I detect enough reverence in your voice. This is my restaurant and while I'm here, I'm a god."

"I must have missed that memo. Could you resend it to me?"

"I'll bring you a copy myself." He glanced around the dining room. "What do you think?"

She followed his gaze. "It's fine."

"Fine? Do you know how much this is costing?"

"Nope. And I don't much care. The front of the store is your business."

He shook his head. "You haven't changed. What happens when you open your own place? You'll have to deal with the front of the store then."

"I'll manage. Naomi has fabulous taste."

"Are you sure she won't want to turn it into some kind of sex shop?"

Penny considered the question. "Good point. Then I'll talk to Reid. I'm sure one of his former girlfriends was an interior decorator."

"Assuming he remembers which one."

"Another good point. You're on a roll this morning."

He sipped his coffee. "You're feisty. When did that happen?"

"A hundred and forty-seven days ago. There was a report on the news."

"I missed that."

"I guess it's hiding with your memo about being a god."

He grinned and she smiled in return. Even as she wanted to lean in and continue the banter, she knew it was far better to keep things completely business-like between them. Her former relationship with Cal had started with fun conversation and had gotten more dangerous by the minute. Although she felt completely immune now, she didn't want to take any chances. Not when it was surprisingly easy to be around him.

"You've been out of the business a while," she said. "How does it feel to be back?"

"Good. Familiar. I didn't think I'd missed it, but there's something about running a restaurant. Everything's changing, with no hour the same, let alone a day. Time is always the enemy. The next crisis is just around the corner."

"Sounds like you've missed it."

"Maybe I have."

"I hope you remember enough to keep this half up and running."

"Your faith in me is overwhelming."

Cal watched Penny lean back as if separating herself from him. He could read her mind as clearly as if she'd spoken.

He hadn't had faith in her.

The statement wasn't true, but he knew she wouldn't believe him. His attempts to protect her from Gloria had only widened the chasm in their rapidly unraveling marriage.

Ancient history, he told himself. Better to forget it.

She reached into a battered backpack and pulled out a folder. "Here are some sample menus. I've marked the items I want to serve at the big pre-opening party. The question marks are in place where I'm

not sure what will be available that particular day.
Inventory changes quickly and my fish people can't
promise the more exotic selections until the day of
the party."

He took the sheets of paper. "The infamous fish
people."

She smiled. "Sometimes they dress in costume."

"I'd like to see that."

She laughed.

The sound washed over him in a wave of unexpected heat. He felt it sink into him, warming him,
arousing him.

Whoa. Not going there. He didn't believe in do-
overs, not in personal relationships, anyway. He and
Penny were simply co-workers, nothing more.

But even as he told himself to back off, sexual energy poured through him, making him aware of the
humor in her eyes and the way her skin seemed almost luminous.

He told himself that the former was at his expense
and the latter was simply the result of damn good
lighting in the restaurant. But even he didn't believe
it.

"Are you even listening?" she asked.

"Yeah. Fish specials depend on the whim of the
fish people."

"No. I was saying that I'll be building my specials slowly. I won't want to dump a bunch of new
items on the menu at once. I also have a few things
in mind for new signature dishes. Once we're estab-
lished, I'll offer them as specials and if they take off,
I'll put them on the menu. I've also been working on

a seasonal menu. Certain fish is available at certain times of the year. I can build around that. The same with produce."

"Berries in the summer, squash in the fall," he said.

She sighed. "I'd like to think I'm more imaginative than that, but yes. That's the idea."

He looked over the menu. There were the basics—steamed and grilled fish, soups, salads, sides.

He'd had her garlic smashed potatoes before and his mouth watered at the memory. She put in a secret ingredient that she'd never shared, even with him.

He flipped to the list of specials. "Corn cakes?" he asked. "I thought we were specializing in Northwest cuisine. Isn't that Southwestern?"

"That depends on how they're prepared."

He shrugged, then shook his head. "Fish and chips? Do we really want to do that here? We're going for an upscale experience, not cheap fast food on the pier."

Her eyes narrowed. "Do I look annoyed?" she asked. "Because you're really pissing me off here. Did you or did you not want a special menu?"

"Yes, but—"

"Did you or did you not hire me to make the dining experience special?"

"Yes, but—"

"Perhaps you'd like to give me a chance to do my job before you start complaining."

"Penny," he said, his voice low and commanding. "I get final say on the menu. That's in the contract."

He could practically hear her teeth grinding.

"Fine. Mark everything you consider questionable.

Then be back here in two days. We'll have a tasting. At that point, you will sample the foods you object to. I will be in the kitchen where you can crawl to me and beg my forgiveness, after which you'll never, ever question my menu selections again."

He chuckled. "I won't be crawling and I will question as I see fit, but the tasting session sounds fine." He pulled out his Palm Pilot. "What time?"

"Three."

"Fine. Of course if I'm not impressed, I'll be calling the shots on the menu," he told her.

"Only if hell has frozen over."

"I hear it's getting cold down there."

She muttered something he couldn't hear, which made him hold in a smile.

She'd gotten tough in the years they'd been apart. He liked that about her. He doubted she would have any trouble controlling the kitchen staff. He thought about what Gloria had told him, that Penny had stabbed someone. He wanted to hear the story, but not just yet.

Cal looked over the menu again. "We should price what we've agreed on," he said. "Somehow I think that will be an argument."

"I have the costs here."

She pulled out several more sheets, these printed out from a computer. They broke down the approximate size of each serving and the cost to prepare it. Store costs—labor, wait staff and the fixed costs of the building were arrived at by estimating the total number of dinners served per night and dividing that into store costs for the day.

"Your portions are too large," he said. "We'll have to charge too much."

"Better that than they go home hungry and have to stop for a burger on the way."

He braced himself for the battle to come. "Who needs ten ounces of halibut?"

"Fish is different from meat. A four-ounce portion isn't normal."

"We're talking about a premium product."

She tapped her pen on the table. "Gee, and I thought this was going to be a premium restaurant. Did I have that wrong?"

Before he could answer, Naomi walked into the dining room with a guy Cal didn't recognize. Penny's friend fell back a step, pointed to the newcomer and mouthed, "I want him!"

Cal groaned.

"It's the wine guy," Naomi said. "Who's going to be ordering?"

"I am," Cal and Penny said at the same time.

CAL WALKED INTO the Downtown Sports Bar a little after nine on Wednesday night. The happy hour crowd had faded with the end of the last game and now there were only the regulars and a few business people who didn't want to go home. Which meant the crowd was about ninety percent female.

His brother, Reid, stood behind the bar, holding court while a dozen or so large-breasted beauties listened, laughed and openly invited him into their respective beds. Or maybe not so respective. With Reid, one never knew.

He'd always been like this, Cal thought with a grin as he waved at his brother and made his way to a booth in the corner. Back in high school, Reid had had more than his share of interested women. Some of it had been because he was the pitching star on the high school team, and some of it was because he was a Buchanan. The Buchanan boys had never lacked for female companionship.

As he approached the booth he saw his baby sister, Dani, already seated. She had a beer in front of her and an expression of betrayal that warned him she'd heard the news.

"How's it going, kid?" he asked as he slid in next to her.

"How do you think? I'm still trying to pull the knife out of my back."

If they'd still been children he would have tugged her close and tickled her until she yelled uncle. Then he would have held her while she cried. That was no longer an option and he didn't know how to make her feel better.

"Hey, Cal."

He looked up and saw Lucy, one of the waitresses, walking toward him.

"The usual?" she asked.

Cal nodded.

"Dani ordered nachos," she added. "Want it for two?"

"Make it three. Reid will be joining us."

"Sure thing."

She turned, giving him a view of her rounded tush in tight khaki shorts. Only Reid could get away with making his staff wear shorts and cropped T-shirts in Seattle in winter.

Cal turned to his sister. He leaned close to kiss her cheek, but she pulled away. Her dark brown eyes sharpened with accusation.

"How could you?" she demanded.

"Dammit, Dani, I didn't have a choice. You know I don't want to get back in the business. I sure don't want to work for Gloria. I knew I could either take the job or watch the restaurant go down the toilet. None of us would want that."

"Ha. Why would you care? You couldn't wait to get away from it all."

"I don't care," he said gently. "But you do. Reid's in the business now. Walker may want to be a part of things when he retires from the marines."

Dani reached for her beer. "All great reasons. You left out kids. Won't we want this great company to pass on to our kids? Not that any of us has them. I don't see them in my future anytime soon, and I'm the only one who's married, but hey, it could happen. Maybe one of you guys could slip up and get a girl pregnant. Then we could have yet another generation in the family business."

He knew she was bitter and he couldn't blame her. Ironically, her words hit closer to the truth than she realized. He *had* gotten a girl pregnant. Seventeen years ago his daughter had been born. Gloria was the only one in his family who knew.

Thinking of his daughter now made him wonder if Lindsey would ever be interested in the family business. Not that she considered herself a Buchanan. She was adopted and aware of the fact but had no curiosity about her birth parents.

"I'm not making a career of The Waterfront," he said, then thanked Lucy as she delivered his beer. "I'm back for four months and I have no desire ever to run the company."

"Too bad, because Gloria would hand it over to you in a heartbeat." Dani tucked her short dark hair behind her ears. "She's a powerful woman. You'd think she'd respect that I want to be just as powerful, although a lot less bitchy. But does she care?"

Before he could figure out how to respond to that, Reid walked over.

"Hey, boys and girls."

Dani glared at him. "You already knew, didn't you?"

"Knew what?" Reid's expression was innocent as he slid in next to Dani and put his arm around her. "That I'm the best looking of the Buchanan brothers? Not that it's a tough competition."

Cal shook his head. "One day your ego is going to come crashing back to earth and crush you like the insignificant bug you are."

"Unlikely. My bevy of beauties will protect me."

"Anything falling from the sky will just bounce off their implants," Dani said. "You need to get him from below."

Cal grinned. "She has a point."

"And so do I," Dani said. She shrugged off Reid's arm. "You knew about Cal running The Waterfront."

"Sure. Penny told me when she came by to say she had the job as executive chef."

Cal winced as Dani slammed her hands down on the table. "Why am I always the last to know?" she asked. "Can't you guys keep me in the loop on anything?"

"Why would you care who's the chef?" Reid asked. "It's not like it's your restaurant."

Cal glared at his brother. "Shut up." He turned to Dani. "I was going to tell you tonight."

Dani stared at him. "You hired your ex-wife to cook at your restaurant?"

"She's good, she has a name that'll bring in customers and she was available."

"Just perfect," Dani muttered. "At least it's late enough that I don't have to worry about my day getting too much worse."

Cal didn't know what to say. He hated that when it came to the family business, Dani always got screwed.

"Penny's a great chef," Reid said. "She'll make the old place a success. Don't you want that? Aren't you the one so interested in seeing the company succeed?"

"That's not the point," Dani said.

Lucy arrived with a massive plate of nachos. They dug in and for a few minutes there was only small talk about who had heard from Walker and whether or not the Mariners would have a decent season.

Cal glanced at his sister. He could feel the tension in her and knew she wasn't happy. Maybe it was because he was the oldest and she was the youngest or maybe it was because she was the only girl, but he'd always looked out for her. Nobody messed with Dani without going through him first, and that went for his brothers as well.

But she wasn't that little girl anymore and he couldn't keep the whole world at bay.

"How are you doing?" he asked.

She shrugged. "Fine. The new low-calorie selections are doing great. We're getting the dieting mom crowd in. The kids can scarf down on burgers and fries and mom can stay on program."

She didn't sound very enthused. Not that he could blame her. Dani had a master's in restaurant management. She'd returned to Seattle, fully intending to work her way up the ranks. But instead of putting her in a junior position at The Waterfront, or Buchanan's, the family's steak house, Gloria had sent Dani to Tukwila to run Burger Heaven. She'd started as a hostess, been a fry cook and two years ago had been made manager. But no matter how hard Dani worked or how many times she talked with Gloria, the old woman refused to move her.

"You let her get to you," Reid said. "If it doesn't matter, she can't hurt you."

"I don't know how not to care," Dani said simply.

Cal knew that was true. Dani didn't have a choice. She lived and breathed the business. Despite everything, she was a Buchanan down to her bones. With Gloria standing between her and success, her choices were to endure and hope to change her grandmother's mind or walk away.

He wrapped his arm around her neck, pulled her close and kissed the top of her head.

"Life's a bitch," he muttered.

"Tell me about it." She straightened and held out her beer. "Change of subject. To Walker. Stay safe and come home to us."

They drank to their brother, currently serving a tour of duty with the marines in Afghanistan.

"At least we can all be together the next time he's on leave," she said.

Cal nodded. "We'll plan something special."

Dani wrinkled her nose. "Oh, please. Because you guys are so into social planning. I'll be the one in charge of that and we all know it."

Reid looked at him. "When did she get to be so bossy?"

"A few years ago."

"I'm still bigger than you," Reid told her.

Dani grinned. "Yeah, big guy, but you were raised to never hit a girl. Not even your sister. So there's nothing you can do about it."

CAL SAT in The Waterfront's main dining room and waited. Right on time, the door to the kitchen swung open and Penny walked out. She wore checked pants, clogs and a three-quarter-sleeve white coat. A blue scarf held her braided hair off her face.

But instead of a tray carrying various dishes, she held only one plate.

He frowned at the fish and chips she put in front of him. "This isn't the only item I questioned," he said. "I want to taste the others, too."

"Try this first," she said, making no effort to conceal her certainty. "Taste it and weep. I'm going to step back a little so you'll have room to come crawling to me."

Yeah, right. She'd served fish and chips. How good could it be?

He was willing to admit she had the presentation nailed. The cream-colored oval plate contained three pieces of fish, waffle-cut fries and brightly colored coleslaw in a cabbage leaf.

"Got any malt vinegar?" he asked.

"Not a chance."

"The diners may want it."

"Not after they taste the fish. I'll allow them to use it on the waffle fries, if they like."

"How generous. Will you be posting a sign explaining that?"

She grinned. "I thought I'd just put it on the menu. You know, an asterisk by the menu item, then a little note at the bottom explaining the rules."

Her confidence grated on him. He cut off a piece of the fish and tasted it.

Crunchy batter, but he'd expected that. Still, it was surprisingly crisp without being too hard. As he chewed, the flavors exploded on his tongue. The fish was nice and mild, yet fresh. There was also a hint of spice… No, wait. It was more sweet than spicy.

He took a second bite to try and figure out what she'd put into the batter. Something Thai? No, but chilies of some kind. And what was that tang?

He swore silently. This was better than good—it was addictive. He had to consciously hold back so he didn't scarf down the entire plate of fish. Instead he deliberately turned to the fries.

The waffle cut made them look more elegant than other fries and he could see they'd been seasoned. He bit into one. Crispy on the outside, but soft and potato-y on the inside. And damn if the spices here didn't add something extraordinary.

He moved on to the coleslaw and that blew him away. He should have known. Penny loved to experiment until she found exactly the right blend of seasonings. No doubt she'd been working on these recipes for months.

He looked at her. She stood just off to the side, her arms folded, her expression patient.

"You win," he said with a sigh. "It's great. I don't know what you're putting in the fish batter—"

"I'm not telling," she said with a self-satisfied smile. "Chef's secret."

"Figures. Put this on the menu, along with everything else I questioned."

Her smile turned smug. "I already did. Naomi called the order in to the printer this morning."

CHAPTER FOUR

"WILL SOMEONE GET THE goddamn salmon off the back burner," Burt growled, his low voice thick with fury.

"It's not my salmon, you sonofabitch," Juan told him, then plunged his knife into a leek and neatly sliced it in two.

Penny ignored the usual high level of profanity, the male posturing and the jostling as her new kitchen staff learned to work together. Over time they would perfect a delicate dance that provided meals at rapid speed, while maintaining taste and quality, but for the first few nights there would be plenty of mishaps.

Nothing huge, Penny thought, willing the fates to smile on her. A cocktail party for five hundred was just the warm-up. Tomorrow they would be serving dinner for real.

Edouard, her sous-chef, whipped up more sauce for the corn cakes. "The salmon is mine," he said, not bothering to look up as he drizzled in extra-virgin olive oil. "You girls leave it alone."

A restaurant kitchen was mostly a man's world. Penny had learned to deal with it in culinary school. At first she'd been shocked by the insults, pet names that would make a hardened criminal blush and the need for even more creative swearing. In time she'd come to see it as little more than the specialized language of the kitchen. She didn't usually participate, but if necessary, she could nail every one of her staff with enough profanity to shock them into silence. Still, she preferred to pick her battles.

Someone dropped a tray of honey-grilled shrimp on the counter. Naomi immediately went to work dressing the plates, first squirting on a dollop of sauce, then adding a sprig of herb and a dusting of green onion. There were demi-cups of lobster bisque, delicately balanced waffle fries with tiny bits of batter-fried fish on top, seared salmon on corn cakes and an assortment of desserts.

Penny couldn't hear much over the hiss of the steamer, the roar of the grill and the chatter of the staff, but a glance at the clock told her the cocktail party had been underway at least thirty minutes.

"I have to go," she muttered, unbuttoning her coat as she headed to her office.

"Yes," Edouard called after her. "If you do not go now, we won't get any of the credit for the food. Go. Mingle. Come back and tell us we are brilliant."

"Sure thing," Penny said, then slipped into her office. She closed the door behind her and shrugged out of her coat.

Underneath she wore a low-cut silk sweater and a black jacket that matched her slacks. She'd traded in clogs for high-heeled boots. Her long hair hung loose, which made her a complete disaster for the kitchen, but her job tonight wasn't about cooking— it was about making nice with Cal's definition of Seattle's beautiful people.

She checked her makeup, then stepped back as her door opened. Naomi stuck her head in.

"There are two waiters I'm considering," her friend said. "I need your help in picking. I'll point them out to you and you can let me know what you think."

"Okay."

Naomi smiled. "You look nervous. Don't be. It's going great."

"You've been in the kitchen. You can't know that any more than I do."

"I have a feeling." She paused. "Wasn't that a song from the movie *Flashdance?*" She hummed for second. "Or is it 'What a Feeling'? I'm dating myself, aren't I? Would it help if I said I was twelve when I saw the movie?"

"Were you?"

"I honestly can't remember."

Naomi had turned forty last December and had celebrated with a long weekend in Mexico and a string of hunky cabana boys. Penny had always admired her friend's ability to make her own fun.

"Nice sweater," Naomi said, nodding at the emerald green fabric.

"I figure I'll show off cleavage while I've got it."

"Good plan. You hardly have any tummy at all, but the jacket hides the little that is there. Come on. You can't stall here forever."

Penny nodded and let Naomi lead her out into the main restaurant. As they walked out of the kitchen, a young blond waiter walked by. Naomi grabbed his arm.

"What's your name?" she asked.

He grinned at her. "Ted."

"Good." She turned to Penny. "That's candidate number one."

Penny was still laughing when she turned to face the crowd.

Her humor faded as she took in the sheer number of people milling in the main dining room. They'd sent out over five hundred invitations and from the looks of things, everyone had decided to show up.

Soft music was barely audible over the general din of conversation. People stood in groups, chatting and laughing, while waiters in white coats circulated with trays of food.

The bar was doing a brisk business, hardly a surprise when the liquor was free. Penny had a brief urge for something to steady her nerves, then braced herself and tried to pick a direction in which to wander.

Just then the crowd shifted and parted, allowing her to see into the center of the room. Cal stood there, tall and studly in a dark suit. Her body reacted, getting all hot and weak and needy.

She used her kitchen experience to call herself several bad names and when that didn't decrease her very inappropriate desire, she reminded herself that she and Cal had already tried the relationship thing and it hadn't worked. He'd let her go without a whimper, leaving her to wonder if he'd ever loved her at all.

"So it's just you and me, kid," she whispered as she lightly touched her stomach. Then she squared her shoulders and plunged into the crowd.

"Nice to see you. Thanks for coming."

Penny smiled, greeted and generally made nice

with the prospective clientele. She made her way toward Cal, who came and collected her before she reached him.

"It's going great," he said. "Big crowd showed."

"Sure they did," she murmured into his ear. "The food is free. Let's see how many of them are willing to pay on another night."

He chuckled, then introduced her to several government officials.

"We used to come here all the time," a petite, pretty lawyer said. "Lately, though…" Her voice trailed off.

Penny waved away the comment. "You can say it was really bad. I wasn't the one cooking."

The woman laughed. "I guess not. I've sampled most of the food. It's terrific."

"Thank you. Obviously we want to offer traditional favorites while helping people branch out."

Cal put his hand on the small of her back, which caused her nerve endings to make a few *Flashdance* moves of their own.

"Have you tried Penny's fish and chips? They're incredible. I made the mistake of saying they weren't important enough for our menu. She won me over with one bite."

Penny glanced at him. "I didn't think you'd admit that."

"I was wrong."

The lady lawyer grinned. "Care to embroider that on a pillow? Women everywhere would love to see it."

"No, thanks."

Cal excused them and they moved to another group

of local business people. He introduced her and then let her explain about her philosophy as far as using local ingredients whenever possible.

"We live in a wonderful part of the country," she said. "Why not take advantage of that?"

A reporter from the *Seattle Times* moved closer. "Are you going to be featuring Washington wines?"

"Of course. And those from Oregon and British Columbia. Obviously, we'll have selections from California, France and other places, but our focus is regional."

The next two hours were a blur of introductions and sound bites to sell the restaurant. Cal stayed close except when she ducked into the kitchen to check on things. When she returned to the dining room, it was to find Naomi leading Gloria Buchanan toward her.

They were an odd couple. Gloria was small, with white hair and piercing blue eyes. Her clothes cost more than the national debt of several small island nations. Naomi towered over her, six feet of Amazon beauty. Her wavy dark hair fell down her back, and her green eyes seemed to laugh at the world. But it was the heart tattoo on her bare shoulder and the way her breasts moved in the black halter top that really caught one's attention.

"Lookee who I found," Naomi said, releasing Gloria's arm and grinning. "Don't you know her?"

Gloria adjusted the sleeve of her winter-white wool suit jacket and sniffed. "Who is this person?" she demanded.

"Hello, Gloria," Penny said, forcing a smile. Gloria had made it very clear she would never forgive

Penny for leaving her precious grandson. After all, in Gloria's mind, marriage to a Buchanan was a pinnacle few could hope to achieve. "Nice to see you. This is my friend Naomi."

Gloria glanced at the other woman, then turned back to Penny. "If you say so."

"Oh, Penny and I go way back," Naomi said cheerfully. "We met while she was still at the culinary institute. I was her next-door neighbor and she came over to complain that I was making too much noise."

Penny winced, knowing what was to come.

Naomi lowered her voice. "It was the sex. I have this thing for younger men and that can get kinda noisy. I felt really bad. But Penny was great about it and we became friends."

Gloria's expression didn't change, but her mouth tightened. It was what gave her away—a trait she shared with her grandson.

Cal joined them. Gloria looked at him. "Do you know this woman?" she demanded, pointing at Naomi.

Cal groaned. "Oh, yeah."

Naomi sighed. "Tell her about the time I saw you naked," she said, then strolled off.

Cal looked from Naomi to his grandmother, then excused himself. Under the circumstances, Penny couldn't exactly blame him. Unfortunately, his action left her alone with Gloria.

"So, Callister hired you," the older woman said, her voice laced with displeasure.

"That he did. I have a three-year contract."

"I see."

"Have you tasted the food?"

Gloria glanced at a passing tray. "I have a delicate stomach."

The insult was so blatant, it was almost funny. Almost. Penny wasn't surprised to hear she wasn't Gloria's first choice. For some reason, the old bat had never liked her and it was hard to feel affection for someone so determined to keep her on the outside.

"Too bad," Penny said. "We're getting rave reviews."

"The food is free, dear. What did you expect?"

Sort of what Penny had thought. Not that she was going to admit it.

"Well, this has been great," she said. "Nice to see you again, but I have to—"

Gloria grabbed her arm. "You won't get him back, you know."

"What?"

"Callister. He's over you. I'm not sure what he ever saw in you."

"Yes, I know. You made that very clear." Penny pulled her arm free and wished her mother had been just a little less insistent on one being polite to one's elders.

Cal might have let her go without a whimper, but Gloria had practically had a party to celebrate the divorce. At least that's what Reid had told her.

"You were never right for him," Gloria said. "You never cared enough. What kind of woman walks out on her marriage?"

The unfairness of the accusation caused Penny to abruptly excuse herself. As she walked away, she found herself wanting to turn around and announce that she *had* cared. She'd loved Cal with her whole heart. She would have done anything for him—anything but not have a child. Having a family of her own was the one thing she wouldn't compromise on.

"Stupid old woman," she muttered, then grabbed a cup of bisque from a passing waiter and drank it down.

"I saw the smoke so I came running."

Penny turned and saw Reid behind her. She leaned against him. "Your grandmother is horrible. I'd forgotten how bad."

"No one ever really forgets about her. You just repressed the memory. We all do. It's how we survive."

He wrapped both arms around her and kissed the top of her head. "The party is great. People are raving about the food. I think you're a hit."

"I hope so."

"How are you feeling?" he asked, his voice low.

"I have a horrible craving for orange sherbet. I'm surrounded by all this amazing food and that's all I can think about."

"Pretty sick."

"That's what I'm thinking."

Cal walked up, dragging Naomi behind him.

"Do something," he told Penny. "She's asking my opinion about waiters."

"There are so many to choose from," Naomi said, suddenly focused on Reid. "Well, hello. You didn't head off to spring training."

"Not this year."

"That's too bad. I always enjoy watching you work. You move really well."

Penny shivered. "Stop it. You guys are my friends. I can't deal with this."

Reid flashed her a grin. "You're going to have to get over it." He held out his hand to Naomi. "Shall we?"

"We shall."

They strolled off together.

Penny watched them go. "I don't know which one to worry about. I suppose it's been inevitable. They've known each other for years. But Reid was always coming or going and Naomi…" She paused. "I'm not sure why she waited this long. At least she'll help keep his mind off the season starting."

"Nothing against your friend, but no woman could do that."

"Then she'll be a distraction."

Cal shrugged. "Probably."

"Naomi can handle him. She can handle anyone."

"She's had the practice."

Penny was about to take offense for her friend when she realized Cal wasn't talking to her. Oh, he'd faced her and was therefore pointing in the right direction, but his attention was far more on her chest than her face.

She'd never had the kind of body that commanded men's attention and it felt good to have it now. Twisted, but good.

"Shall we?" she asked, pointing to the crowd.

"Why not?"

They dived back in.

CAL WOKE UP in a great mood. The party the previous night had gone well and he was expecting a lot of positive press from the event. Even more important, people would talk about Penny's food and that would bring in customers as much as any article. If the opening went as smoothly as the party, then he would have achieved the success he wanted in four months and he could bow out and return to The Daily Grind.

He showered, shaved and was about to pick out his clothes for the day when his phone rang. He glanced at the clock. Who the hell would be calling at ten past seven in the morning?

He instantly thought of Walker. Had something happened to his brother? He reached for the phone.

"Dammit, Cal, this is your fault," Penny yelled before he had a chance to say hello. "Get down here right now. To the restaurant," she added. "I mean it. You have twenty minutes." Then she hung up.

A push, but he made it with forty-five seconds to spare. Whatever the crisis was, he planned to have a little talk with her about manager-chef relationships. She might be in charge of the kitchen but that didn't make her boss of the world.

He pulled into the parking lot and circled around back. As he'd suspected, the morning deliveries were stacked outside the rear of the building. Penny stood there with a very tousled Naomi at her side.

He didn't want to think about what Naomi had done with her night. Not when his brother was involved. So he parked and climbed out of his car. Penny saw him and raced toward him.

"Smell this," she said, thrusting a large piece of fish in his face. "Smell it."

He inhaled, then wished he hadn't. Good fish shouldn't have a smell at all. Old fish smelled fishy. This fish smelled as if it had died three weeks ago.

"It's all crap," she said, her eyes bright with temper, her cheeks blazing as red as her hair. "You could tie the celery in knots and it wouldn't break. The shallots are practically a liquid. Crap. Did I tell you? Did I say there was a reason this restaurant had closed? Did you listen?"

She sucked in a breath. "Do you know how many reservations we have for tonight? The house is full. Full. Starting at six and going through until ten, we have every seat taken. We're talking about dinner for just over three hundred. You want to know how much food I have? None. None! I have a damn box of cornstarch and three leeks and I have to provide dinner for three hundred."

"Penny—"

She ignored him. "I said they could screw up one time. Well, they have. I'll get my own people in here, which is great, but I still have dinner for three hundred tonight. I want someone's head on a platter. I want it now and I want it raw. I'll cook it myself."

With that she turned on her heel and stalked into the restaurant.

He was equally torn between admiring her spirit and dealing with the disaster at hand.

Naomi stared at him. "Don't go there, big guy. You already screwed that one up once."

Cal ignored that. "Tell the guy to pack up and send

it all back." He would call later and cancel the contract, but right now there was a bigger problem. Dinner for three hundred.

He went into the restaurant and found Penny in the cold storage, taking inventory.

"I have shrimp," she said, a note of hysteria in her voice. "Great. If we cut them in half, then everyone gets a serving. Fabulous. Come to The Waterfront and enjoy half a shrimp." She turned and saw him. "Get out of my way."

"I want to help."

"You will. Tell me you drive something bigger than that expensive toy."

"I have a full-sized truck."

"Good. Go get it. Dress dirty. We're going to Pike Place Market. But first I'm calling my fish people and finding out what they can do for me." She winced. "They're going to charge a lot for a last-minute order."

"We'll pay." He moved close and grabbed her shoulders. "I'm sorry the delivery was crap, but we'll handle this. We can do an opening night chef's menu and pretend it was our plan all along."

"I know, but you have the easy part. You just have to print it out on the computer and slip it into the menus. I have to figure it all out and then make sure we have enough food, then cook it."

"You can do it."

"There's an assumption."

He saw the doubt in her eyes.

He felt her pain and annoyance and couldn't think of a damn thing to make her feel better. She deserved more. Worse, he was partially to blame. He'd insisted on keeping the old vendors.

"I…"

"Yes? Any solution would be welcome."

When he was silent, she sighed. "Yeah, I don't have a miracle up my sleeve, either. Okay, meet us at the market in forty-five minutes," she said. "We'll check out what's available and I'll come up with a menu. Then we'll put it all together and pray that it works."

CHAPTER FIVE

CAL WALKED THROUGH THE dining room at eight-thirty on opening night. Every table was full and there wasn't an empty seat at the bar. Quiet music blended with conversation and laughter from the guests. He could smell the various foods and hear the comments of surprise as people tasted one of Penny's many special dishes.

The disaster had been averted.

Three hours at the market, with everyone running around buying mushrooms, shallots, fish, shellfish and ingredients for salad had produced a Chef's Menu that should fool everyone. He couldn't believe she'd pulled it all together so quickly, but she had.

He crossed the floor and pushed through the swinging door. In contrast to the quiet elegance of the dining room, the kitchen was a loud, bright, crazy house of activity.

"Fire up!" one of the cooks yelled. "Fire up, you skinny-assed sonofabitch."

"Puta," the other man replied without looking up from his pan where he sautéed shrimp with various vegetables.

"Table three. I'm waiting on bisque," Naomi yelled from the front. "Bisque, ladies. How hard is that?"

Another chef pushed a full bowl toward her. She grabbed it, put it on a tray, expertly turned, then hustled out into the dining room.

Cal moved next to Penny who watched everything anxiously. She fingered the orders lined up and then turned to him. "What's the next seating?" she asked.

"Two tables of four are going to open up in about five minutes."

"Okay, once they're seated, switch the menu." She shook her head. "I hate this."

"I know. I'm sorry."

"Ha. Like that helps me now."

He was just as pissed as she was, but figured there was no point in showing it. One of them screaming was enough. But the contracts with the old supplier had already been canceled and the new company would start in the morning. He would be there himself to make sure everything was up to standard. If it wasn't, there would be hell to pay.

"I've never had to do this," Penny said. "It's opening night, Cal. I'm playing fast and loose with the menu. One special order could sink me. I don't need this kind of pressure."

The small printer in the corner spat out three more orders. Penny lunged for them. He sidestepped her and started out of the kitchen. On his way, he passed Naomi.

"She still threatening to kill you?" the other woman asked.

"Not to my face."

"You should have been here earlier." Naomi lowered her voice. "Orange sherbet. Bring her some and she'll be eating out of your hand. Assuming you're into that sort of thing."

He looked at Naomi. "Why are you being nice to me?"

She grinned. "Because sex with your brother was so amazing, I'm feeling at one with the world. I'd say that you should try it, but that's a place neither of us wants to go."

"You got that right."

He left the kitchen and made his way to his office. Leaving the store wasn't an option—not on opening night. But he was management, he knew how to delegate. Once there he picked up the phone and called Reid. "Do me a favor," he said. "Stop at the store on your way over and pick up some orange sherbet."

IT WAS AFTER MIDNIGHT before the last guests had left, the kitchen had been cleaned and the staff clocked out. Penny sat at a round table for six, her feet propped on a chair, her lower back aching.

Every cell in her body groaned with exhaustion. She'd been at the restaurant since shortly after six. Eighteen-hour days weren't all that uncommon in the business, but she was pregnant and apparently that changed things.

"You did good," Dani told her. "I was impressed."

"Thanks. I just never wanted to have to replace menus partway through the evening."

Talk about doubling the work in the kitchen. But they'd done it. Their first night in business was a hit.

Hugh, Dani's husband, raised his glass of wine in her direction. "To Penny—chef extraordinaire."

"To Penny."

Everyone joined in. Penny smiled. "Thanks. I appreciate it. Now one of you volunteer to take care of my shift tomorrow and I'll be really grateful."

"Not a good idea," Naomi said from her place next to Reid. "You're the talented one."

"That is the rumor."

Penny picked up her glass of water. She'd been fake-drinking her wine for nearly half an hour and was ready to give up the game. Half the people at the table knew the truth. She did, of course. Naomi and Reid. Which left Dani, Hugh and Cal as the only ones who didn't.

Penny looked at Dani and her husband. Dani sat on her husband's lap, her legs hanging over the arm of his wheelchair. Hugh was tall and muscled, a former star football player at the University of Washington. He'd been injured his senior year, a hit gone wrong paralyzing him from the waist down. Dani had stuck by him through his recovery and rehab, her love never wavering.

Penny didn't know anything about their sex life, although with Hugh's injuries it was unlikely to be completely conventional. What would happen when they wanted children?

On the off chance word of her pregnancy might send Dani to a bad place, Penny decided to keep the news to herself for now. She would have to come clean with Cal sooner rather than later, but not tonight.

Speaking of Cal—she turned her attention to her ex-husband. She was still pissed off that he'd insisted she use his suppliers who had then totally screwed her, but she had to admit he'd taken the fall like a gentleman and had done everything he could to help. He'd always been a great guy to have around in an emergency. It was the day-to-day stuff he wasn't so good at.

"Your fish and chips were a hit," Cal said, with a nod of his head. "I bow to your superior cooking skills."

"As you should," Naomi told him.

"It's our first victory," Penny said. "Let's hope there are others that follow."

He stood. "I need some more wine," he said. "Anyone want any?"

There was a chorus of *no*s. Cal had a feeling the party was going to break up soon. Both Dani and Hugh had to be up early, and Reid and Naomi were looking at each other like sharks eyeing bait. He guessed they'd be heading out shortly to do things he didn't want to think about.

He nudged Penny's chair. "Come into the kitchen for a second," he said.

She pushed herself to her feet and followed him. "If we've got rats, I don't want to know."

"It's a restaurant in an old building. What do you think?"

She shuddered. "I know it's inevitable, but I don't want to see them."

"I've got a great exterminator."

"You'd better. I hate rats. It's the tails. They're so scaly looking. Why can't their tails be furry?"

"Not my department."

He crossed to the freezer and stepped inside. The carton Reid had brought earlier was right where Cal had left it. Orange sherbet didn't sound the least bit like anything Penny—the queen of fussy eating— would want, but Naomi was too happy with Reid to lie. So he pulled out the container and slapped it on the counter.

"I heard you had a taste for this," he said. "It's my way of saying thanks for doing a hell of a job tonight."

Penny took a step back. "Who told you to buy this?"

"Naomi. I think she felt bad because I heard you planning to kill me."

Penny grabbed a bowl and a spoon. "I only threatened to take out your liver. There's a difference."

"It's a subtle one."

"Want some?"

"No, thanks. Not my favorite flavor."

"More for me."

She scooped out the sherbet and pushed the carton toward him so he could put it away. When he stepped back into the kitchen, she'd raised herself onto the stainless-steel counter and was happily chowing down on sherbet that was a very unnatural color of orange.

"Couldn't you just drink juice?" he asked.

"Not the same."

"If you say so." He leaned against the counter opposite hers. "You did good tonight."

"Thanks. You did okay, too."

He chuckled. "Gee, thanks. You still mad?"

"Not so much. Everything worked out." She raised

her head. "I'm good at my job, Cal. That's why you hired me."

"I know."

"Then stay the hell out of my way. Do I come into the dining room and tell you how to fold napkins?"

"There's more to my job than that."

"You get my point."

"I do and it's well taken. The kitchen is your responsibility."

"Except for the rats."

"Fine. The rats are mine," he said.

She licked her spoon. "Gloria didn't come. I thought she might."

"She was here last night."

"Oh, I know."

He frowned. "Did she bother you?"

Penny shrugged. "Was she breathing?"

"Want to talk about it?"

"Not really. She's a cold old woman. That hasn't changed. She didn't exactly scare me when we were married, but I never wanted us to be best friends."

"She's not my favorite person."

"That makes me sad," Penny said.

"Why?"

"Because she's family. Your folks are gone. She's the last living member of a previous generation. It's too bad she makes it so hard to love her."

As nothing about his family situation had changed since he and Penny split up, she was dead on in her assessment.

"I think she needs to get laid," Penny said.

Cal winced. "Tell me you're not talking about Gloria."

"It's true. When do you think was the last time the old bird got any?"

"I am *not* going to think about that."

"I'm not asking you to stand in the room and watch. I'm saying she's lonely. It's sad."

"You're being nicer to her than she deserves."

"I have very little to do with her, so it's easier for me. Although last night she really got on my nerves."

"What did she say?"

"What did who say?" Reid asked as he and Naomi walked into the kitchen. "Dani and Hugh bugged out. They said to say good night. We're heading home, too."

"Thanks for coming, baby cakes," Penny said to Reid.

He walked over and kissed her cheek. "You, too, knife girl."

Penny laughed. "Night, Naomi. See you tomorrow."

"Bright and early."

Reid put his arm around her. "Early, at least. I don't think your assistant is going to be getting any sleep tonight."

Naomi smiled. "I like that in a man." As she passed Cal, she patted his arm. "Want to know how many times we did it last night?"

"Not even for money."

Reid made a fist. Cal did the same. They bumped them together.

"Later," Reid called as they left.

When the front door of the restaurant closed, Penny grinned. "So do you think they'll wait until they get back to his place or do you think they'll do it in the car?"

"What is with you? You're on a roll with the sex talk tonight." Was she feeling an itch? He would admit to a need to scratch. After all this time, Penny could still get to him just by being in the same room. "Someone else might think you were issuing an invitation."

She narrowed her gaze. "Don't go there. This is my kitchen and I know where all the knives are. It's just interesting to speculate. Okay, not about Gloria, because I don't want to think about her naked. But with Naomi and Reid. Come on—you have to wonder. They're both out to break the land speed record for most partners in a lifetime."

"Doesn't it get old after a while?"

Penny's eyes brightened. "Are you saying sex gets boring? How interesting."

"No. I'm saying switching partners all the time would get old. I gave up counting conquests about the time I turned twenty-two. The sex is more fun when I'm in a relationship."

He hadn't had any complaints about Penny. She'd been caring and responsive and just adventurous enough to keep him guessing about what was going to happen next.

"I think they both do it because they can," she said. "I'm not sure Naomi's ever met a guy who didn't want her and Reid is just, well, Reid. Women flock to him."

"Not you."

"I know. I always saw him as a friend."

"And after we split up?"

He'd wondered. Had his brother offered comfort?

He'd told himself it wasn't possible. That neither of them would do that to him. Except Reid didn't play by the rules and Penny had wanted revenge.

"Yuck," Penny said, sounding both sincere and annoyed. "Why on earth would I sleep with your brother? It's gross and tacky. It would be like you sleeping with Naomi."

"No, thanks."

"That's my point. Besides, I wouldn't have done that to you."

"Why? I thought you hated my guts."

"I did. But I didn't want you punished."

He thought about the angry fights, the things she'd said to him. "Could have fooled me."

Penny put down her empty bowl. He hadn't understood then and she doubted he would understand now, but she meant what she'd said. She didn't want Cal punished—she'd wanted him to get it. She'd wanted him to love her enough to want to have a baby with her. She'd wanted them to be a family.

Deep in her heart, she believed he loved her but with Gloria always ready to pounce at any sign of emotional weakness, he'd been afraid to show his tender side. Leaving had been a last-ditch attempt to get him to admit that she was important to him. The plan had backfired. Instead of coming after her, he had let her go and decided that being apart permanently was the best course for both of them.

"It was three years ago," she said. "Does it really matter now?"

"Probably not. But speaking of the past, I heard an interesting story about you the other day."

Uh-oh. "From who?"

"Gloria."

"Then it's probably not true."

"She said you'd stabbed one of your cooks when he wouldn't do what you said."

Penny laughed. "Actually, that *is* true." She giggled at Cal's shocked expression. "Well, sort of."

"What happened?"

"This guy was bugging me. He didn't like that I'd been promoted over him. You know how guys are in the kitchen. Every word is profane and it's a giant power play. The guy had been backing me into the corner and touching me. I told him to stop it or I'd make him stop it."

She paused as Cal stiffened. "Don't get all macho on me. I mean it. I took care of him."

"How?"

There was anger in that word. His hands curled into fists and he looked ready to take on the world.

His reaction was that of a man to a woman in jeopardy. She liked that he was still one of the good guys, even if he wasn't good for her.

"I didn't exactly have a plan. One day I was cutting up chicken. Someone called to me. I turned, just as the guy moved close. I don't think he meant to do anything. It was a small kitchen and really crowded. Anyway, I was holding the knife and someone bumped me from behind. I fell forward, so did the knife, which slid neatly between his ribs."

She shrugged. "I didn't hit anything vital and even though I told the police it was an accident and everyone backed me up on that, all the guys in the kitchen thought I'd done it on purpose. Including him."

"What happened when he came back?"

"He called me ma'am."

Cal grinned. "Good for you. Now you have a reputation for being a tough boss."

"Now I have a reputation for being a dangerous bitch who'll take out your eye if you talk back to her. I like that. It makes my job easier. I wonder how Gloria heard about it?"

"She hears everything."

"Ah. A network of spies to admire."

Penny was suddenly aware of the quiet of the evening. Except for the guy cleaning up the dining room they were alone. It was late, she was tired and that made her vulnerable to Cal's appeal.

Dangerous, she thought. It was past time for her to head home.

"It's late," he said.

"So I was just thinking."

"You head out. I'll lock up."

"Okay."

She jumped down from the counter. He moved toward her.

It was one of those moments when good sense seemed highly overrated.

"What are you thinking?" he asked.

"Nothing."

"Liar."

Despite the tension, she grinned. "Yeah. But I'm cute when I do it."

They moved closer until they were almost touching. And then they were in each other's arms, his mouth on hers.

Several things occurred to her at once, the foremost being that the man could still kiss like the devil. Even with his lips only lightly pressing hers, she felt shivers and heat and need. Second, her breasts were so exquisitely sensitive—probably from a combination of abstinence and the pregnancy—she suspected if he'd simply touch her tight nipples she would explode into orgasm.

She wanted to throw her arms around him and give in to the moment. She wanted to crawl inside of him and see how much two-become-one they could muster. But then that pesky third thought crept into her brain.

This was not a good idea.

She wanted it to be, but it wasn't. Smart people did not get involved with their ex-husbands at work. Not even ones who were only sticking around for a few months.

She gathered every ounce of strength and stepped back.

His arms looked inviting and she wouldn't mind more pressing her sex-starved body against his. But then what? Did she really plan to get naked with him? Ignoring the whole working together issue, the second he saw her without clothes, the secret would be out. She might be able to disguise her condition behind loose shirts at work, but in the nude, she was obviously pregnant.

Not exactly how she wanted to tell him, she thought.

"You still have it," he said, his eyes dilated, his voice low.

"You, too."

"Not a good idea. Mixing work and..."

She nodded. "So I guess I'll, ah, go."

She headed for her office where she grabbed her purse and keys. "See you in the morning."

He walked her to the back door. "Come in later. I'll be here at seven to check on the delivery. If there's a problem, I'll call. Otherwise, you get some sleep."

The concept was too heavenly to ignore. "Thanks. You have to check the fish. Sniff it. You shouldn't be able to smell anything."

He smiled. "I know how to buy fish, Penny. I've done this before."

"So you say."

She hesitated, suddenly wanting something more but not sure what it was. A connection? Closure?

Whatever it was, she and Cal had already had their chance and messed it up big time. There was no going back.

TWO WEEKS LATER Cal ran the numbers a second time, then tossed the report in the air. "Damn, we're good," he said. They were already thirty percent above their income projections. Profits were only up eighteen percent, but that was because Penny insisted on large portions of expensive ingredients. As much as he hated to admit it, she was onto something.

Someone knocked on his open door. He glanced up, then waved in the young woman standing there.

Tina was still in street clothes, her coat and handbag over her arm. She held her punch card.

"You said you wanted to see me?" she asked.

Rather than asking her to sit, he stood, then pointed at the clock on his wall.

"Care to tell me what that says?" he asked.

"Five-fifteen."

"Right. Your shift starts at five."

Tina sighed heavily. "I know, but there was traffic."

Something that happened every night, he thought. "You know the rules. No unexcused tardiness, Tina. You call and give us notice or you show up on time."

She stared at him. "Are you kidding? You're mad 'cuz I'm fifteen minutes late?"

"I'm not mad. You're not in trouble. You're fired."

Her mouth opened, then closed. "For fifteen minutes?"

"You were told the rules when you were hired. You had to sign a copy of them along with your application. Call if you're going to be late or lose your job." He bent down and picked up her paycheck. "I'll walk you out."

"Don't bother."

She jerked the check from his hand and sailed out. He heard grumbling, which he ignored, then returned to his seat. Penny walked in.

"Someone's unhappy. One of the waiters just left in a huff."

"Tina. She was fired."

"For what?"

He nodded at the clock.

Penny took the chair opposite his and sighed. "I do that, too. Fire 'em for being late. You have to or no one believes you mean it. Call and let me know what's going on, just don't leave me hanging. I sure can't afford to be wondering if I'm going to be short-handed for the night."

"So we agree."

"About that." She smiled. "Don't get your hopes up. I'm here to complain."

Why wasn't he surprised? Penny had earned her reputation as a perfectionist. Three days ago she'd come in saying that the flowers on the table smelled too much—their scent interfered with the aromas from the food. She demanded excellence and wouldn't accept anything less.

"What's wrong now?" he asked.

"The wine list sucks."

"Agreed, but I'm working on it."

She leaned forward. In her white chef's coat and headscarf, she looked both professional and completely feminine. An intriguing combination.

"I have a plan," she said, her voice low.

"I'm not going to like it."

"You don't know that yet." She glanced over her shoulder, as if checking to make sure no one was eavesdropping, then smiled. "Raid the wine cellar at

Buchanan's. I sent someone over to check it out and it's fabulous."

"I'm not cannibalizing from one of the family's restaurants."

"Why not? We don't care about them. The Waterfront is what matters. Just take half of all the good stuff. The wine list here is too young. We don't have any really expensive wines. You know how diners love to impress each other with the pricey stuff. We're going to lose their business, along with the serious wine lovers. Come on, Cal. You have pull. You could do it."

"I could, but I won't. And before you start calling me names, read this."

He took a piece of paper off his desk and handed it to her. Then he leaned back and prepared to enjoy the groveling.

She scanned the sheet, then looked at him. "What happened?"

"Two restaurants went out of business. I heard about them first and bought up their wine lists. Both were excellent. And you wanted to say what about that?"

She grinned. "You're the best."

"And?"

She sighed and reclined in her chair, the back of one hand to her forehead. "You're smart and funny and I'm just so lucky to work for you. Oh, I can barely breathe from the excitement of just sitting close to you."

"Yeah, yeah."

She straightened. "Seriously, this is very cool. I'm impressed."

Her compliment pleased him. She wasn't a woman who impressed easily and she had no reason to be especially nice to him.

Things were so different now, he thought. While he'd liked being married to Penny, she hadn't been very strong back then. He'd worried about her getting hurt. Ironically, he'd been the one to hurt her the most. Now she was tough, and he admired her ability to take charge.

If she'd been like this back then, would they have made it? Or would his secrets still have screwed up things?

Probably the latter, he thought. Penny could forgive a lot, but he doubted she would have understood why he'd been unable to risk loving another child.

Penny pulled a sheet of paper out of her pocket. "I can meet with you tomorrow morning about the group bookings. I'm open to the idea, but I want to start slow. We have to be up and running in the kitchen, with all the kinks worked out before we start feeding fifty at the same time."

"I thought we'd start with a very forgiving crowd. The Daily Grind has an awards luncheon every year in July. We can have that here. I've had calls about a few other things. Two more over the summer and three in September."

"Get me the details on everything and I'll let you know what we can do. The summer ones are fine, and I'll cook for the Daily Grind event as long as I can stand in the back and watch."

"Why would you want to?"

"Professional curiosity. It's your other life."

Why would that interest her? "Sure."

"But we can't schedule anything in September."

He frowned. "Why not?"

"I won't be here."

"For the whole month? You can't do that. We'll only have been open five months."

"I know, but I'm still going to be gone and you can't stop me." She held up a hand to silence him. "This isn't by choice, Cal. Well, technically, I guess it is. I'm not going on vacation. I'm going on maternity leave. I'm going to have a baby."

CHAPTER SIX

CAL'S EXPRESSION DIDN'T CHANGE, but as always, his mouth gave him away. His lips thinned into a line of displeasure while a muscle in his jaw twitched.

"Congratulations."

There was a world of anger in that single word, Penny thought, doing her best not to react. She'd known the news would throw him. The smart thing would be to give the guy a couple of minutes to get used to the idea.

"Thank you."

"I didn't know you were seeing someone." His mouth tightened. She had a feeling he was thinking about their kiss.

"I'm not. There isn't anyone in my life right now."

"What about the baby's father?"

"He isn't involved."

He looked both angry and disapproving, which really annoyed her.

"My condition doesn't have anything to do with you," she told him. "I'm fully capable of doing my job while pregnant. It's been a couple of centuries since women had to disappear from public life while in a delicate condition."

"Doing your job is the least of it."

He stood and walked toward her. She rose so they remained eye to eye…sort of.

"You deliberately kept this information from me when I offered you the job," he said.

"I didn't mention it because I knew you'd freak out if you knew."

"I'm not freaking out. I'm pissed off. How far along are you?"

"Four months." She glared at him. "Me being pregnant doesn't change how good I am in the kitchen."

"As a chef, you're on your feet for twelve hours a day. You can't do that pregnant. How are you supposed to taste the dishes? Aren't there certain types of fish you should avoid? What about wine?"

"I can taste both the food and the wine. One bite or one sip isn't the issue. I'm perfectly capable and I'm doing a damn good job, so get off of me."

He loomed over her. "You lied to me. You withheld material information. I can fire your ass for that and we both know it."

She opened her mouth, then closed it. He had a point. If she'd been in his position and had learned an employee lied about something this big, she would escort them to the door without thinking twice.

"I'm the reason this place is successful," she said, deliberately lowering her voice. "I do good work. Yes, you can fire me, but then what? You think this place can survive losing its chef two weeks after opening?"

She stared at him, willing him to understand. "I have this all figured out. I can do the job and be pregnant. We're in this together, Cal. Don't get weird on me now."

"Don't pretend we're a team when you're keeping secrets like this," he said. "Anything else you want to spring on me?"

"No."

"Fine. I'll be back in a couple of hours."

"But we've just opened. It's dinner."

"So? According to you, you have a plan. Deal with it." Then he turned and walked out.

CAL DROVE without thinking and he wasn't surprised when he found himself in front of Reid's place. He tossed his keys to the valet, then stalked into the crowded bar.

What the hell was going on? Penny pregnant? He knew she'd always wanted kids—she'd made that clear enough times. But now?

He saw his brother behind the bar and waved him over. Reid spoke to one of the women serving with him, then walked out and joined Cal.

"What's up?" he asked.

Instead of answering, Cal led the way to Reid's office. He pushed inside, then closed the door when his brother had entered.

"You knew about the baby," he said, making the words a statement instead of a question.

Reid looked amazingly unconcerned. "So she finally told you, huh? I warned her you wouldn't take it well. Looks like I wasn't wrong."

"Not take it well? You're right. I didn't. What the hell happened? Did you encourage this?"

Reid frowned. "Hey, slow down. Why does it matter to you that Penny's pregnant? You let her go a long time ago."

"That has nothing to do with this." He didn't care who his ex-wife slept with, or what she did with her personal life. He was just furious that she would go and get herself pregnant.

Reid leaned against the edge of his messy desk. "Look, it's no big deal. Penny's been thinking about having a baby for a long time. She's always wanted a family."

Cal knew exactly just how long she'd been thinking about it. He didn't even have to close his eyes to see her curled up next to him on the sofa, her hand on his thigh as she leaned close and whispered, "Let's try again, Cal. Let's have a baby."

"She hit thirty and realized she'd better get going," Reid continued.

Cal grabbed him by the front of his shirt. "Is it you? Did you sleep with her?"

His normally laid-back brother instantly stiffened. Reid's hand covered his own in a grip that both punished and threatened.

"I'm going to give you ten seconds to take that back, then I'm going to wipe the floor with you," Reid growled.

"What makes you think you could?"

The two men glared at each other. Reid backed off first. He released Cal and raised both hands in the air.

"No one slept with Penny," Reid said. "It wasn't like that."

Cal released him. "What do you mean?"

"There's no guy. Penny went to a sperm bank.

You know, one from column A, one from column B. She picked the sperm out of a computer list. Crazy if you ask me, but she didn't." Reid poked him in the chest. "Why didn't Penny tell you about the in vitro fertilization herself?"

Cal shrugged.

Reid poked him again. "You didn't give her a chance, did you? You jumped to conclusions. Dammit, Cal, why do you always think the worst of people?"

"I don't."

"Sure. You're a regular ray of sunshine. You have to trust people to do the right thing. Penny would never get involved with a guy who would abandon a child, okay?"

Cal took a step back. He didn't know what to say to his brother. Somehow Reid had gotten right to the heart of the matter. That's what Cal couldn't deal with—the thought of a man walking out on his own child. Because an adult would have choices—choices he hadn't had at seventeen.

"You're right," Cal said. "Good point. I, ah… thanks for explaining things."

His brother leaned back against the desk again and folded his arms over his chest. "You're pretty screwed up, you know that?"

"Tell me something I don't know."

"We all are. Thanks to Gloria." Reid shook his head. "That bitch. The things she made us do. Always threatening us. So many damn secrets." He looked at Cal. "Penny wants this baby. She'll be a good mom."

"That's not the point."

"Isn't it? Are you all jacked up because of Lindsey?"

Cal stared at his brother, unable to believe what he'd just heard.

"You know?" he asked, his voice harsh with shock. Reid nodded.

It had been seventeen years and Cal had never discussed his daughter with anyone in his family. Gloria had known—she always knew everything. While his high school girlfriend had been content to give the child up for adoption, Cal had wanted more for his daughter. He'd wanted to take care of her himself. But he'd been a senior in high school, with no way to support a kid, let alone raise one.

Then Gloria had offered. Cal could keep his child, but she, Gloria, would raise the infant.

Every fiber of his being had rebelled against that. She'd forced his hand and he'd given in to the idea of adoption.

He still remembered signing the papers. How wrong everything had felt. He'd been a few weeks shy of his eighteenth birthday—too old to cry. But he'd wanted to. He'd wanted to take the baby and run. Only the kindness of the adopting couple had allowed him to give Lindsey away.

"How did you find out about her?" Cal asked. "No one knew."

"Maybe no one was supposed to, but Walker and I both did. We heard you arguing with Gloria about it. I don't think Dani knows. She was pretty young."

"You never said anything."

"Why would we? It was your decision. Walker

and I talked about what we would do if it was us. We agreed we both would have given up the kid without a second thought."

"Easy to say when it hasn't happened to you."

"Maybe." Reid shrugged. "Then it was done and we figured it was your secret to keep. If you wanted to talk, you knew where to find us."

Reid seemed casual enough, but Cal wondered if there was more to it. A sense of betrayal that he hadn't trusted his brothers with a decision that big.

"I was the oldest," he said awkwardly.

"Right. Set a good example. Don't tell your younger brothers you knocked up your girlfriend. We got that. We both became poster guys for safe sex. Don't worry, big brother. Your experience served us well."

Cal supposed that was something.

"How old is she now? Fifteen? Sixteen?" Reid asked.

"Seventeen. She's a senior in high school."

"You keep in touch with the family?"

"With the parents. They send me pictures and letters a couple of times a year. Lindsey knows she's adopted, but isn't interested in her birth parents." Not that her birth mother cared. Alison had given birth, graduated and moved back east. Cal had never heard from her again and suspected she had no interest in the child she'd given away.

"I always felt bad," Reid said. "You didn't want to let her go."

Now it was Cal's turn to shrug. "I didn't know how I could take care of her."

"You did the right thing. You always do. It was a hell of a characteristic to have thrown in my face over and over again."

"Thanks for not holding it against me."

"No problem. But here's the thing. Maybe it's time to do the right thing for Penny. She didn't get pregnant just to mess with your mind."

"I'm sure she sees that as a fun bonus."

"Maybe. But she wants this baby. You should respect that and get off her ass about it."

His brother had a point. "I'll think about it."

"You do that. Want a beer?"

"No, thanks. I need to get back to the restaurant."

He made a fist. Reid did the same, then they banged them together.

"Hang in there, big brother," Reid said. "This isn't your kid. You don't have to sweat what goes on this time."

"Yeah. Thanks."

Cal walked out of the office and headed for the front door. When the valet had retrieved his car, Cal drove back toward the restaurant.

Too much had happened too fast, he thought. Penny being pregnant. Learning that Reid and Walker knew about his daughter.

He remembered the fights he and Gloria had had back then. How he'd screamed at her with all the fury of a seventeen-year-old being denied something precious. It was amazing everyone in the neighborhood hadn't heard. But his brothers hadn't said anything. They'd waited for him to go to them, and he never had.

He should have. They would have understood. Especially three and a half years ago when his marriage had been unraveling. Penny had been pressuring him to emotionally engage, to have a baby with her, to be in their marriage. He'd been holding her as far away as he could while he dealt with the horror of knowing his only daughter had been diagnosed with acute myeloid leukemia.

For three months he'd waited to hear what would happen. Lindsey's adoptive parents had kept him informed at every stage of her treatment. He remembered the agony of not knowing if the chemo would work. Wondering if his daughter was going to live or die and then the joy when Lindsey had beaten the disease.

Should he have told Penny about her? At the time he'd known he couldn't. She would never have understood how he could care so much about a child he had with someone else and yet be unwilling to have a baby with her. He hadn't known how to explain he was afraid of losing Lindsey all over again.

So she'd pushed for more and he'd retreated until eventually she'd walked out. Her leaving had seemed like the best thing for both of them.

He entered the restaurant and spoke with his assistant manager, then he walked to the kitchen. As always, the level of noise filled his head with shouts, the hiss of the steamer, the roar of the grill.

"Three more salmon," one of the waiters called as he put down a tray. "The lady wants to know what you put in the sauce."

Penny looked up, saw him and turned her attention to the waiter. "Sorry, it's a secret. But I promise if I ever publish a cookbook, I'll put the recipe in the first chapter."

When the waiter left, Penny glanced at Cal. "You left during dinner."

"I know."

Her expression told him not to do it again, but she didn't say the words. Penny was too good for that. She wouldn't chew his ass in front of her staff.

But she wanted to and under the circumstances, he couldn't blame her.

"We need to talk," he told her. "Around ten?"

"Sure. I'll be the one in the chef's coat."

BY NINE-FIFTEEN, things had quieted down. They'd worked through all their reservations and there were a few empty tables in the dining room. Cal retreated to his office to catch up on paperwork before his meeting with Penny. He wasn't sure what he was going to say to her. He wanted to apologize for overreacting, but he couldn't tell her about Lindsey. Not when she'd just told him she was pregnant. He wanted to make things right with her before he dropped that bombshell.

He sat at his desk, but instead of turning on his computer, he leaned back in his chair and remembered the first time Penny had told him she was pregnant. Neither of them had planned for it. Sometimes birth control failed.

He'd been stunned—first by complete happiness and then by guilt. Because he would get to keep this child. He would experience everything he'd missed with Lindsey. What if he loved his child with Penny more than Lindsey?

He hadn't known where to get answers to his questions, or who to trust with his confusion. So he hadn't said anything. Eventually Penny had noticed that as time went on, he seemed less and less thrilled. She couldn't understand why he'd held back. But then she'd never held back in her life.

"Knock, knock."

Cal turned and saw Gloria standing in the doorway to his office. He held in a groan. Yeah, right, because he needed more stress in his day.

"You're not supposed to be here," he told his grandmother.

Gloria swept into the small space and claimed the only other chair. "I don't know why you think I spend my life micromanaging. Nothing could be further from the truth. I'm just here because I want to see my grandson. Is there anything wrong with that?"

There wouldn't be, if he believed her. But he didn't. Gloria always had a purpose and a motive.

"Fine," he said. "If this is strictly a social visit, then you won't have anything to say about the restaurant."

She pressed her lips together. "I did notice a few things."

He stared at her. She exhaled slowly.

"I won't mention them. Although why you don't want constructive criticism is beyond me. I would think you would *want* the restaurant to be the best it can be."

"Nice try, but I'm not biting."

"Oh, all right." She shrugged out of her coat. "I just wanted to let you know that Daniel quit."

He stared at her. "Who's Daniel?"

"Daniel Langstrom. The president of the company. Honestly, Callister, can't you even pretend interest? He wouldn't say why he left. It's very inconvenient. He's the third one to leave in fifteen months. The executive searches are very expensive. Not to mention time-consuming. One would think the search firms could bring better candidates."

"The search firms aren't the problem, Gloria," Cal said. "You are. You're hell to work for."

Gloria stiffened. "I beg your pardon. You can't talk to me like that. It's rude and vulgar."

"Maybe, but it's true. You add new intensity to the term *micromanage.* You've never met an order you didn't want to tweak or change or countermand. You get in the way, you change your mind fifteen times a day and you make everyone around you wish they were dead."

She paled. "That's not true."

"Haven't you noticed how difficult it is for you to keep an executive assistant, let alone a company president? You drove me away years ago. Reid and Walker never even bothered to try. You need to back off or there won't be anyone left at the company."

"That's ridiculous. You're exaggerating. Regardless, I want you to take over the job as president."

He would rather be shark bait. "No, thanks. I have a job."

"At that coffeehouse." She made it sound as if he sold acid milk shakes to children.

"You got it. I like it there, Gloria. I'm proud of what I do." He stopped, reminding himself he was never going to convince her.

"This is your heritage," she said. "You're a Buchanan."

"Not interested. No one is, except Dani. God knows why you haven't been able to scare her off, but she's still hanging on. Give her a shot."

Gloria sniffed. "That's impossible. She's not one of us. Not a Buchanan. She is her mother's daughter and I will never forgive her for that."

"My mother had an affair nearly thirty years ago. You need to let it go."

"Never." Gloria's eyes blazed with anger. "She betrayed my son. Don't you care that she made a fool of your father?"

He wasn't happy about it, but he found it hard to get worked up about it after all this time. "Move on," he said. "Mom and Dad are dead."

"But the proof of your mother's affair lives on."

"You might want to enter this century," he said. "Dani is your granddaughter."

"Never. She's nothing. I allow her to believe she's a Buchanan as a kindness."

"Is that what you call it?"

When he'd graduated from college, Gloria had told him the truth—a twisted sort of present. She'd used the information to blackmail him into going into the family business.

He hadn't wanted to be part of the empire, but she'd threatened to tell Dani she wasn't really one of them. He'd taken that first job at Burger Heaven to make sure his sister didn't know the truth.

Gloria glared at him. "I have been a part of this family since I was eighteen years old. I have sweated blood so that you could have this legacy. I'm the reason this family has wealth."

"We would have been a whole lot better off if you'd simply let it go."

She stood. "You may not care about family, but I do. Your mother destroyed my son with her lies and her deceit."

"None of which is Dani's fault. She's the only one who gives a damn about the company. She's paid her dues. She's good at her job. So cut her a break. Move her up the food chain. Let her prove herself at Buchanan's, or here."

"Never."

Cal felt like punching something, but he'd put his fist through a wall once and it hadn't been a smart idea. "I should tell her myself," he said, more to himself than Gloria.

"But you won't." His grandmother resumed her seat. "You would never hurt your sister like that."

She was right. He wouldn't knowingly hurt Dani. Although he was starting to wonder if not telling her was causing a different kind of pain.

"On a different subject, did you know your executive chef is pregnant?"

He swore. How had she found that out? Less surprising was her need to make trouble.

"Of course," he said, not mentioning he'd only been told that day.

"Oh." Gloria sounded disappointed. "Do you know who the father is?"

"Why does that matter?"

"She's not right for you, Callister. I always thought so. I thought you'd seen it, as well."

"My personal life isn't your business."

Her small eyes zeroed in on his. He knew she was wondering if he was telling her to back off because there was something between him and Penny or just on general principle.

"You never liked her," he said. "Was it something specific about Penny or the fact that you didn't get to handpick my wife?"

"I'm sure I would have done a better job than you did."

That was it. Old lady or not, he'd had enough of her. He stood.

"It's time for you to go."

She collected her coat and rose. "Think about the president's job," she said. "It's an excellent opportunity."

"Not going to happen."

"But, Callister…"

He walked her to the hallway, then firmly closed the door in her face.

CHAPTER SEVEN

PENNY SET OUT HER MEAL in a corner table of the dining room. The kitchen cleanup was nearly finished and while she was tired and ready to head home to bed, she was starving.

At first she'd been so angry at Cal for walking out at the start of dinner, she hadn't been able to think about eating. Then she'd gotten busy and then the evening had been over. So she planned to make up for lost time.

She had a large plate of the batter-fried fish from her infamous fish and chips, a second plate with garlic smashed potatoes and a huge bowl of salad made with every vegetable she'd been able to dig up. There was enough to serve six or eight people, but sometimes she forgot how to cook for one.

She'd kind of thought Naomi would join her, but her friend had rushed off to warm Reid's bed. Penny had always known they would eventually hook up and when they did, she would feel the temporary loss as her two closest friends entered a world of their own. She just hadn't been expecting it now.

Cal walked into the dining room. She ignored him and began to fill her plate. He walked toward her.

"We had a good night," he said.

She nodded.

"Numbers are still above projections."

"You sound surprised," she said.

"I am. I hope we can sustain the momentum."

"No reason we can't. The location is good, the food better. What's not to like?"

He grinned. "You always did look on the bright side."

"Beats the alternative."

"Want company?"

She looked at him then, at the handsome lines of his face and faint curve of his mouth. He wasn't mad anymore and neither was she. Oh, she could pretend. Given a few minutes, she could work herself into a temper, but to what end?

"Only if you're hungry," she said. "I made a little extra."

"So I see."

He sat next to her and took one of the empty plates. After filling it, he picked up a fork and took a bite of potatoes.

"Still the best," he said.

She shrugged. "Potatoes, garlic, butter, a few spices. You're too easy, Cal."

"I know what I like."

That statement had danger written all over it, so she decided to change the subject. "I saw Gloria was here earlier. Mercifully, she stayed out of my kitchen. What did she want with you?"

"She's trying to badger me into accepting the job of president of the corporation. The third guy in fifteen months just quit."

"If he reports directly to her, I can see why."

"That's what I told her. I said she had to loosen up or she was going to lose everything."

"You'd never do it," Penny said confidently. "You'd hate working for her and you wouldn't want to give up your work with The Daily Grind."

He stared at her. "How do you know that?"

"Am I wrong?"

"No."

She smiled. "Cal, you're a guy. Most of the time, you're not very complex. Although there were a few times you confused the hell out of me." She didn't want to talk about them now. "So what's the big deal? She should offer the job to Dani. She'd jump at the chance to run things and I think she'd do a good job."

"That's what I said, but Gloria won't have any part of it."

Typical, Penny thought. "Gloria's always been horrible where Dani's concerned. What's the problem? What does she have against your sister?"

She expected Cal to brush off the question or say he didn't know. He surprised her by putting down his fork and leaning toward her, then lowering his voice.

"She's not a Buchanan."

Penny couldn't have been more surprised if Cal had morphed into a dancing squid. "Excuse me? She's your sister."

"Half sister. Same mother, different father. My dad was always really distant. He drank—I think having Gloria as his mother drove him to it. I don't remember all that much about their marriage, but they never seemed happy or like other couples. At some point, she met someone else and had an affair. Dani was the result. I first found out about it when I graduated from college. I'd never guessed. None of us had."

Penny instinctively reached for his hand and took it in her own. "That's not possible. Of course Dani is one of you."

"No. She's completely different. Her looks, her personality. Also, look at how Gloria treats her. Dani thinks it's because she's a girl, but it's more than that."

Penny thought about the years she and Cal were married and interacting with the rest of the Buchanan family. Gloria was rude and difficult with everyone, but there was a special level of awfulness in her contact with Dani. It was almost…contempt.

"No," Penny said, more to herself than Cal. "Family is everything to Dani. Being a Buchanan defines her world. The only thing she wants outside of her marriage is to run the corporation."

"Gloria's not going to let that happen."

Penny squeezed his fingers. "Do Reid and Walker know?"

He nodded. "Gloria told them, then used the information to threaten them. Do what I say or I'll tell your sister she's not really part of this family."

Penny's chest tightened. "That's awful. I never liked Gloria, but I never thought she was evil. Poor Dani. You have to tell her."

Cal pulled his hand free and shook his head. "No way. I'm not screwing up her life."

"Her life is already screwed. You're keeping secrets from her, Cal. It's not a good idea. I speak from personal experience."

His gaze dropped to her belly. Without her white coat, her condition was fairly visible. While she doubted he'd noticed her breasts were larger than usual, there was no way he could miss the distinct roundness of her belly.

"I can't tell her. It would hurt too much," he said.

"It's going to hurt more when she finds out another way."

He bit into a piece of fish. She recognized the stubborn set of his mouth and sighed. Fine. She couldn't make him tell Dani, but she could keep on him until he caved.

"I will say this," she told him. "Talking about your family always makes me appreciate my own a lot more."

"How are your folks?" he asked.

"Good. My dad is still busy with the dealership and making both his sons-in-law sweat about who is going to be left in charge."

"Do they know?" he asked, glancing at her midsection.

She touched her stomach. "Yes. I told them about the baby. Actually I told them when I started thinking about getting pregnant. Mom wanted me to wait to get married, but it wasn't a big argument. They've stopped expecting me to be conventional."

"Because you didn't decide to be a stay-at-home mom like Emily and Julie?"

She nodded. Both her sisters had married within two years of finishing high school. Penny had never seen the point of hooking up with a guy, then locking herself in a house and popping out babies. Of course she'd never planned on being a single mom, either.

"I've made my way in a man's world," she said brightly. "As soon as word gets out about the baby, everyone will be really nice to me and if they're not, I'll have Naomi to protect me."

He glanced around the empty restaurant. "She's with Reid tonight?"

"That's my guess. I'm sure they're off having hot monkey sex even as we speak."

Cal grimaced. "Don't go there. It's not an image either of us want in our brains."

She grinned. "You have a point. Naomi is far more sexual than anyone I've ever known."

"Tell me about it. That time she walked in on us, I was sure she was going to offer to join in."

Penny laughed. "If we hadn't been married, I think she might have. Later she told me you were much more impressive naked than she'd ever suspected."

"Great. Not something I needed to know."

"But Naomi is practically a legend," she teased. "Don't you want to know what all the fuss is about?"

"No."

"But, Cal…"

He glared at her. "I'm not interested in having sex with your best friend. Okay?"

"Fine. It's your loss."

"If you want details, ask Reid. I'm sure he'll share."

"No, thanks." Penny enjoyed teasing Cal about Naomi, but she didn't actually want to know what her friend was like in bed. That would just be too weird.

"So if you're not interested in Naomi," she said, "who are you interested in?"

"Asking about my love life?"

"Uh-huh." She suspected there wasn't anyone right now. Cal wasn't the type to have kissed her if he'd been involved.

"I'm between women. And you?"

"You talked to Reid," she said, knowing it was the only place he could have disappeared to so he could get answers. "You know there isn't anyone."

"That's why you chose in vitro?"

"Sure. I got tired of waiting for Mr. Right to show up. Apparently his flight was delayed or he married someone else by mistake."

Cal didn't like the sound of that. Once he'd been her Mr. Right. Of course, that had changed when their marriage had ended.

"Is that what you want?" he asked. "A traditional marriage?"

"Sure. Being a single mom was never part of my master plan. I'm not afraid to do it on my own, but I would have preferred to be part of something more. Still, I can do this."

Penny had always been stubborn about achieving her goals. He didn't doubt her for a second.

"You said September. When?"

"The twelfth. I have the advantage of knowing the actual day I got pregnant."

"Are you okay in the kitchen?"

"Sure. I'll need to sit a little more after my seventh month, but I can still handle things. The pregnancy is one of the reasons I wanted Naomi with me.

She'll help pick up the slack. I'm going to take a short maternity leave, then come back after three weeks."

That surprised him. "Don't you want to stay home longer with the baby?"

"I'm bringing the baby to work with me. Why do you think I took the larger office?"

A baby? Here? "You can't."

"Really? Why not?"

He stared at her and couldn't think of a single reason.

"That's my point," she said. "Why can't I bring in the baby? At least for the first few months. I'm going to be breastfeeding, so I'll need the baby around. I've already lined up a fabulous nanny. She looks like Mrs. Claus. By the time my son or daughter is ready for preschool, I'll have my own restaurant."

She'd always been a planner. "The kid's going to know what a sauté pan is before he or she can walk."

"I hope so."

He ate a forkful of potatoes. Four months along. No wonder her breasts were larger. He held in a grin. Penny would accuse him of being a typical guy for noticing that first.

There would be other changes, he thought, remembering the first time she'd been pregnant. They'd both been so excited. Scared, but happy. Then the guilt had set in and he hadn't known how to handle it.

Telling her about Lindsey made the most sense, but he'd never found the right time or the right words. He'd distanced himself from Penny and the baby growing inside of her. He'd done his best to ignore her increasing size until one day she'd called in tears, her voice thick with terror.

"You were about four months along before," he said, not sure if he should mention the past.

She put more salad on her plate. "I know. I've been thinking about that. My doctor says what happened then was just one of those things. There was probably something wrong with the baby, which was why I lost it. She swears I'm perfectly healthy and there's no reason to think I'll lose this one."

"Are you past the date…?"

"In two weeks."

He didn't have to ask if she was worried. He could see it in her eyes.

Before, she'd been devastated. He remembered holding her as she sobbed for the tiny life lost. He'd felt both stricken and relieved. He wasn't going to have to choose who he would love more—Lindsey or the new baby. But Penny's pain had been too big for her to contain and she'd been inconsolable.

Time had healed, as it always did. Eight months later she'd said they should try again and he'd told her he didn't want children. It had been easier than telling her the truth. That he couldn't deal with one more loss—not with Lindsey battling leukemia.

"We used to do this all the time," Penny said. "Stay up late and talk while the rest of the world went to bed."

"Restaurant hours," he said. "The world is a different place at night."

"I always used to feel sorry for those poor people who had to get up early. I liked staying awake until two or three in the morning. Of course, back then I didn't have to be here to check on deliveries and plan my specials for the day."

He glanced at the still-full serving dishes. "Want to take that home with you?"

"Of course. I'll have it for breakfast."

"Fish? That's disgusting."

"My fish, big guy. And it's delicious."

"Have it."

He stood and walked into the kitchen to collect to-go containers. After she'd scooped everything off the various plates and bowls, they carried the dirty dishes back into the kitchen, then grabbed their coats.

"You need anything?" he asked as he locked the back door and escorted her to her car.

She looked at him. "Oh, great. I told you I was pregnant and you're going to get all mental, aren't you?"

"If mental means worrying about you, then yes."

She paused by her Volvo and leaned against the driver's door. "Not your responsibility."

"You're on my staff."

"You wouldn't be this concerned if your hostess turned up pregnant."

"I didn't used to be married to my hostess."

"As she's barely eighteen, that would have caused talk."

He knew what Penny meant. She was all grown up and didn't need anyone to take care of her. Funny how her independence was so appealing. Before she'd needed so much—and now she didn't.

The lights from the parking lot brought out the red

in her hair. Her blue eyes looked black and mysterious. Her skin seemed lit from within.

"Pregnancy agrees with you," he murmured.

"Don't you dare sweet-talk me. I'm immune."

The challenge made him smile. "Really?"

"Oh, yeah."

After that, he didn't have much choice. He bent down and brushed his mouth against hers.

He half expected her to pull back. Instead she slipped her hands inside his open coat and rested them on his waist. He leaned closer and put the bag of leftovers on the roof of her car, then cupped her face in his hands.

She tilted her head in a silent invitation he had no desire to ignore. Even as he lightly touched his tongue to her bottom lip, she parted for him. He slipped into her mouth and found himself in a sensual paradise he remembered all too well.

She was soft and hot and sweet. Need heated his blood before racing south and making him hard. The wanting increased as he swept his tongue against hers and she shuddered in response.

The fingers at his waist tightened. He heard her moan low in her throat, then the light pressure of her belly and her breasts as she leaned into him. He dropped his hands to her shoulders and squeezed.

The kiss went on until he felt her melting in his embrace. He'd made love with her enough times to know what the quickened breathing meant and to read the invitation in the way she struggled to get even closer. He was hard and getting harder, which didn't seem possible. She was willing, and neither of them were involved.

"Cal," she breathed, pulling back slightly from the kiss.

He slid his hands from her shoulders to her chest, then to her heavy, full breasts.

Her nipples were already hard. He brushed them with his fingers and she groaned. Her eyes slowly closed, her body swayed.

"Don't stop," she whispered. "Oh, yeah. Just like that."

He rubbed his thumbs and forefingers against her nipples, teasing them until her breath caught. Her eyes opened.

"You were always really good at that," she whispered.

"I spent most of my teenaged years practicing through visualization."

She smiled and covered his hands with hers. "There are about fifty reasons why this is a bad idea."

He shifted so he could cover her whole breast, then lightly kissed her mouth. "Give me five."

"I work with you. Fraternizing with the staff is never smart."

He kissed her again. "Is that one or two reasons?" he asked against her mouth.

She bit down on his lower lip, which made his erection pulse painfully.

"Two."

"Okay, three more."

"I'm your ex-wife. Do you really want to go there with me?"

She probably had a point, but right now he didn't care about anything but getting them both naked and easing the ache.

"I'm also pregnant with another man's child," she said, her voice shaky as he dropped his hands to her hips and slid them around so he could cup her ass.

"You being pregnant just means we get to be more creative," he breathed into her ear before nibbling on her lobe and making her squirm.

"We're standing on a parking lot your grandmother owns, there's a question about your sister's paternity, my two best friends are sleeping together and one of them happens to be your brother."

He got the message, even though he wanted to ignore it. Parts of him were very insistent that talking was highly overrated and that they should just get to the naked part. But the mature, intelligent part of him was bigger, and slightly more in charge. He dropped his hands and took a step back.

"You're saying there are complications," he said.

She laughed. "You think?"

He smiled. "You have a point." And of all of them, her being his ex-wife and them not going there made the most sense.

It was strange. Two months ago, he'd never given Penny a thought. Now she was back in his life, if only temporarily, and he was—for the moment at least—interested in getting her into his bed. What did that mean?

Okay, part of what it meant was that he hadn't had any for a while, but part of it was about Penny.

He liked who she'd become and he'd always enjoyed her in bed.

"I'm tempted," she said, raising herself on tiptoe and lightly kissing him. "Very tempted."

"Good."

He stepped back as she climbed into her car. After passing her the leftovers, he waited until she'd driven off before getting into his own car and heading home.

The streets were empty, the drive quick. Good news, because he didn't want too much time to think. Not about Penny or wanting her, or Lindsey or even Dani. He wanted to clear his mind and fall into bed. Tomorrow he would have more answers. Tomorrow—

Cal rounded the corner and saw his house. There were several lights on in the windows and a strange car parked in front. As both Reid and Dani had a key, he figured it could be either one of them. Not Reid, he thought, hoping his brother hadn't brought Naomi over so they could do it in a new location. His cleaning service had just changed the sheets.

But when he pulled into the garage, the door to the house opened. The man standing there was tall and muscled, with a military-short haircut. Cal grinned.

"Walker," he called as he got out of his Z4. "When did you get home?"

"About three hours ago. I picked up a rental car at the airport and drove here. Hope you don't mind me crashing at your place for a few days."

"Stay as long as you like."

They hugged, then walked into the house. Cal led

the way to the kitchen and saw the bottle of Scotch already on the counter.

He grinned at his younger brother. "Just like I raised you."

Walker picked up the bottle and poured his brother a glass. After handing it over, he picked up his own. "You always did keep the good stuff around. I respect that."

They toasted each other silently, then moved into the living room. As always, Walker took the club chair that faced the door and allowed him to sit with his back to the corner of the room.

Cal studied his brother. There were no new visible scars, which was good. Walker looked tired and there was something in his eyes. He'd seen things, done things. It came with a career in the marines.

While Cal had taken a job in the family business after college, both Walker and Reid had escaped. Reid had lived and breathed baseball—when he wasn't living and breathing women—and had never looked back until he'd blown out his shoulder last year.

Walker had gone from his high school graduation straight to the marine recruitment center. He'd shipped out a few weeks after that. Gloria had been furious—not only had she lost another Buchanan, but Walker hadn't gone to college first. He'd entered the military as a grunt.

"How are you?" Cal asked after they both had a chance to sip the Scotch and appreciate the fire Walker had expertly built.

"Good."

"You seeing much action?"

"Some."

Walker had spent much of his past tour in Afghanistan. He sent regular e-mails that didn't say much more than he was fine. There were no details about his day or his assignments.

"How about you?" Walker asked. "You said you'd taken over The Waterfront."

"Only for four months. The place was such a disaster, Gloria closed it."

"Then called you in to rescue her."

Cal shrugged. "It's four months," he repeated. "Then I go back to The Daily Grind."

"Dani and Reid okay?"

Cal nodded. "Dani's still frustrated because Gloria won't let her leave Burger Heaven. Reid's settling into The Downtown Sports Bar. He's popular, which brings in the customers."

"All the waitresses still built and nearly naked?"

"You know Reid."

Walker grinned. "I'll have to stop by."

"We should all meet there. How long's your leave?"

Walker sipped his drink, then put it on the side table and leaned forward. "I left the corps."

Cal stared at him. "Retired?"

"It's been fourteen years, so that's what they're calling it."

Cal couldn't imagine his brother doing anything else. "Why?"

Walker shrugged. "It was time."

"What are you going to do?"

"I'm not sure. I thought I'd stay here for a few days, then go get my own place."

"Sure. Stay as long as you like. I'm working twelve, fifteen hours a day, so I'm never here. And my love life sucks, so you won't get in the way of that."

Walker picked up his drink. "Not seeing anyone?"

"Not in a while." He thought of the kiss he'd shared with Penny and decided that didn't count. If he couldn't explain it to himself, he sure as hell wouldn't be able to explain it to Walker.

"I thought you'd be in until they kicked you out," Cal said. "Are you all right?"

"Fine."

Cal wasn't sure he believed him. There was something about Walker's eyes—something dark.

"Want to talk about it?" he asked.

Walker looked at him. "Have I ever?"

"No. Want to get drunk?"

Walker grinned. "I wouldn't say no."

"Good. I'll call Reid."

"Won't you be interrupting?"

He thought about Reid and Naomi. "Probably," he said cheerfully. "But why shouldn't he suffer, too?"

CHAPTER EIGHT

"I WANT TO SAY it's the salt," Penny said as she picked through the bowl of nuts and fished out the hazelnuts. "But I think it's more than that. If it was just about salt, then any nut would do. The craving is very specific."

She glanced up to see Reid shudder.

"What?" she asked, holding in a laugh. "You don't want to hear about my cravings?"

"Not especially. Some of them have grossed me out."

"This from a guy who used to spit on national television."

Reid wiped another glass and set it behind the bar. "I never spit."

"All baseball players spit."

"Some don't."

"What is up with that, anyway? Why all the spitting? Don't the mothers call and say it's disgusting? Because it is. Yuck." She touched her stomach. "Okay, change of subject. I'm making myself queasy."

"Fine by me."

Lucy came out of the kitchen and walked toward the bar. "Here you go, hon."

Penny took the large root beer float and sighed. "You're a goddess. Thank you."

"Don't thank me. I just turned in the order." Lucy looked at her boss. "Want anything?"

"Not right now. Thanks."

Lucy smiled and walked toward the lone table of customers in the bar.

It was three—that quiet time between lunch and happy hour. Penny knew she had to get back to The Waterfront fairly soon, but she fully intended to indulge herself first.

While Reid watched and pretended to gag, she dumped the hazelnuts into the float, then dug in with a spoon. The combination of cold, fizzy liquid, smooth, melting ice cream and crunchy, salty nut was pure heaven.

"You're just jealous," she said after she swallowed, "because you didn't think of this combination."

"Uh-huh. That's me. Jealous." He leaned back and folded his arms over his chest. "You seen Walker yet?"

"No, and I can't wait to. I was so surprised when Cal told me he'd left the marines. I didn't think that would ever happen." She glanced around the empty bar. "Is he coming here?"

"At some point. You sure are happy about him being home."

She grinned. "I am. And don't worry. I'll never love Walker the way I love you," she teased.

"Like I care about that."

He probably didn't. She and Reid had been friends too long for him to sweat she would ever leave him.

Sometimes she thought that she and Dani were the only consistent females in his life.

"Your real problem is Naomi," she said as she scooped another spoonful of ice cream. "She's never met Walker. You know how women fall for guys in the military."

"It's very possible she'll be interested."

She glanced at Reid. "That's it? You don't care if the woman you're currently sleeping with wants to move on to someone else?"

"Naomi and I understand each other. We have a good time together." He grinned. "A very good time."

She winced. "I don't want details."

"Your friend is very—"

"Stop!"

He chuckled. "Okay. I'll play nice. Naomi and I are the same. We want to be involved as long as it's good. When it stops being fun, or one party loses interest, it's time to move on."

She'd seen them in action long enough to believe he was telling the truth. But seeing and believing weren't the same as understanding.

"Don't you ever want something more familiar?" she asked.

"Why? Variety keeps things interesting."

"For a while, but people are hard-wired to pair bond."

"Cal always said I had a screw loose."

She stuck a straw into her float. "Reid, I'm serious. I worry about you. Doesn't the series of one-night stands get old? Don't you ever want to settle down?"

"No. Not even a little. Look around, Penny." He

waved at the bar. "I can have a different woman every night of the week. No one expects me to show up at a certain time, eat dinner and then watch TV. I can come and go as I please, my life is always interesting. Why would I trade that in for one woman, a couple of kids and a mortgage?"

"Because you fell in love." It was a familiar discussion, but no matter how many times they had it, she never understood. "Don't you want to be a part of something? Don't you want to leave your mark on the world?"

"I'll be in the history books."

"Not because you were a great pitcher. Because you cared about someone. Because you—" She stopped. "Sorry. I know we agreed not to talk about this anymore. We always fight."

He stepped toward her and briefly touched her cheek. "*We* don't fight. You get upset because I don't want what you think I should have."

"I worry about you. I don't want you to grow old alone, with no one to care about you."

"I'm okay with that."

Was he? How was that possible? While his lifestyle might sound fun to the average eighteen-year-old guy, she couldn't help thinking that in the bright light of morning, it wasn't all Reid made it out to be. But maybe that was just wishful thinking on her part.

None of the Buchanan men had been very successful at love. Only Dani had a happy, stable relationship, and she wasn't even a Buchanan. A fact Penny still had trouble comprehending.

"How's Junior?" Reid asked.

She suspected he was trying to change the subject and she figured that was probably a good idea.

"Good. I'm having a textbook pregnancy, although I still manage to freak out about everything." She put her hand on her growing stomach.

"How much longer?" he asked, his eyes dark with concern.

"A week," she said. "I know that crossing the date where I lost the baby before doesn't mean anything, but it still feels like I'll be able to relax a little once it happens."

"It makes sense," he said gently. "You want to break the streak."

He was right.

"I keep telling myself I'm fine. The doctor says the same thing."

"You'll believe it when it happens," he told her. "So what's going on with my brother?"

She sipped on her float. "What do you mean? Cal's fine."

"He came in here ready to tear off one of my arms when he found out you were pregnant. He wanted to know all about the guy."

Penny felt her cheeks heat and she was careful to focus all of her attention on the tall glass in front of her. "I doubt he was that upset."

"You weren't here. He wanted to beat the crap out of me."

Unable to help herself, she looked at Reid. "I know that's not true."

"It may be an exaggeration, but there's something going on."

She thought about their last encounter. Their last, very personal, encounter. Funny how three years ago she'd been so angry and so hurt, she'd never wanted anything to do with Cal. But now...

"We work together," she said. "We're becoming friends."

"Then why are you blushing?"

Guilt made her cheeks heat even more. "I'm not. It's just..."

Reid waited patiently.

"It's just..." She repeated, then sighed. "I can't explain it. We're getting along. It's nice. We seem to appreciate each other now in a way we couldn't before." She held up a hand before he could say anything. "I mean that in a nonromantic sense. We're different people. It's as if the stuff I really hated about him is gone and only the good stuff remains. Or maybe I'm the one who changed."

"Sounds like a lot of hooey to me," Reid told her. "You're not falling for him, are you?"

"What? Of course not. I'm pregnant."

"How do those two concepts relate?"

"I'm only thinking about the baby. Cal doesn't want children."

Something flickered in Reid's eyes. "He might. Like you said, he's different."

"Not interested, even if it is true," Penny said. "I don't need a man in my life."

"So why are you all fired up to get me a woman?" he asked.

"I've committed to people in the past. You never have."

"I'm committed to my family."

True enough. He'd also committed to baseball, but she didn't want to go there. She'd seen the pain in his eyes when the games came on television.

"I find it very interesting that you and Cal are getting along so well now," he told her. "And that neither of you were interested in getting serious while you were divorced."

Penny did her best to look innocent. "Really? Cal didn't have any long-term relationships?"

"No. There were a few women, but nothing that mattered."

"A few? How many?"

Reid grinned. "Why do you care?"

"I don't. I'm curious." More than curious. What women? Who had Cal dated?

"Sorry," Reid said. "I don't tell on my brothers. Not even for you." He looked toward the front door. "Hey. What's up?"

Penny turned and saw Dani walk into the bar.

She claimed the seat next to Penny. "Hi. How's it going?" She peered at Penny's float. "What *is* that?"

"A root beer float with hazelnuts."

Dani winced. "Does that fall under the craving category?"

"Nope," Reid told her. "It's just plain gross."

"Men don't appreciate these sorts of things," Penny said.

"I'm not sure I appreciate them either," Dani told her. "How are you feeling?"

"Good. Getting a tummy." She tugged at her sweater to show off her bump.

Dani eyed her stomach, then looked at Reid. "Can I get a Diet Coke?"

"Sure. Want anything to eat?"

"No, thanks. I just need the caffeine."

"Busy day?" he asked as he handed her the glass of soda.

"Oh, yeah. Lunch was standing room only."

She didn't sound very happy about the fact, but Penny couldn't blame her. Dani had only ever wanted to be successful in the family business and Gloria had stood in her way at every turn.

She remembered what Cal had told her, about Gloria threatening to tell Dani the truth about her father if he didn't toe the line. Penny knew it wasn't for her to decide, but a part of her thought it would be better if Dani knew the real reason Gloria wasn't on her side.

She looked at her former sister-in-law. Dani was short, with light-brown hair and hazel eyes. Her features were more delicate than her brothers' and completely feminine. She looked enough like them that no one would ever guess the truth, yet there was much that was different.

Her lighter coloring, her petite build. Dani wore her hair in a short, stylish bob. Her tailored slacks and cropped jacket suited her slender body. Looking at her, Penny felt like a cumbersome giant.

Dani sipped on her drink, then smiled at Reid. "I'm going to change the subject to something very girly that will probably make you uncomfortable."

He instantly took a step back. "Thanks for the heads-up. You two have fun." He quickly moved to the other end of the bar.

"Men are so predictable," Dani said. "I really like that about them."

"It does help. What's up?"

"I wanted to talk to you about the in vitro fertilization you went through. Not now," she added. "But would you be comfortable talking to me about it at some point?"

"Sure. You can ask me anything you'd like. Are you thinking of doing that yourself?" she asked, not sure if she was treading in dangerous territory.

Dani nodded. "Because of his injury, there are some things Hugh can't do and that's one of them." She wrinkled her nose. "We do other stuff you probably don't want to hear about."

Penny grinned. "I'd like to be drunk first and I can't drink right now."

Dani laughed. "Fair enough. Anyway, that's in our future, so I thought if you wouldn't mind telling me about it, that would be great."

"Sure. I'll give you the name of my doctor, too. She's fabulous. Very easy to deal with and completely understanding of the panic that goes with the whole process."

"It's expensive, right?"

"Oh, yeah. The cost seriously cut into my 'open my own restaurant' fund, but I knew I wanted a baby before my eggs turned to raisins."

"Good plan."

Penny fished out another hazelnut. "You have a few years before you have to worry about the eggs to raisins thing."

"Not that many." Dani rubbed her fingers against

her glass. "Why didn't you…" She glanced over her shoulder as if checking to make sure Reid was still at the other end of the bar. She lowered her voice. "Why IVF? You could have picked some guy to sleep with you. It would have been cheaper."

"The very question my mother asked me," Penny admitted, remembering her parents' distress when she'd first told them what she wanted to do. "But with IVF I could get more information about the father's family, see how the various traits looked, that sort of thing." She thought for a second.

"I didn't want the hassle," she admitted. "I didn't want to risk the father coming back to lay claim on his child."

"You could have had him sign papers," Dani said.

"Sure, but he could change his mind. What if in ten years he came back and said he wanted some visitation? I didn't know how the courts would rule and I didn't want to deal with it."

"What about Reid?" Dani asked. "He wouldn't have come back for visitation rights."

Penny stiffened. "Sleep with my ex-husband's brother? No, thanks. Talk about a giant ick."

"Is that how you think of him? As Cal's brother?"

"Only when someone talks about us having sex. And I believe he'd agree with me on that."

Dani laughed. "Okay. Fair enough. Hugh and I talked about waiting a couple of years to get our lives in order before we started a family. He's doing well at the university and I'm…" She sighed. "Anyway, I think this might be a good time. Maybe having a baby would distract me from other things."

Penny touched her arm. "You mean being stuck at Burger Heaven?"

"Yeah. Gloria's driven away the third president in about fifteen months. The thing is, I'm willing to deal with her. But does she ask me? Does she even give me a chance? I'm not saying I should run the company, but there has to be another way for me to contribute."

"Like running The Waterfront?" Penny said, feeling sympathetic.

"Not to take away from Cal, but yeah. I could have done it."

Penny smiled. "He's only there for four months. Why don't you start a campaign now to take over when he's gone?"

Dani's eyes widened. "But you're the chef there— we used to be related. Wouldn't you be more comfortable with someone else as general manager?"

"I think we'd work well together," she said. "I know you'd do a terrific job."

"Really? Wow. That's great. Maybe I'll talk to Cal and see what he thinks."

"Cal will think it's a fabulous idea," Penny said. The real problem was going to be Gloria.

"Then I'll start campaigning," Dani said. "I swear if I didn't need the incredible medical insurance for Hugh I would have quit Burger Heaven years ago. As soon as he gets tenure, I'm leaving the company. Well, unless I'm running The Waterfront."

"So you have a plan."

"Pretty much." Dani sipped her drink, then put the glass on the bar. "I know it's none of my business, but how are you and Cal working together?"

"We're doing really well." Penny shrugged. "I guess we had to get divorced and spend three years apart before we could become friends. How twisted is that?"

"I'm not sure. It's just too bad you couldn't work things out before."

Penny nodded as if she thought so, too, but it wasn't true. There was no way she and Cal could have remained married. Not when he'd broken her heart so completely.

Before getting married, they'd agreed to have children. The only fight had been over how many—three or four. When she'd first gotten pregnant, he'd been as delighted as she. They'd held on to each other, excited, scared and determined to do the best for their baby.

Over time, Cal had changed. By her fourth month, she'd started to wonder if he wanted children with her at all. He wouldn't talk about the baby or even come with her to the doctor. And then she'd miscarried.

The first cramps had terrified her. She'd rushed to her doctor, but by the time she made it to the examining room, it was all over.

Cal had said all the right things, he held her while she cried, but she hadn't believed him. In some ways, he'd seemed more relieved than sad.

She'd told herself it was wrong to judge him—that people expressed grief in different ways. But her suspicions had been confirmed a few months later when she'd suggested they try again.

She still remembered how he'd sat at the other end of the sofa, staring at the wall rather than looking at her. He'd told her flat out he didn't want children. Not now, not ever. And he wouldn't say what had changed his mind.

Wondering if he still loved her, she'd done all she could to get his attention. But somehow he slipped further and further away until she couldn't reach his heart. In a last-ditch effort to get him to admit he still cared, she'd left. Her hope had been he would come after her and beg her to return. Instead he'd told her it was for the best.

CAL RAN THE TOTALS for the day. They were still ahead of projections and the reservations showed no signs of slowing. He wanted to claim the new dining room or advertising was responsible, but he knew it was a whole lot more about Penny's menu.

"Got any leftovers?"

He glanced up and saw Walker in the doorway to his office. "Sure. I'll have Penny get you something."

He buzzed the kitchen. Naomi picked up.

"Why are you calling?" she asked by way of greeting. "Because you're too important to walk the twenty or thirty feet from your office to the kitchen?"

"Exactly. Ask Penny to come out, would you?"

"It's not like she works for you," Naomi said.

"You might want to check the contract. She does and you do, too."

"Oh, fine. Throw your authority around. Penny. You've been summoned."

The phone went dead. Cal looked back at his brother. "She'll be right out."

The door to the kitchen opened. Penny walked out, a dishtowel in her hand. "You're buzzing me?"

she asked as she turned toward his office. "There's nothing in the contract about buzzing—"

She broke off when she saw Walker. Her face lit up, her mouth curved in a wide, open smile and she ran as if being chased by wolves.

"Walker! You're back!"

She launched herself at him with the confidence of a woman who knows she's going to be caught. Walker grinned and wrapped his arms round her.

"Hey, Penny," he said and leaned his head toward hers.

She did the same, so their foreheads touched. "You're back. My favorite ever marine is back."

Cal knew that Penny adored his brothers. She claimed it was because she grew up with two sisters and was desperate for some male point of view in her life.

Until that moment, Cal hadn't cared one way or the other. But right then, watching Walker turn in a slow circle, Penny in his arms, her feet kicking behind her, he felt a definite need to growl.

He told himself he didn't give a damn what Penny did in her personal life. She wasn't his wife anymore. One or two kisses didn't give him any rights, and he didn't want any. He even told himself that Walker would never be interested in his ex-sister-in-law. But that didn't take away the feeling of discomfort low in his gut.

Walker lowered Penny to the floor. She beamed at him. "Cal said you're out of the marines. Are you really? For good?"

"It was time."

"Yeah. I get to see you more. Okay, you have to come taste some stuff. I have the best fish and chips. You'll die. And then you'll beg me to tell you what's in the recipe, but I won't."

Just then the kitchen doors opened and Naomi strolled out. She was dressed in black jeans and a tight red sweater that set off her long, wavy dark hair. She looked like a sexy Amazon on the prowl. Cal watched her gaze settle on Walker and gave his brother maybe thirty more seconds of freedom before Naomi claimed him.

"So this is Walker," she said as she approached. "I've heard a lot about you but I was starting to think everyone had made you up."

Penny sighed. "Oh, great. Another conquest. Walker, this is my friend, Naomi. Naomi, Walker. Be gentle, though. He's just out of the marines."

Cal held in a laugh at the thought of Penny trying to protect his tough baby brother. Then he wondered what Reid would think to know he'd been replaced.

"Ma'am," Walker said, releasing Penny and offering his hand.

Naomi winced. "If you call me ma'am again, I'm going to have to take you down."

"All right. Naomi."

"Much better."

Cal moved closer to watch the show.

Naomi looked Walker over. "If you're just back from overseas, you might want someone to show you how Seattle has changed. I'd be more than willing."

"I appreciate the offer, but I understand you're seeing my brother."

"Reid?" Naomi shrugged. "I was. But you know Reid. Fifteen minutes is about his attention span."

"You don't seem too broken up about it."

She smiled. "That's because my attention span is two minutes shorter. No bruised hearts. I'm not into getting serious, just getting involved."

The invitation was clear. Cal had to admit that Naomi embodied sexual availability in a way that called to men.

Penny looked between them. "Whatever you decide, I still expect you to eat dinner with me, Walker," she said.

"I wouldn't do anything else," he said, tugging on her long braid.

"Please have something to eat." Naomi sighed. "You'll need your strength."

Walker looked at Naomi for a long time. "I appreciate the offer," he began.

Her eyes widened. "You're turning me down?"

"How about if I take a rain check?"

Cal braced himself for the explosion. To the best of his knowledge, no one had ever turned Naomi down. Then she surprised him by laughing.

"Your loss, soldier. If you change your mind, and you will, Penny has my number."

She strolled back into the kitchen. Walker watched her go.

"Interesting lady," he said.

"That's the rumor," Penny told him. "Are you really not interested, or are you playing hard to get so you can have her full attention?"

Walker's expression shuttered. "I don't play games."

"Ha! It's hard-wired into your gender. Okay, go find a seat. I'll bring out food."

"I don't get to pick what I want?"

"Oh, please. On what planet?" She glanced at Cal. "Are you hungry? I can get another plate together."

"Thanks."

She returned to the kitchen and Walker looked at him. "Yours?"

Cal figured he meant the baby. "She would be my *ex*-wife."

"You wanted to punch me out when she launched herself at me."

Cal didn't see how Walker could have known what he was thinking. He would have bet money it hadn't shown. "No idea what you're talking about."

"Right. So you just hired your ex-wife because she's a great chef?"

"Have you forgotten the year she cooked our Christmas dinner?"

"Good point. So how's it going?"

"Good. Better than I would have thought."

"And the baby?"

"She decided it was time. Went to a sperm bank. There's no guy."

Walker's dark gaze locked with his. "Lucky break."

THE THREE OF THEM SAT at one of the tables by the kitchen. Penny served two different salads, her famous fish and chips, a poached salmon dish, smashed potatoes, green beans with a mustard sauce and she promised something special for dessert, although she wouldn't say what.

"Do you have any idea what you're going to do now?" Penny asked after all three plates were full.

"Get my own place," Walker said. He looked at Cal. "Not that I don't love living with you."

Cal chuckled. "You're welcome to stay as long as you like."

"I appreciate that, but I want my own place. An apartment at first. Until I figure out where I want to live."

"Are you rich?" Penny asked.

Cal and Walker both looked at her.

"What?" she asked. "It's a serious question. I'm curious. Didn't you invest in The Daily Grind?" she asked Walker.

"Uh-huh. Cleaned out my savings account for my big brother."

"And you made a fortune," Cal reminded him.

Five years ago Reid had been on his second multi-million-dollar contract and had offered to bankroll the whole thing. Cal had refused and instead had taken on multiple investors. Walker had been one of them.

"I did okay," Walker said, then shrugged. "I don't have to go to work anytime soon."

"Will you get a job?" Penny asked.

Walker nodded.

Cal figured he had to. Walker wasn't the kind of guy who enjoyed sitting around doing nothing.

"But first I have to find someone," Walker said.

"Who?" Penny asked.

"A woman named Ashley."

Cal looked at his brother. "A girlfriend?"

"Yes, but not mine. One of the guys in my unit was killed. Ben. He was a good kid. Not a great marine but he had a lot of heart. Ashley was his girl. He planned on marrying her when he got out. I have a letter to deliver to her, so I have to find her."

Penny set down her fork. "You have more than just her first name, right? His family can help you locate her."

The darkness returned to Walker's eyes. "Ben didn't have any family. He grew up in foster care. Four high schools in four years. I know she lived in the Seattle area when they were in high school and that her name is Ashley."

Cal leaned back in his chair. "That's not enough to go on."

"Sure it is." Walker picked up his glass of wine. "I can go through high school yearbooks until I find where Ben went to school, then get the names of all the Ashleys."

"Couldn't you hire a private detective or something?" Penny asked. "That's a huge amount of work."

"I have time," Walker told her. "I want her to have the letter."

Cal knew his brother well enough to recognize his stubborn expression. "Don't argue, Penny. His mind is made up."

"Good luck," Penny said.

"Thanks." He cut off a piece of the battered fish. "Great meal. The best I've had in nearly a year."

"Thank you. I thought you'd like it. So why did you turn down Naomi?"

Cal winced. "Very smooth transition. Subtle."

Penny shrugged. "I'm curious. You've been away a long time. I'm guessing there wasn't a lot of, um, well, you know."

"Sex," Walker said calmly. "You're saying there wasn't a lot of sex to be had on my tour."

"Something like that. Naomi is attractive and from all accounts, very skilled."

"You're offering me your friend?"

"No. I'm curious. Is it because she's older?"

Walker shrugged. "She's what? Thirty-eight? Thirty-nine?"

"Forty."

"Perfectly seasoned," he said. "It's not the age thing."

"Then what?"

"Then none of your business."

She held out her fork like a weapon. "I'm pregnant. You have to be nice to me."

Cal decided his brother needed rescuing. "Mariners should have a good season this year."

"I heard that," Walker said.

Penny rolled her eyes, then said, "The infield looks promising. Now if only we can come up with the hits."

Conversation shifted to baseball, then the success of the restaurant, then to possible neighborhoods for Walker's apartment.

Cal watched his brother skillfully dodge any personal questions. Walker might love Penny, but he wasn't going to share more than he wanted to.

Secrets, Cal thought. They were a family who kept secrets.

CHAPTER NINE

FRIDAY MORNING PENNY FOUND herself pulling into The Waterfront shortly before seven.

"This is just plain wrong," she muttered as she climbed out of her car and hurried toward the rear of the building. There hadn't even been time to shower. As she wasn't allowed caffeine anymore, due to her pregnancy, a shower was the only thing that perked her up in the morning.

"I know, I know," Naomi said from her place just outside the open back door. "It was your turn to sleep in. I'm sorry. I thought you'd want to see."

Penny and Naomi traded off predawn times, alternating who had to get in to go over the delivery.

Penny stared at the water pouring out the back door. "Shouldn't we be able to turn that off?"

"We're working on it." Naomi gave a half smile that didn't look the least bit convincing. "First the pipe cracked, then the shutoff broke. That's when I made the executive decision to rip out part of the wall to see if we could get to any other kind of shutoff."

Penny had a bad feeling there wasn't a happy ending to the story. "And?"

"Rats."

Penny took a step back and shuddered. "This isn't your attempt not to use bad language, is it?"

"Sorry. No. There's not a lot. Obviously the exterminator has been doing his job, but still, there was a family of them."

It was too early to deal with rodents. "Great." Penny started for the kitchen.

Naomi clutched her arm. "There's more."

"Because a broken pipe, no ability to turn off the water pouring through my kitchen and out into the alley and rats in the walls isn't enough?"

"We haven't had the produce delivery. The truck was in a big pileup. Three cars and the truck. No one was injured but…" Her voice trailed off.

Penny shook her head. "Something tells me my lettuce didn't survive."

"That's what they're saying."

"Great." She had special orders due in today for her new chef's special. "You know we have three parties of ten in tonight."

Naomi nodded.

"And I would kill for cilantro, which we're now not getting."

"You mentioned that," Naomi said. "I'm really sorry."

Penny stepped close and hugged her. "None of this is your fault." She reached for her cell phone. "Time to call in the troops."

She punched in Cal's number. "You'll never guess what's happened here," she said and told him what was going on. "Naomi has already called the plumber, but we have to do something about the rats. They're going to totally gross me out."

"I'll call the exterminator and then be in."

"Yeah. You wouldn't happen to have any cilantro, would you?"

"No. Want me to stop and get some?"

"No. I'll call the produce company and see what they can do about delivering something to me. Although it won't be their best. That's in the pileup."

"Gotta love the business," he said.

"At least it's not boring. See you in a bit." She hung up and looked at Naomi. "Cal's on his way. He's calling about the rats." She glanced at the door. "Do I have to go in there?"

"The rats are all scattered. You don't have to worry about them."

"Okay." Penny tried to tell herself they were just really big, ugly mice and she liked mice. They were small and cute and reminded her of Cinderella. But rats? She shuddered.

She stepped inside and immediately found herself ankle-deep in the raging river that went right through her kitchen. "The plumber's on his way, right?"

"Shouldn't be too long."

"Good." Because there wasn't going to be any prep work while this was going on. And even after the water was turned off, the floor would need some time to air out. And there were those three parties of ten, not to mention a full house, tonight.

At least her office was dry, she thought as she shrugged out of her coat and moved back into the main area of the kitchen.

"We have fish," Naomi said helpfully. "That's something."

Penny put a call in to the produce company. They read off what they had available and she checked it against her order. "Send it," she said, then hung up. She quickly scribbled out another list and handed it to Naomi. "I'll need this stuff by one. But before you go, let's brainstorm a new special for tonight."

An hour later they had a special and a modified menu. Edouard strolled into the kitchen. Her sous-chef looked especially male and self-satisfied as he surveyed the flowing water.

"There is a broken pipe," he announced.

Naomi grinned. "Gee, Eddie. Thanks. We weren't sure what all this water was."

Edouard smiled. "You are crabby. Should I ask why? Man trouble? I, of course, have no trouble with the men in my life. They adore me."

"Of course they do," Penny said. "We're all delighted you had a good night. Now let's talk about what's going on."

Naomi moved next to Edouard and rested her chin on the top of his head. "I never have trouble with my men, either, my little friend."

Just then, a strange man stuck his head in the back door. "I'm the plumber," he said with a grin. "Looks like you have a broken pipe."

As he was well-muscled, young and good-looking, Penny wasn't surprised when Naomi hurried toward him.

"I'll deal with this," she said.

"Of course you will," Edouard told her. "He looks innocent. Be gentle."

Penny glanced at the clock. It was barely eight in the morning. She didn't want to think about how the rest of the day was going to go. Was there a chance she could sneak home in the late morning for a nap? Just a couple of hours of sleep. Not like she'd be doing anything else in bed. Yup, that was her. Sexless girl.

She tuned out Edouard and Naomi's banter as she realized she couldn't actually remember the last time she'd been with a man. As in naked. As in skin on skin, kissing, touching and the ever thrilling moment of climax.

"So unfair," she said, still caught up in the revelation. "Everyone is having sex but me."

Her two assistants stared at her. The plumber shifted uncomfortably. "Ah, maybe someone could show me that pipe," he said.

Naomi patted her shoulder in sympathy, then led the guy out.

"You could be getting some," Edouard said.

Penny accepted the comment in the generous spirit in which it was given. "I'm pregnant. Trust me. No one wants to see me naked."

"*Au contraire.* Many men find the lushness of the flower at full bloom most appealing."

"Who's blooming?" Cal asked as he walked into the kitchen. He had a grocery bag in one hand and a huge pet carrier in the other.

"Penny. She's upset because she's not getting any," Edouard said, staring at the carrier. "What do you have in there? A dog? There will be no dogs in my kitchen. Go. Shoo."

He waved his hands toward the door, as if that would make Cal retreat.

No such luck, Penny thought, knowing her cheeks were on fire. Kitchens were rowdy, randy places where no one had secrets and every weakness was a target. She knew that and accepted it. But why did Edouard have to announce her lack of sex to Cal? And why was her ex-husband grinning at her?

"What?" she asked. "Did you have something you wanted to say to me?"

He held out the grocery bag. She took it and looked inside. Instantly her stomach growled.

"You brought me cilantro."

He shrugged. "You said you needed it." He set down the pet carrier and opened it. "This is for the other problem," he said as a massive black-and-white cat jumped gracefully out.

"A cat!" Edouard sounded so horrified, Penny half expected him to jump on the counter. "No. No! They shed. The hair would be everywhere."

"I agree," Penny said. "No cats in my kitchen. It's not sanitary. We won't even discuss the health code violations."

"Better a cat than rats," Cal said. "He's not an indoor cat. He's a hunter. Guess what he likes to eat?"

That was something. She eyed the creature. "How much does he weigh?"

"Twenty-eight pounds. The lady at the shelter said he was clean, friendly and always on the prowl. He's big enough that rats shouldn't be a problem."

The cat looked around, then strolled over to Penny. He rubbed against her leg and started to purr. She bent down and petted it. "Nice kitty." She looked at Cal. "Does he have a name?"

"No idea."

She felt the muscles in his back. "I hope he really does eat what he catches, otherwise he's going to be damned expensive to feed."

Edouard continued to eye the cat as if it would attack him. Suddenly the cat's ears perked up and it took off toward the open wall. It slipped inside and there was silence.

"Seal up the wall quickly," Edouard said. "While we still can."

Penny shook her head. "The cat stays. The building is old. There have been so many remodels, I'm sure there are dozens of places the exterminator can't get to. A cat is a good idea."

At least she hoped it was.

A low rumble told her the second produce truck had arrived.

"It's all going to be crap," she muttered as she made her way outside. "The good stuff was in the crash."

"Can't you sort through it?" Cal asked, falling into step beside her.

"I'll have to."

"I'll help." When she looked at him, he added, "I know what decent lettuce looks like. I might not be a trained chef, but I'm not an idiot."

"I'll accept that." She was grateful he was

going to ignore what he'd heard earlier. Maybe he would even—

"Not getting any, huh?" he asked with a grin. "Bummer."

PENNY STOOD and chopped cilantro. Her back ached, a fairly new event in her pregnancy, but one she was willing to live with. In an effort to ease the pressure, she scrounged a footstool and rested her left foot on it. The new position helped and she resumed her chopping and imagined forty-seven ways she could use cilantro in various dishes.

If she—

"Penny!"

She winced when she heard Cal call her name. It had been nearly a week since Edouard had announced she wasn't "getting any" and she was still feeling a little self-conscious. Not that Cal had been anything but the perfect gentleman. She couldn't complain about that. But still, it was embarrassing.

She looked up. "We're fine in here. All the orders are out. Do not tell me we have an unexpected party of twelve showing up."

"No. We've cleared the reservations. We're done for the night."

"Good."

He walked toward her, all tall and good-looking in slacks and a sweater. Gloria might be a bitch on wheels, but her grandsons came from a mighty fine gene pool. Just looking at Cal, at the way his body moved and the slight smile on his lips, made her knees wobble. Not a good thing when she was holding such a sharp knife.

"You're off tomorrow," he said into her ear.

His warm breath tickled and aroused in equal measures. There hadn't been any repeats of their hot kisses. She'd told herself she didn't care. She'd told herself it was better this way. She'd been lying both times.

"Is that a question or a statement?" she asked.

"A question."

She kept her gaze on her cilantro. It had been delivered fresh and smelled heavenly. "Yes."

"Good." He tucked a piece of paper into her jacket pocket. "My place. Tomorrow. Sixty-thirty. I'm cooking. Here are directions."

"What if I have plans?" she asked, turning her head so she could meet his gaze. His dark eyes made her want to jump without looking. A divorce and being many years wiser than the last time she'd jumped made her less sure.

"Do you?"

She was tempted to say she did. Except she was curious about why Cal was inviting her over. Plus the man was offering to cook. Most people assumed chefs hated to eat anyone else's food or that they were critical. Maybe others were, but Penny loved having someone else take responsibility for the food.

"No."

"Then I'll see you there."

How hard could fajitas be? Cal had picked the dish deliberately. He'd bought beans, rice, salsa and guacamole from his favorite Mexican restaurant. All he had to do was chop up a few onions, peppers and cilantro, along with the steak and chicken and throw on the spices.

He'd already set the table and he had a blender of virgin margaritas in the freezer, so why wasn't the meal coming together? Here it was, less than fifteen minutes before Penny was due to arrive and he'd suddenly realized he had no way to heat the beans.

"I need more pots, dammit," he yelled as he flung open cupboards. Except he never cooked and he wouldn't know a good pot from a bad one.

He finally found a casserole dish and dumped the beans into that. He would use the microwave and be done with it.

Just then the doorbell rang. He walked to open it.

"Right on time," he said, before he got a look at Penny. Then he stepped back and jammed his mouth shut before his jaw dropped and he just stared like an idiot.

Penny looked great. A black-and-purple sweater clung to her newly impressive breasts and her round tummy. Black jeans made already long legs seem to go on forever. Her hair was loose and hung nearly halfway down her back. The soft waves made him remember other times when her hair had been falling over his belly and thighs as she—

He slammed the door on that train of thought and invited her inside.

"You look great," he said.

"Thanks. I'm really starting to show, but I'm still too small for maternity clothes. It's hard finding things to wear. Love the house. Queen Anne is such a cool neighborhood. I saw you have a view. I'm jealous." She shrugged out of her coat and handed it to him. "I stopped by the restaurant on my way over. Everything is fine. The cat is really settling in. We have to name it. Maybe we can hold a contest. With staff, I mean. Not customers. They don't need to know about the cat or the rats."

He closed the door and waited for her to talk herself out. The babbling meant she was nervous. Knowing he wasn't the only one made things a little easier.

"So, ah, why am I here?" she asked as he hung up her coat.

"Because I asked you and you said yes."

"I know *that.* Why did you ask me?"

"You passed the date."

Tears filled her eyes. She blinked them away. "Hormones," she said thickly. "I didn't know you were keeping track."

"It wasn't hard. You only told me about the baby a couple of weeks ago. So when Naomi said you got the all clear from your doctor," he said, "I wanted to celebrate."

The idea had popped into his brain and he hadn't been able to shake it loose. He'd decided to give in to the impulse and see what happened.

"You didn't have to do this, but I'm glad you did," she said, heading down the hall. "Is the kitchen this way?"

"Yeah. Turn right."

He rounded the corner and plowed into her. She'd stopped just inside the room.

"What?" he asked, feeling the criticism rolling off her. "It's big. There's plenty of light. It's a good stove."

She eyed the six-burner stainless steel appliance that had come with the house. "Better than good, but jeez, Cal. It's red."

He nodded. "They'd just painted before they put the house on the market. I'll change it."

She winced. "You should do it soon. A red kitchen isn't a good idea. You'll never get the color right on your vegetables and it's not appetizing. But I can live with it."

"I'm glad, because I'm not painting today."

She walked over to the stools at the island and plopped down. "So what are we having?"

"Fajitas. Steak and chicken."

"Cool."

As she seemed to have settled in for the evening, he knew he wasn't going to get out of cooking in front of her. "Want something to drink?" he asked, when he really wanted to offer her something to read, or a movie on TV. Anything so she wouldn't see him fumbling around in the kitchen.

"Sure. What do you have?"

"Virgin margaritas."

"Perfect."

He poured them both drinks, then turned on the heat under the grill pan. He could see her eyeing the flame but didn't know if he had it too high or too low.

"You want to do this?" he asked.

"No. I do it for a living. I like having you cook for me. It will be fine."

"Any pointers?"

She smiled. "Cal, it's nothing more than a simple stir-fry on a grill pan. You'll do great."

"Yeah." He was already sweating. Why had he thought this was a good idea?

"I didn't see another car in the driveway," she said. "Has Walker already moved out?"

"A couple of days ago. Reid offered him a bedroom on his houseboat, but Walker's determined to have his own place."

"I'm surprised he moved out of here," she said after taking a sip of her margarita, "but who on earth would want to move in with Reid? There would be too many women coming and going. I heard he already has a new chickie. He and Naomi lasted what, two weeks? Maybe three?"

"They burn hot and bright," he said as he dropped the meat onto the grill pan. "Then it's over."

"I know. Naomi's already making moves on one of the busboys. She's amazing."

"I hear Edouard has a new man in his life," Cal said, throwing on peppers and onions.

"That's the rumor."

He glanced at her, remembering what Edouard had said about her not getting any. Did she want to?

Her eyes narrowed. "I know what you're thinking. Stop it."

"What am I thinking?"

She sniffed. "I'm gestating right now. Sex isn't important to me."

"Good to know." He thought about how she'd responded to his kisses. She might be pregnant, but it wasn't keeping her completely occupied. If he asked, would she say yes? Did he want her to?

Penny sniffed again. "Ah, is that burning?"

"I'M IMPRESSED," Penny said as she made another fajita. "This is great."

"Thanks." Cal accepted the compliment, although he looked a little suspicious.

"I mean it. I love when someone cooks for me and this is really delicious. You used plenty of cilantro."

"I knew you were having a craving."

"That seems to come with the territory. At least I haven't run into a food I can't either buy or fix."

They were eating in Cal's dining room. He'd put her with her back to the kitchen, so she wouldn't have to look at the red walls. A sweet gesture, she thought. Any more like that and in her present hormonal state she would start sobbing.

There was also something familiar about their dinner. Just the two of them at a table, talking about restaurants, food, life. How many evenings had they spent together around a table? Their world had been food, work and each other.

Where had their relationship gone wrong? She knew Cal changing his mind about wanting a baby was a big part of it, but there had been plenty of cracks before the crumble.

"Why did you start The Daily Grind?" she asked. "How much of it was wanting something of your own and how much of it was getting away from Gloria?"

He shrugged. "It was about equal." He leaned

toward her. "Oh, I see. Now you believe me about Gloria."

She smiled. "I never had to work with her before. I'll admit that when we were first married I thought you exaggerated her personality. I've had a few recent encounters with her that have changed my mind. She's the most controlling person I've ever met."

"Tell me about it."

"Speaking of telling, have you thought any more about telling Dani the truth about her father? I know it would hurt her initially, but I suspect that after a while she'd find the information very freeing."

"I don't know what to do," he admitted. "I've always looked out for Dani. I always wanted to protect her from the world. Now she's all grown up and I still find myself wanting to shield her from things."

He kept talking, but suddenly Penny couldn't hear him. There was an ache deep inside that told her his words confirmed what she'd always believed: Cal would have been a terrific father.

He instinctively took care of those who weren't as strong. Those in need. She could imagine him adoring a toddler while teaching him or her how to go forward in the world.

Why had he changed his mind? Why hadn't he wanted children with her?

She opened her mouth, then closed it. The evening was going too well. She didn't want to spoil the mood by fighting—and discussions about children and babies always led to fights.

He picked up his margarita. "I've been thinking about what you said," he told her. "Better the information come from me than from Gloria. I just have to figure out the best time."

Penny wasn't sure there was a good time to shatter someone's view of their world, but she trusted Cal to be sensitive about the whole thing.

"She'll want to leave Burger Heaven," Penny said.

"I know. Maybe I could offer her a job at The Daily Grind. We're always looking for good managers. I've tried to hire her before but she claimed one incident of nepotism in her life was enough. I told her I would have hired her even if we weren't family, but she didn't believe me."

Penny had a feeling Dani would want to escape family-owned businesses for a while, but she didn't say that.

"You've done well for yourself," she said instead. "The company is really growing."

He grinned. "It's even more impressive when you consider we're in the city where Starbucks started. Talk about competition."

"Good point. Obviously you've filled a niche and we're a society of obsessive coffee drinkers." She sighed. "I miss coffee. And before you remind me I can have decaf, I'll tell you that it's just not the same."

"I know. Only a few more months." He eyed her stomach. "Is your mom going to come out and stay with you when you have the baby?"

"Yes. She says she was there with all her other grandchildren. She'll be here for the birth of this one." Penny rested her hand on her belly. "I can't help thinking she's disappointed."

Cal frowned. "At having another grandchild? Not possible."

"Oh, I know she'll be happy about the baby. It's me being pregnant this way. My two sisters did everything exactly right. I bounced around for nearly five years before I figured out what I wanted to do with my life. I flunked out of college twice, worked at dozens of jobs. I know my parents were frustrated. Now I'm pregnant by a man they'll never meet and about whom we know nothing. I have a list of characteristics and a brief medical history."

Cal leaned close and took her other hand. "You waited to find out what made you happy instead of settling for a career you'd hate. How many people have the courage to do that? You weren't willing to compromise. That's a good thing."

"Don't be nice to me. I'll start to cry."

"Anything but that," he teased. "Guys hate tears. It's too much like blackmail."

She smiled. "I was always very good about that."

"Yes, you were. You played it straight."

Except for changing his mind about having children, Cal had played it straight, too. They'd been good people who had been in love. So what had gone so wrong in their marriage?

"Why didn't we make it?" she asked quietly.

"Hell if I know."

"It seemed as if everything was fine one day and the next there were cracks everywhere. They had to have started sometime. They didn't just appear."

"Maybe we were too young," he said.

"We were both in our twenties. Hardly kids. But

maybe you're right. Maybe we weren't ready for the stresses of marriage." She stared into his dark eyes. "I never hated you."

"I'm glad. I didn't hate you, either."

Was it her, or had it just gotten hot in here?

"At least we can be friends now," she said, knowing she should pull her hand free of his. There was something intimate about sitting next to each other, staring into each other's eyes and holding hands. Way too intimate. And sexual. Because she was suddenly aware of his body—the hard planes, his broad shoulders. She knew exactly what he looked like naked. How to touch him to make him stiffen with pleasure.

"Wow, look at the time," she said, drawing back and tugging her hand free. "Where did the time go?"

He glanced at his watch. "It's eight-thirty."

"I know, but I'm tired and, you know, tomorrow's a work day. Friday, even. A busy work day. And I should call Naomi and check on things. Just to be sure."

"What's wrong?" he asked. "What are you afraid of?"

"I'm not afraid." She stood and looked at the mess on the table. "I should help you clean up."

"Screw that. Why are you running away?"

"Do I look like I'm running? I'm standing in place." She raised one foot to show him. "See?"

He rose and moved close. "Did I say something to upset you?"

Nope. Not a word. She'd upset herself without any help at all. And upset wasn't even the right word. She was…uncomfortable. And sexually aware. And seriously pregnant. Hardly circumstances to turn Cal on.

"Okay, this was great," she told him as she backed toward the door. "The dinner. The conversation. All of it. Really, really great. Thanks. I appreciate it."

She grabbed her coat and purse, then opened the door and ducked outside. Thirty seconds later she'd started her car and was zooming out of his driveway.

Free at last, she thought, unable to slow the pounding of her heart.

The worst part of it was she couldn't explain what had just happened. She'd become aware of Cal on a sexual level and she'd been afraid she would act on it. Frankly, doing without was a whole lot better than getting rejected. Still, running felt wrong. Maybe she should have explained.

"Oh, yeah. *There's* a conversation I'm dying to have with my ex-husband and boss."

She drove across Seattle until she reached her own small rental house. After she inched her way inside the single-car garage, she turned off the engine. It was only then she noticed a car pulling in behind her. A familiar, small, two-seater sports car.

She walked out of the garage just as Cal climbed out of his Z4.

"What are you doing here?" she asked.

"Making sure you got home okay," he told her. "And trying to figure out what has you so spooked."

"I'm not spooked. I'm not anything. I'm tired. It's late. I had a good time and then I left."

He grabbed her arm, pulled her hard against him and lowered his mouth close to hers.

"I don't think it's that at all," he said, right before he kissed her.

CHAPTER TEN

PENNY FULLY INTENDED TO protest, right up until his lips touched hers. But the second she felt the warm heat, the soft pressure, wanting exploded inside of her. Powerful sexual need blocked anything close to common sense. She gave herself up to the kiss and knew she would have to deal with the consequences later.

Instinctively, she tilted her head, parting her mouth even before he asked her to. But instead of responding as he should, and plunging inside, he continued to kiss her chastely, nibbling on her lower lip before flicking his tongue against her upper lip without actually doing anything more.

Okay, he was being a gentleman. Under most circumstances, that was a good thing. She decided to give him a few more hints. She wrapped both arms around him and pressed her body against his. Her stomach made it hard for her to rub her breasts against his chest, but she rounded her shoulders and kind of leaned in so that he would get the message.

Or not, she thought several seconds later when he'd done little more than kiss her like a brother and rest his hands on her shoulders.

"What's wrong with you?" she asked as she drew back. "Why are you here?"

He reached up and tucked her hair behind her right ear. "I'm seducing you."

Seducing? With those chaste little bird kisses? "I don't think so. If this is about what Edouard said, you can forget it. I don't need mercy sex."

He had the nerve to grin at her. "Actually, you do, but I'm interested in more than that."

She wasn't sure what to do. On the one hand, she longed for physical intimacy, to touch and be touched. That part of her relationship with Cal had always worked extremely well. But there were complications. Not only the fact that she worked with him and that they had once been married, but also how she looked.

"This is dumb," she said and started for the garage.

He followed her up to the entrance to the house and pushed the button to close the garage door. "No, it's not," he said. "I want you, Penny, and I think you want me. What's dumb about that?"

His words made her knees go weak, even as she glanced down at her stomach and panicked.

"There's the whole baby thing," she said.

"We'll be careful." He opened the door of the house and pushed her inside. "You can tell me what to do. You like doing that."

"There's not a safety issue, if that's what you mean," she said as she dropped her purse onto the table in the hallway and turned to face him. "But there are other things."

He stepped forward and rested his hands on her stomach. "You mean the fact that you're so beautiful, you practically glow? Or maybe you're talking

about your breasts, which are much bigger than I remember."

She couldn't help smiling. "You've noticed?"

"I've obsessed."

"Really?"

He nodded. "Especially before I knew you were
pregnant. I couldn't figure out what you'd done to
make them bigger."

She liked knowing that.

He rubbed her stomach in slow, sensual circles.
"Your body is different and that's okay." He leaned
over and lightly kissed her. "Or are you going to make
me beg?"

"Begging would be good. I would encourage—"

And then she couldn't talk because he'd pushed
his tongue inside her mouth.

He kissed her deeply, claiming her with a mastery
that left her breathless. Sensations washed over her as
he ran his hands up and down her arms, then did the
same on her back. It was as if he had to reacquaint
himself with every inch of her.

She wrapped both her arms around him. He angled
his head, then circled her tongue with his.

There was heat between them. A melting warmth
that made her want to be naked and on her back with
him filling her. The combination of kissing and thinking caused her body to swell. Her breasts tightened
and her nipples got so sensitive she could barely stand
the pressure of her bra. Between her legs, everything
dampened in anticipation.

He broke the kiss so he could nibble along her jaw

to her ear. He sucked on the lobe, then licked the skin right below her ear. Goose bumps broke out all over.

"Bedroom," he whispered in her ear.

Oh. Right. That would make things easier.

She began backing up down the hallway. At one point, she managed to flick on a light so they wouldn't bump into anything.

As they continued to move, Cal reached for the hem of her sweater and tugged it up and over her head. He waited until they entered her bedroom to toss it on a chair.

She didn't bother turning on a lamp. Enough light spilled in the open door. He moved close and then stepped behind her where he moved her hair to the side and bent down to nibble on the back of her neck.

"I remember your breasts were really sensitive the last time," he murmured against her skin. "Is that still true?"

She was surprised he remembered anything from her previous pregnancy.

"I think so," she said. "They haven't seen a lot of action."

He chuckled. "I'll be gentle."

Part of her wanted him to be fast. Seduction was all fine and good, but she *ached* for her release. Still, when he kissed his way across her shoulders even as he unfastened her bra, she decided to put up with his attentions for just a few more minutes.

He threw the bra on top of the sweater, then reached around her to cup her breasts. Even as he kissed his way down her neck, he cupped her curves.

It was five kinds of heaven, she thought as her eyes

fluttered closed. He held her gently, barely touching and yet touching just enough. He rubbed his fingers against her sensitized skin, moving in slow circles that brought him closer and closer to her nipples. Then, as he lightly kissed the side of her neck, he brushed his forefingers against her nipples.

The contact was exquisite. She arched back, wanting more. Needing more.

"Again," she breathed and he obliged her. Over and over he touched the tight tips, pressing a tiny bit harder each time. Fire shot through her and made her burn from the inside out. Between her legs, her muscles clenched in anticipation.

It felt too good, she thought hazily.

He released her and turned her so she faced him. Then he claimed her with a kiss that stirred her soul even as he found her breasts again and squeezed her nipples between his thumbs and forefingers.

Her body shuddered as pure liquid pleasure poured through her. She clung to him, caught up in an unexpected moment of release.

This couldn't be happening. She'd never come that way. But there it was. And as he continued to touch her, she continued to come.

But it wasn't enough. The minireleases only made her want more. She pulled back and reached for his shirt. "Take this off," she demanded.

He grinned. "You're my kind of woman."

While he took care of his clothes, she removed the rest of her own. She had a brief thought that her stomach seemed huge, then she pulled back the covers and climbed into bed.

Cal was beside her in a heartbeat. She wondered if this could get awkward, but then he reached for her. Even as he kissed her, he slipped his hand between her thighs. The second his fingers moved into her swollen heat, she forgot everything except the potential for pleasure. Her legs fell open, her hips began to pulse and she couldn't catch her breath.

"You're already close," he said against her mouth.

Close didn't describe it, she thought as she dug her heels into the mattress. Tension filled her. Need grew until it swallowed her whole.

He found that single spot of pleasure and began to rub. His fingers moved over slick, swollen flesh, bringing her closer, higher, tighter with each quick circle.

He shifted so that he could continue to touch her there with his thumb, then he slipped two fingers inside. It was good, she thought desperately. Then he lowered his head and took her nipple in his mouth. The gentle sucking pushed her over the edge.

Her orgasm claimed her with the subtlety of an explosion. Wave after wave of pleasure crashed into her, taking her breath away and making it impossible to do anything but absorb the wonder he created in her.

On and on, her body released months of abstinence until she thought she might never stop.

Still feeling the rippling contractions, she forced her eyes open and stared into his face.

"Now," she whispered.

Cal wasn't about to refuse an invitation like that. He kept his fingers inside of her as he shifted between her legs, then he quickly replaced them with his erection.

The second he pushed into her hot, wet, swollen body, he felt her orgasm contract around him. Talk about a sensual massage. Just being inside of Penny had always been enough to send him over the edge, but thrusting into her while she was still coming was indescribable.

The rest of the blood in his body rushed into his arousal, making the already sensitive hardness even more aware of the feel of her body clutching his.

He swore as she came again. "You're going to have to stop that or I won't be able to hold back," he ground out.

He opened his eyes to find her smiling up at him.

"You're complaining because I'm coming too much?" she gasped. "Poor guy."

He laughed, then groaned as she came again and his control slipped.

Inventory, he told himself. He would think about inventory. Even as he put his hands on her raised knees and buried himself inside of her, he thought of the stockroom. How much…

Oh, God. Too late. His body took over. Faster and faster, he pushed deeper and deeper. He opened his eyes and found her watching him. Another contraction, then another and then he was coming.

They stared at each other, pleasure filling them. Even as he emptied himself into her, he felt her body squeezing his again and he was lost.

CAL WATCHED LIGHT creep across the bedroom wall. The space was unfamiliar, as was the bed, but he knew exactly where he was and what he'd done. Beside him, Penny slept, her body warm and feminine as she curled up against him.

He was tired—they'd stayed awake long into the night making love—but content.

He waited for the need to bolt that usually followed spending the night, but his only pressing emotion was one of confusion.

Technically he and Penny were both single, consenting adults. They liked each other, obviously found each other attractive. So they'd taken things to the next level. It happened all the time.

In reality, though, things weren't that simple. He and Penny weren't dating. They worked together, and he'd always done his best to keep his personal life very separate from his work environment. And even if they'd once loved each other enough to commit to forever, he didn't believe in do-overs, so why was he here?

Penny stirred, then opened her eyes. "Morning," she said. "What time is it?"

"Nearly six."

She groaned. "It's my day to check in the order. I'm going to be late." She sat up, then smiled. "I'll be tired all day and it's your fault."

"Sorry."

Her smile widened. "No, no. Don't apologize. It was so worth it."

She stood and stretched, her naked body his to admire. The proof of her pregnancy jutted out toward him, making her seem more lush. Her breasts were definitely bigger. He'd already touched every inch of them and wouldn't mind doing it again. Then he glanced at the clock and groaned. He was running late, too.

Five minutes later, she walked out of the bathroom in a robe. Her face was washed, her hair tied back in a braid. "I'll have to sneak back at some point so I can shower," she said, pausing to give him a kiss. "Take your time. Just lock the door behind you, okay?"

"I will."

She stepped into the closet, reappearing minutes later fully dressed. "See you at the restaurant," she called as she hurried down the hall.

He watched her go, then sat up. As easy as that, he thought.

He stood in his ex-wife's bedroom, after making love with her most of the night and wondered what on earth he'd been thinking.

PENNY ARRIVED thirty seconds before the delivery truck. She checked everything in, then stored what needed immediate refrigeration. The sky was bright, the birds were singing and the new cat had left two dead rats by the back door. It was a very good day.

She walked through the quiet kitchen and felt at one with the world. It was as if every cell in her body had just taken a big breath and relaxed. Sex was a very fine thing and something she should do more of. Especially if it could be as good as it had been last night.

She supposed that made Cal the perfect lover. Not only did he know what pleased her, he knew without being told. They'd already worked out the kinks in their physical relationship and they didn't have an emotional one.

Oh, sure, she liked him. He was a decent guy. But not for her. They'd already tried that once. Him not wanting kids was too big a hurdle to overcome.

But he sure could make her toes curl.

She went to work on her menu for specials that evening. Sometime around eight-thirty, Edouard showed up. The unnamed cat appeared shortly after, looking fat and sleek and wanting plenty of scratches and petting.

"I don't want to know what you've been doing," Penny told him. "But I haven't seen a single rodent since your arrival."

The cat purred louder.

Naomi strolled in around ten. "Morning all," she said. "How is everyone do—" She stared at Penny. "Oh. My. God."

Penny half turned in her seat at the counter, fully expecting to see a large alien hovering behind her.

"What?" Penny asked.

"What happened?" Naomi demanded as she walked toward her. "There's something. I can tell." Her friend started to laugh. "You did it. You had sex!"

Penny glanced around and was grateful when she didn't see Edouard. None of their cooks were due in until later, which meant there was time to do damage control.

"I have no idea what you're talking about," Penny told her, not sure it worked, what with her inability to stop smiling.

"Oh, please. You're glowing, and not in a pregnant

way. This is far more earthy. I can't believe it. And
after all this time. But who? You——"

Naomi froze. Her eyes widened, her mouth
dropped open. "Holy shit. You had sex with Cal."

"Because I *needed* to know that?" Reid asked as he
stepped into the kitchen. He walked over and leaned
against the counter. "Say it isn't so."

Penny returned her attention to her menu. "I have
no idea what either of you are talking about but if
you're not going to do work, then get out of my way
because I'm busy."

"It's true," Naomi said. "Look at her. The half
smile. The fact that she hasn't showered."

Reid leaned on the counter next to his former lover.
"What do you bet Cal spent the night at her house?"

"You think they did it there? They could have done
it at his house."

"I don't know if Penny could. You haven't seen his
kitchen, but it's bright red and she'd really hate that."

Penny slammed down her pen. "Would you two
please stop it? I'm right here."

"We know that," Naomi said. "Having this conversation when you weren't here wouldn't be nearly
as much fun."

Penny stood. "My private life is just that. Private.
So I'm not going to talk about it."

Naomi raised her eyebrows. "Did you see that?
She's not denying the sex thing."

"I know. You think they're getting back together?"
Reid asked.

Penny groaned. "Fine. Talk about me. I'm going
to my office where I will——"

She froze, barely daring to breathe. Naomi was at her side in a heartbeat.

"What happened? Are you okay?"

"Shhh."

Penny waved her hands and waited. Seconds later, she felt it again. A fluttering on the inside of her stomach, followed by a definite jab.

The menu and pen fell from her fingers. She grabbed Naomi's arms. "I felt the baby!" she cried. "I felt the baby move."

The two women jumped around together. Reid got pulled into the group hug. Penny pressed both hands against her stomach.

"Do it again," she said. "I want to feel it again."

The baby obliged with a slight stirring.

"Good job," Reid said with a grin.

"Thanks. I'm excited. Wow. Movement. I'll have to get out my baby book, but I think I'm right on schedule." Penny laughed. "It's really a baby."

"Did you think it was gas?" Naomi asked.

Penny grinned. "No." She bent down and picked up her paper and pen. "Okay. Now I have to do the menu." Even though she wasn't in the mood. "Maybe I'll call my mom first," she said. "She'll want to hear."

Penny walked into her office and reached for the phone. Oddly enough, the person who came to mind wasn't her mother. Instead she found herself wanting to call Cal and tell him the good news.

"Bad idea," she told herself. Cal didn't want children and three years ago, he'd made it clear he didn't want her. So expecting him to share in this was foolish.

So why was that the first place her mind went?

PENNY CHECKED the bandage on her hand. The bleeding had stopped, proving her theory that she didn't need stitches. It was Friday night and the kitchen was moving at top speed. Nothing less than a severed limb was going to get her out of the restaurant until the orders were through.

"The table for eight has been seated," she yelled. "You know they're going to want the special so brace yourself."

Edouard glared at her. "Did you have to offer two different reductions? On a Friday?"

Penny shrugged. "I thought you were up to it."

She offered bravado to her staff because it was expected, but on the inside, she winced. She hadn't been thinking when she'd planned the specials for that evening. Unfortunately, they required too many burners. Which meant if several came in at the same time, there was a delicate dance to be performed, along with a strong-armed game of "who gets the open burner."

She wanted to make a general announcement that the baby had moved and that had distracted her, but she doubted anyone would care. So she put up with the complaints and vowed not to screw up again.

Naomi blew into the kitchen looking like she was ready to choke someone.

"The wine inventory is wrong," she announced. "I can't believe it. On the tasting dinner, they're out of the pinot. Just like that. Randy just announced it in hushed tones, as if by whispering no one would notice." She stood in the middle of the kitchen and raised both her fists. "Where the hell is Cal? I want him dead. I mean that. Seriously, not breathing, dead."

Penny stared at her. "What do you mean, we're out of pinot? We can't be out of pinot. Next to my fish and chips, the tasting menu is the most popular item. Dammit all to hell, I told Cal we needed to double-check the wine inventory. Did he have Randy do it?"

"That's what I'm guessing."

"And Cal's not here?"

Naomi shook her head. "I haven't seen him in about an hour."

Great. It was a Friday night. The restaurant was packed, they were out of wine and Cal was missing.

"Nobody screws with my tasting menu," Penny muttered as she headed for her office.

The tasting menu—a five-course *prix fixe* meal that offered everything from appetizers to dessert— came either with or without wine. The "with wine" selection offered a different glass of wine with each course, including a very nice Pinot Noir with the salmon.

Penny had been very specific about the pairing. Some pinots were sweeter than others and she'd wanted the exact balance of sugar with her salmon.

She jerked off her jacket and stepped out of her clogs. If she was going to have to walk through the dining room, she didn't want everyone noticing that she was the chef.

After slipping into loafers and tugging on a black blazer she kept hanging on the back of her door for just such occasions, she pulled off her head scarf and raced toward the dining room.

Once there, she moved slowly, acting as if she were simply one of the staff. She smiled at various diners as she walked toward the wine room that was clearly visible from the front of the restaurant.

The cold hit her at once. The room was kept at a constant fifty-five degrees. She ignored the momentary discomfort and quickly walked to the pinots. Sure enough, the bin in question was empty. The wine room door opened.

She turned and saw Randy there. Cal's assistant was young, tall and very blond. He rubbed his hands together in a signal of worry that reminded her of her grandmother.

"We're out of the pinot," he said, his voice shaky and weak. "I don't know what to serve with the tasting menu. Naomi wouldn't help. She just threatened to kill me."

"I know. Right now I'm all that's standing between you and certain death."

Penny scanned the various pinots, then grabbed three and walked back to the kitchen. Randy followed.

"What are you going to do?" he asked in a whine.

"Taste them and figure out what works best with my salmon," Penny said.

"But then we'll have three open bottles. Plus, what about costs? We haven't calculated if these wines will still allow us to meet our margins on the tasting dinners."

Penny did a quick change of clothes again, this time emerging as chef. She found Naomi holding a very large chef's knife to Randy's throat—and Naomi looked more than capable of taking him down.

Ignoring the tableau, Penny collected three wine-glasses, then quickly opened the bottles.

"Salmon," she yelled.

Burt dropped a piece of salmon onto a plate. Edouard topped it with the reduction and slid it toward her. She poured, careful to line up each glass with its appropriate bottle.

"Taste," she yelled.

"Do I have to let him go?" Naomi asked.

"Yes. This is more important. You can beat up the assistant manager later."

Naomi released Randy, who squeaked, then raced from the kitchen.

Penny grabbed a fork and took a taste of the salmon. She let the flavors meld on her tongue.

"Damn, I'm good," she muttered, then studied the wines. She picked up the middle one first and took a sip. "Not enough flavor."

The first wine blended well. She took another sip, tried the third wine, then scrawled her initials on the first bottle's label.

Naomi went next. She liked the first and third bottle equally. Edouard agreed with Naomi.

"Then I'll break the tie," Penny said. She grabbed the first bottle and handed it to Naomi. "Give this to Randy. Don't hurt him until the shift is over. Understand?"

"Oh, be that way," Naomi grumbled.

Within five minutes, the kitchen was back on track. Penny left the two open bottles of pinot in the

kitchen for her staff to indulge in later. It would serve
Cal right to lose the money. He shouldn't have left
such a green assistant in charge of something that
important.

And where the hell was he, anyway?

He didn't appear, but shortly after nine there was
another visitor in the kitchen. Penny glanced up as
Gloria entered. The older woman was well-dressed
and looked very happy. The latter was never good
news.

"Penny, I wanted to stop by and say how wonderful everything was tonight. I'm here with friends who
are very impressed."

"Thanks," Penny said. "The special is doing well."

"Yes. I noticed that. Although it seemed a little
overpriced. Still, you and Cal are making the decisions these days."

Penny forced herself to keep smiling. She'd felt her
baby move for the first time that day and nothing the
old bat was going to say could upset her.

"Speaking of Cal," Gloria said, "I don't know if
you noticed he's not here."

"I had noticed. Did you want me to give him a
message?"

"Oh, not at all. I know where he is."

Uh-oh. Penny recognized potential trouble when
she heard it. "Good. I'll tell him you stopped by."

"If you'd like, dear. But you're the reason I'm here.
I thought *you'd* want to know where Cal is tonight."

Penny had been curious, right up until Gloria had
offered to tell her. Now she felt a little queasy.

"I'm really busy," she said. "Maybe another time."

"This won't take but a moment," Gloria said, pulling a piece of colored paper out of her purse. She smoothed the paper on the metal counter. "It's a flyer for a local high school play. They're doing a musical—*The King and I*. Look at the girl playing Anna. Isn't she pretty? Her name is Lindsey. She's seventeen. Do you know about her?"

Penny couldn't speak. She could only stare at the picture. There was something about the teenager—something familiar.

"Cal's daughter," Gloria said. "Didn't he mention her to you? I would have thought he might have, seeing as you were married. Hmm, maybe not. She's a lovely girl with a beautiful voice. So lovely. She was sick a few years ago. Cancer, I believe. But she's fine now. She'll be going to college in the fall. Cal adores her. He's never missed a school production. He hated giving her up, but he was just a teenager himself. What choice did he have? Still, he's been a wonderful, caring father. He always wanted children. Just not with you, dear. Just not with you."

CHAPTER ELEVEN

CAL WALKED INTO THE WATERFRONT a little before ten. The dining room was surprisingly full, with three couples still waiting to be seated. It was going to be a late night.

He nodded at the hostess, then looked around for Randy. His assistant was a little new to have been left in charge on a Friday night, but Cal hadn't had much choice. He wanted a report, then he wanted to check in with Penny.

As he crossed the dining room, he saw Randy race out of his office. The younger man slowed his pace slightly as he approached. He grabbed Cal's arm and pulled him to the side.

"We ran out of wine," he said, his voice low and thick with tension. "For the tasting dinner. Penny's really mad. I mean really mad. She picked a different wine and wouldn't let me run the numbers, so I don't know if we're losing money or not."

Cal groaned. "We ran out of the pinot? How did that happen?"

Randy shrugged.

"Great. Let me go calm Penny down, then we'll get through the evening and sort it out in the morning. There's a decent pinot for the dinner now, isn't there?"

"I think so. Penny didn't want me involved in the decision."

"Okay. I'll take care of things."

He patted Randy on the back, then started for the kitchen. He stepped through the swinging door and into the madness that was a kitchen at capacity.

"Penny, I heard there was a—"

Something whizzed past his head and slammed into the door frame. He turned and saw a meat cleaver sticking out of the wood. Except for the hiss of the steamer and the roar of fire at the burners, the kitchen went silent.

"What the hell?" He turned and saw Penny standing by the counter, glaring at him.

"Oops," she said, not sounding the least bit sincere or concerned. "I must have slipped."

He couldn't believe it. "You threw a knife at me," he said, more stunned than furious.

She shrugged, a casual enough gesture, but he could see the rage in her eyes.

She'd thrown a knife at *him* and she was mad? "What the hell is wrong with you?" he demanded.

"Gosh, I don't know. Like I said, it slipped."

She turned back to the plates she was assembling. Conversation began again in the kitchen. Cal stared at her, not sure what was going on. Penny couldn't be this mad because they were out of wine.

Penny thrust the plates at him. "Table sixteen. Did Randy tell you we're out of the pinot for the tasting menu?"

"He mentioned it."

"Next time you take off on our busiest night of

the week, you might want to leave someone compe-
tent in charge."

She turned her back on him and began calling out
the new orders that popped out of the small printer.
Cal stared at her for a second, then walked out into
the dining room. Something was up, but he didn't
have any idea what.

After delivering the meal and chatting briefly
with several guests, he walked toward his office. He
stepped into the small space and found Naomi waiting for him.

"You okay?" she asked.

"Why do you care?"

She shook her head. "I don't know what happened,
but you're in big trouble. Penny's never gone ballistic
like that before. What did you do?"

"I haven't a clue. Everything was fine when I left,
and now she's crazy. She threw a meat cleaver at my
head."

"I heard. Good thing she's got a decent aim."

He didn't want to think about what would have
happened if she'd slipped.

Naomi looked at him. "Gloria was here. What do
you want to bet the old bat made trouble?"

It was more than possible, but what could Gloria
have said to set Penny off? "As soon as things slow
down, I'm going to talk to Penny. Would you give me
a heads-up if she tries to sneak out?"

Naomi hesitated. "All right. But just because I'm
worried about her. Don't expect me to get in the habit
of siding with you against her."

PENNY FELT AS IF she'd been awake for five days and had just finished a marathon. Her body ached, her head throbbed and she longed for hours and hours of sleep. Maybe then she would be able to forget what Gloria had told her.

She didn't want to believe, but the proof was folded in her jacket pocket. The teenager looked so much like Cal. And knowing he'd had a child and then had given her up explained a lot. But it hurt to finally know the truth.

"You're not leaving without talking to me first."

She glanced up and saw Cal standing in the doorway to her office. He seemed larger than normal, as he filled the space and cut off her only escape route.

Hearing him out was the mature thing to do, although she wasn't in the mood to do much more than throw a tantrum—something she'd sort of already done with the meat cleaver. She hadn't meant to do that. One second she'd been holding it after chopping some beef, the next she'd heard his voice and the knife had somehow slipped from her fingers to go sailing through the air.

She sank onto her chair and drew in a deep breath. There was so much to say, yet she didn't know where to begin. Or how to explain what she was feeling.

"You tried to kill me," he said as he walked into the room and took the seat opposite hers. "Want to tell me why?"

"I reacted without thinking."

"That's a relief. I would hate to have you planning my death."

She really could have hurt him. "I'm sorry. I shouldn't have done that."

He folded his arms over his chest. "You won't have your cooks arguing with you about anything."

"A happy by-product."

She tried to smile and couldn't. Her eyes burned, as much from unshed tears as from exhaustion.

"Naomi told me Gloria stopped by," he said. "So I know she has something to do with what happened. I can't think of what she could have said that would piss you off so much."

"Really?" Did he mean that? Could he possibly have spent the evening watching his daughter in a school play and not have any clue what his grandmother had said? "Then let's clear things up right now."

She reached into her jacket pocket and pulled out the playbill. After smoothing it, she slid it across the desk so he could see the picture. She watched him carefully as he studied the paper. His expression didn't change, but his mouth tightened.

It was as if he'd hit her.

Somewhere in the back of her mind, in the deepest, darkest corner of her heart, she'd hoped Gloria had been lying. That despite the physical similarities, there was another explanation. She didn't want to know that the man she'd loved and married had kept such a big secret, that he'd been willing to have a child with someone else, but not, as Gloria had said, with her.

"She told you about Lindsey," he said quietly.

Penny leaned back in the chair and didn't speak.

She wasn't being difficult—she knew that if she tried to open her mouth, she would start to cry.

He looked at her. "She's my daughter. I was seventeen when she was born. I should have told you before."

"You think?"

"Penny, I'm sorry. I didn't know how to tell you. When we were dating, it didn't seem important. Then we were married and I didn't know what to say or how. The longer I waited, the harder it was to explain. I never meant to keep this a secret."

"We were *married*. I got pregnant. Never once did it occur to you to say 'been there, done that'?"

"I wanted to."

"Apparently not very much. No one stopped you."

"I know. I'm sorry. I guess I hated what it said about me. That I'd given up my kid. It was a pretty typical story. My girlfriend, Alison, got pregnant. She didn't want to keep the baby, but I did. I wasn't sure how I could support us both, but I was willing to try. Then Gloria got involved and she said she would be there to help. We both know what that means."

Her head was spinning. Wait a minute! He'd wanted to keep the baby? He'd been willing to turn his world upside down and keep his child? Her stomach tightened and she felt as if she might throw up.

"I couldn't let her get her hands on my daughter," he said. "So I agreed to adoption. Under the settlement, the parents were to keep me informed of her progress and tell her about me if she ever asked. They've been great about sending me updates and pictures. But while Lindsey knows she's adopted, she's not interested in her birth parents."

He leaned forward. "She's seventeen. Going to college. God, she's pretty and smart. And just about grown up. I can never be her father. All that time is over. But I still like knowing she's okay."

Penny wanted to bolt. It hurt to breathe and she couldn't think. Each word was a blow. He loved this girl so much. She could see it in his eyes, hear it in his voice. He loved Lindsey and yet he hadn't cared when she, Penny, had lost their baby. He'd barely acknowledged its passing.

"Is she the reason you didn't want children with me?" she asked, barely able to keep her voice from shaking.

"Partly. I felt guilty." He shrugged. "I know that sounds crazy, but I couldn't help thinking it was wrong to have another child I could keep when I'd had to give up Lindsey."

"Because she was the one who mattered," she whispered.

"Yes."

Penny did her best to keep breathing. "You knew I wanted children, Cal. Yet you never told me this. You never bothered to explain what was going on. Everything you did was for Lindsey. But what about our marriage? Didn't that matter?"

"I'm sorry. I know it was wrong to keep everything a secret."

That wasn't her point. And he hadn't answered the question.

"I thought I could do it," he said earnestly. "I

thought I could have more children. Then you got pregnant and at first it was great. But then I thought about us being a family and I couldn't stop thinking about giving up Lindsey. I didn't know how to reconcile what I'd done with the life we were planning. I never meant to hurt you."

"But you did. You changed the rules." She stood. "You were happy when I lost the baby, weren't you?"

He rose. "No! Never. I wanted us to have children."

"No, you didn't. When I wanted to try again, you told me you'd changed your mind. You said you didn't want a family. But that's not true, is it? You did want a family, but only if Lindsey could be your daughter. No other child was going to be good enough."

"Penny. Stop. It's not about being good enough. It was about my guilt."

His words didn't make any sense. Then her breath caught and she realized she was crying. She brushed away the tears. "I have to know everything. Just tell me it all now. I don't want any more secrets."

"There aren't any."

"Did you even love me? When I left, when I threatened to leave, I was trying to get your attention. I wanted you to wake up and notice that our marriage was dying. But you weren't even shocked. You let me go without saying a word. I remember thinking you were relieved. Did you love me at all?"

She had to know. Maybe it was wrong. Maybe she would regret it later. But for now, the information was essential.

Cal shoved his hands into his pockets and hung his head. "I'm not sure I knew how I felt," he began.

"Oh, please. At least have the decency to tell me the truth."

He looked at her. "I didn't love you the way I should have. You're right. I was torn between what we had and what I wanted to have with Lindsey. That's why I let you go."

Her body began to shake so hard she thought she might collapse. This wasn't happening. All those years they'd been dating and then married, she'd loved him. Loved him completely, and with such hope for their future. She'd trusted him with her heart, her life, her very being.

"I'm sorry," he said. "I cared about you."

"I'll be sure to hold on to that."

She grabbed her purse and started for the door. He reached for her arm. "Don't run out like this."

She jerked free. "How should I run out? You've just told me that our marriage meant nothing. You weren't willing to have children with me because you couldn't get over giving up your first child. Tell me, Cal. Are Lindsey's parents so horrible? Is she abused in any way?"

"What? No. They're great."

"So there isn't any reason for your guilt, except selfishness. You don't care about what was best for your daughter, you never cared about me. You only cared about what *you* felt. I don't know what kind of game you were playing, but I'm sorry it took me so long to leave. I can't believe how much time I wasted."

Was still wasting. To think she'd made love with

him, had wanted him. That she'd started to think maybe he was one of the good guys.

"You don't understand," he told her.

"I think I do. You couldn't forgive yourself for giving up your child, even though it was the best thing for her. You'd rather live in guilt than have a real life, which is your choice. Only you pulled me in with lies and promises you had no intention of keeping. It was a game. I gave you everything I had and you were just playing."

"You're wrong," he said.

"No, I'm not. You're a fool, Cal. You missed out on something great with me. I don't know if you're afraid to love or just plain stupid. All I can say is I was lucky to get away from you."

WALKER SAT alone in a corner of Reid's bar and enjoyed the rowdy crowd. Since returning to Seattle, he'd found life too quiet. The military was a noisy place and after fifteen years, he'd grown used to the sounds of war.

He'd spent the day on the Internet, looking for class lists of graduates in the Seattle area. So far he'd managed to place Ben at two different high schools for two years, which meant he had more work to do.

He took a drink of his beer. As he set the bottle back on the table, he saw a tall, curvy brunette stroll into the bar.

In heels, she cleared six feet. A soft-looking sweater clung to every curve. Black leather pants left little to the imagination on the lower half of her body. Walker could picture her naked, her head leaning back, her long hair swaying as she rode him home.

His body tightened at the image and once aroused, it wasn't about to let go so easily.

He told himself not to think about her or sex, although the two ideas were intertwined. Was that because of what he knew about her or was it the woman herself? Did it matter?

She glanced around the bar. He waited until her gaze settled on him, then he smiled. He didn't do it often, but he knew how to curve his mouth in invitation. Someone more innocent might not understand, but he was willing to guess Naomi could more than hold her own.

She raised one dark eyebrow, then walked toward him.

She maintained eye contact, her gaze promising she would make it more than worth his while. Anticipation filled him, making him harder and willing to consider clearing the table with a single sweep of his arm and taking her right there.

"Hey, soldier," she said. "Why are you all alone?"

"I was waiting for the right kind of company."

"And who would that be?"

"You."

That single eyebrow rose again. "I thought I wasn't your type."

"I never said that. I wanted a little time between me and my brother."

"I can respect that."

He rose and pulled out a chair. "Have a seat. What are you drinking?"

She moved close but instead of sitting down, she grabbed the front of his sweater and pulled him close.

Her mouth claimed his in a brief kiss that was all fire and promise and need. He felt her heat, tasted her sweetness, then straightened, just as she pulled back.

"Vodka tonic with a lime," she said as she sank into the chair. "Which means you'll be driving."

He returned to his seat and picked up his beer. "My first of the evening."

They were in a relatively quiet corner of the large bar. The round table was small and Naomi leaned close as she spoke.

"I wouldn't have thought to find you here," she said.

"Were you looking for me?"

She smiled. "Darlin', I'm always looking."

"Why is that?" He waved at one of the waitresses and gave her Naomi's order.

Naomi stared into his eyes. "You're one of those guys who likes a little relationship with his sex, aren't you? You're going to want to get to know me."

He grinned. "Right down to your favorite color."

"All right. But just this once. And don't go telling anyone. It'll ruin my reputation."

She shifted so that her forearms were on the table, with her breasts resting on top of them. The position pulled down her sweater, giving him an eyeful of curves that just begged to be explored.

He deliberately stared into her eyes. "You're trying to cheat."

"A little. Is it working?"

"Of course. But we're still going to talk first."

She frowned. "Why is that so important to you?"

"Because I don't get a lot of it in my life."

Her eyes softened as her mouth twisted. "Dammit, Walker, don't you start cheating, too. You're going to tell me you've been in a war and there wasn't any time for soft talk. Probably not any time for sex, either. You're playing on my sympathy."

"Is it working?"

The waitress arrived with the drink. "Here you go, hon."

When she left, Naomi took a sip. "Okay—stop trying to manipulate me. We can talk. Why did you leave the marines?"

He opened his mouth to tell her what he'd already told Cal and Reid, but what he said instead was, "I owe a guy."

"What? Money?"

"No. There was this kid, Ben. Lousy marine but a great guy." He explained how Ben hadn't had any family. "When he died, I'm the one who wrote the letter. I need to find his girlfriend so I can deliver it to her."

"Why?" she asked. "What's so important about a letter?"

"It's all that's left of him."

She touched his arm. "There has to be something else. You don't leave a career to deliver a letter. Why do you owe him?"

"He took a bullet for me."

Walker stared at the table. He could still see everything about that moment as clearly as if it had just happened. It had been cold in the village. There'd been snow the night before and he and some of his men were following tracks. Insurgents had been spotted in the area. Everyone was on alert. Walker had been the most experienced and he knew they were going to have trouble, but even he hadn't expected gunfire to come from the caves.

"There weren't any tracks," he said, more to himself than Naomi. "I'd checked the caves myself the previous evening and no one had been there. How could they have gotten in without leaving footprints?"

"Walker?"

He shook his head. "Ben heard something. I don't know what. Suddenly he pushed me aside and then he was dead. The bullet caught him right in the heart. He didn't have a chance to say anything."

He finished his beer and leaned back in his chair. "I owe him. I'm going to find Ashley and tell her he died bravely. I want her to have the letter. Someone, somewhere has to care about that kid."

She still had a hold of his arm. She moved her hand down until their fingers laced together.

"I'm sorry," she said. "I know that's lame and meaningless, but I'm really sorry. I won't say anything."

"Keeping my secrets?" he asked.

She nodded.

Tears filled her eyes. She might be forty, but she was damn beautiful. Her full mouth quivered. A single tear rolled down her cheek. He brushed it away.

He'd always thought it must be a good thing to be able to cry. To ease the pain that built up inside.

He never managed it himself. Not even when he'd crouched there, holding Ben's body.

"I know how much it hurts," she whispered.

He appreciated the sentiment, even as he dismissed it. She squeezed his hand.

"Walker, I *know*," she told him. "I was married once. A long time ago. I had a child. A son. He was great. Smart and funny and curious and just the greatest kid ever."

Another tear rolled down her cheek.

"I loved him. I didn't know it was possible to love that much until I had him and then it was as if my heart couldn't hold all that love. I would have done anything for him. I would have died a thousand times for him."

There was another tear, then another. She brushed them away.

Walker wanted to bolt from the room. He wanted to be anywhere but here, because whatever Naomi had to tell him, he didn't want to hear.

But he stayed because he knew if he left, she would be alone, and he couldn't bring himself to do that to her.

"He was twelve," she said. "We were in the car, just talking and having fun. I went to put a tape in. I'd done it a thousand times before. The tape slipped, I reached down to pick it up. It just took a second."

Her breath caught. She pulled her fingers free and covered her face with her hands.

"Just one second. And then there was a car. It plowed right into us, hitting his side. He was killed instantly. I walked away without a scratch and my baby died. Not even in my arms. Just there, in the seat. I screamed and reached for him, but he was already gone."

Walker shifted in his chair and pulled her against him. He could feel her sobs. He didn't try to comfort her with meaningless words. Instead he held her tight.

"So I know," she said against his chest. "I know how much it hurts. I know what it's like to never forgive yourself, because I couldn't. Everyone said it was just one of those things. That it wasn't my fault. Even my husband. But they were wrong. It *was* my fault. It was me. I wanted to die. I took some pills and they locked me away for a while. When they let me out, I got in a car and I drove and I drove until the road ended. I was here, in Seattle. I lived in my car for a while, but no matter how much I suffered, I couldn't forget what I'd done."

He touched his fingers to her chin and forced her to look at him. Tears trickled down her cheeks.

"God, it hurts," she said. "Every minute of every day it hurts."

He felt her pain. It mingled with his own.

"I loved him," she whispered. "Why couldn't I save him?"

"We can never save the ones we love," he told her.

Then he stood and pulled her to her feet. After tossing a twenty on the table, he led her out to his car.

As he opened the door, she stared at him. "That's why I do it. To help me forget."

The men. He'd figured there was a reason. "Does it help?"

"For a little while. And then I remember and my heart breaks all over again."

"I'd like to forget," he said and pulled her close.

She went willingly into his arms. He kissed her with a desperation borne of far more than just sexual need. She clung to him, responding as if she would die if she didn't have him.

Perhaps she would, he thought, as desire took over and clouded his mind. Perhaps they both would.

CHAPTER TWELVE

TWO DAYS LATER, THINGS weren't much better with Penny. Cal appreciated that she'd stopped assaulting him with deadly weapons, but she still wasn't speaking to him. After thinking over their conversation he realized that admitting he hadn't really loved her while they'd been married had probably put him at the top of the list for idiot of the year.

He parked next to Reid's Corvette and climbed out of his car. The day was sunny but he could feel the dampness of the lake in the chilly morning. Still, the view was impressive as he stared east toward Bellevue and Kirkland.

He walked along the dock, then stepped onto his brother's houseboat and knocked on the front door.

"It's Cal," he called in warning. "Don't answer the door naked."

Reid pulled open the front door and grinned. "Don't want to be intimidated, huh?"

"Like that would happen."

Reid, dressed in sweats and barefoot, led the way into the kitchen. "Let's not have that conversation. Coffee?"

"Sure."

Reid poured them each a cup from the pot. Without speaking, they walked into the living room and sat down.

Houseboat didn't fully describe the remodeled twenty-two-hundred-square-foot luxury home on the water. There was every modern convenience and the added pleasure of being directly on Lake Washington.

"Penny wants you skinned alive and served with salsa," Reid said conversationally.

"She mentioned that, huh?"

"She ranted and yelled. Then she cried." Reid looked at Cal. "You get that one for free this time, but don't let it happen again."

Cal knew his brother wasn't kidding. "You were right. I should have told her about Lindsey."

He waited for the crowing "I told you so," but Reid only sipped his coffee. The silence told Cal how bad things were.

He wondered if his brother knew that he and Penny had slept together. That night had been spectacular— and not just for the hot sex. There had been something about being with her again....

Warning signs flashed on and off in his brain. No emotions allowed, he reminded himself. No feeling. It wasn't smart, it wasn't safe and in the end, every-one suffered.

"I hate that bitch," Reid said.

It took Cal a second to realize he meant Gloria. "She loves to screw with us."

"It's because we won't do what she wants."

"I have," Cal said. "More than once."

Reid glanced at him. "That's because you were the oldest and were trying to protect the rest of us."

True enough, but that didn't make him feel any better about his decisions. "Gloria's been on my ass about taking over the company," he said. "Why would she pull something like this? She has to know it'll piss me off."

"She wants to make sure you don't get back together with Penny more than she wants you to run the corporation. She can't forgive Penny for walking out on one of her precious grandsons."

Made sense, Cal thought. "Still, it's my fault Gloria had ammunition in the first place. If I'd told Penny about Lindsey, Gloria couldn't have fucked things up."

"We've all made bad choices," Reid said. "Now you'll deal with yours."

He regretted having to make the confession more than he could say. "She thinks I'm glad she lost the baby. I'm not. I wasn't back then, either. I never wished anything bad would happen to our child."

"Maybe not, but you were relieved."

Cal opened his mouth and closed it. His brother spoke the truth. He remembered his initial happiness fading as a sense of being trapped took over. How was he supposed to have another child and care about it when he'd simply walked away from Lindsey? He'd been confused and hadn't had anyone he could talk to. Or so he thought. Now he knew he could have discussed it with his brothers. Or Penny. He hadn't trusted her to understand. What if she had? What if they'd been able to pull together instead of being pulled apart?

"I didn't have all the answers," he said at last.

"No one ever expected you to. Except you. Cal, none of us is perfect. It's time you stopped trying to be. Get over it. Yes, you had a kid. You didn't want to give her up, but you did. She's great. Happy, living a good life. Move on."

Advice he should listen to. "Penny has. She's excited about the baby."

"Of course she is. She's always wanted kids."

Cal knew that. In some ways, that was his greatest sin. "She was right—I changed the rules. When we were first together, I wanted kids as much as she. It was the reality of having a baby I could keep that screwed me up. When I told her I'd changed my mind..." He could still see the disbelief and hurt on her face. "I owe her."

"Big time. But that's the past. Let it go. She's moved on." Reid looked at him again. "Your timing sucks."

"What do you mean?"

"Friday, when all this hit the fan, she'd just felt the baby move for the first time. She wanted to tell you. How's that for a kick in the teeth? There she was all excited and doing the happy dance."

The baby moved? "She never felt that with ours. She lost it too soon." He could imagine her delight and excitement. "Did you feel it, too?"

"I tried, but it was too faint. There she was, all happy and then Gloria dumps the first load on her and you dump the second. Way to go, big brother."

Cal swore. He felt like shit. "I never meant..."

Right. Because meaning or not meaning didn't matter to anyone. Penny didn't deserve any of this from him. She hadn't done anything wrong. All she'd done was show up every damn day of their marriage. She'd taken a whole lot longer to give up than she should have and he'd let her go without a word.

"You should beat the crap out of me," Cal muttered.

"That would only make you feel better and right now I'm not interested in doing that. She has a doctor's appointment in a couple of days. An ultrasound. She's pretty sure she doesn't want to know if it's a boy or a girl. And jeez, the names she's talking about. Poor kid. But I think she'll come around. Penny's pretty smart."

Penny was a lot of things, Cal thought, fighting a sudden aching sense of loss for all he'd missed with her.

He reminded himself that he was fine with that—being a part of something wasn't his goal. Love didn't last. Hadn't he had that proved to him over and over?

"Naomi was in last night," Reid said. "She left with Walker."

"You okay with that?"

Reid shrugged. "Sure. Why not? There were never any promises between us."

Not wanting a permanent commitment was one thing, but Reid's lifestyle made no sense to him. "Don't you ever want more than a parade of women through your life?"

His brother frowned. "No. Why?"

"But you don't care about the women you sleep with."

Reid grinned. "For that night, she's the most important woman in the world."

Cal snorted. "Yeah, right. And in the morning you can't remember her name. Don't you ever want more than that?"

"Not even on a bet."

"ARE YOU SICK?" Penny asked.

Naomi continued to chop leeks. "No. I'm fine. Stop bugging me. You're getting on my nerves."

Penny knew she should back off, but she couldn't help worrying. "You're not yourself. You've been quiet for a couple of days. Is it a guy?"

Naomi turned to her, holding the knife in her hand. "I learned from an expert, okay? I'm fine. I have stuff on my mind."

"But I'm worried about you."

Naomi put down the knife. "You're sweet to worry, but don't. I'm fine. Just thinking. It's not something I usually do, so it's hard for me."

Penny could see emotions swirling in her friend's eyes. "I want to help."

"You can't. Now let it go before I start foaming at the mouth."

"Okay. But if you want to talk, I'm here."

"I know."

Cal walked into the kitchen. "The wine delivery is here. I was able to get more of the original pinot for the tasting dinner, but it's an '02 instead of an '01. I'm going to open a bottle to see how different it is."

The implied question was did she want to join him?

Did she want to participate in this joint venture, because they were both responsible for the restaurant.

She knew the right answer. As her goal was to run her own place, she had to be interested in all aspects of the business. Hiring a good general manager would help, but in the end, the decisions would be hers.

She knew she should agree for another reason—to show Cal he didn't matter. That she wasn't crushed by their fight last week. Okay, maybe crushed was strong, but she was still hurt. Worse, she felt stupid. She hated feeling stupid.

She walked past him and headed for the wine room. Three cases stood on a dolly. The top case was open and a single bottle rested on the counter.

She reached for the bottle opener sitting there and quickly cut the foil. After twisting the corkscrew into the cork, she turned and pulled in a quick, expert movement. Cal set out two glasses. She poured a small amount in each.

Penny picked up hers and swirled. She held the glass to the light to check the color, then swirled again and inhaled.

The scent alone was delicious. She took a sip and allowed the flavors to settle on her tongue.

Good, she thought. A hint of sweetness, but not too much. Plenty of berry.

"It's fine," she said.

"I agree."

She put her glass on the counter and turned to leave. Cal moved in front of her.

"Wait," he said. "I want to say I'm sorry about what happened on Friday. All of it. Gloria telling you about Lindsey, our fight afterward. I should have told you myself. Years ago, before we got married. I grew up keeping secrets and it's a hard habit to break. And I was afraid of what you'd think of me."

"I appreciate the apology, but it's not necessary. We're divorced, Cal. None of that matters."

"It does. We work together. I want us to be friends."

Friends. Right. She wanted to point out that she didn't usually sleep with her friends. That by having sex with her, they'd crossed the line and now everything was different between them. Except she didn't understand how it was different or what it all meant.

"I shouldn't have allowed Gloria to have information you didn't," he said. "She wanted to hurt you and she succeeded. I'm sorry about that."

Without wanting to, she remembered a conversation from their past. When she'd wanted the entry-level job at Buchanan's and Cal had done his best to keep her from getting it. At the time he'd said he didn't want her near Gloria. She'd laughed off his concern. How could the old woman hurt her? Now she knew there were probably a thousand ways.

"I can take care of myself," she said. "Then and now."

"Now I believe. But back then…"

"You're acting as if my being hurt would have bothered you."

"Of course it would have. You were my wife."

The one you didn't love. Only she didn't think she could say that without him knowing she was still bruised inside.

"Look, Cal. We didn't do well on the personal front

when we were married and we obviously can't do it well now. Let's just keep things strictly business. It will be better for everyone that way."

"But I want us to be friends."

"Sometimes we don't get what we want. Deal with it."

PENNY PACED in the parking lot. Where was he? Reid was many things, but late wasn't one of them. She glanced at her watch and groaned. If she didn't want to miss her appointment, she was going to have to leave in the next two minutes.

Cal walked out of the restaurant. She eyed him suspiciously, especially as he had a coat on and was heading in her direction.

"Let's go," he said. "You want me to drive?"

She planted her hands on her hips. "What, exactly, are you talking about?"

"Your doctor's appointment. You're getting an ultrasound. I'm going with you."

She glanced at him. As she hadn't told him about the appointment, he must have been talking to Reid. Was this a conspiracy?

"Is Reid even going to show up?" she asked.

"I don't know. He's not here now, you need to leave and I want to come with you."

"I'd rather go alone."

His dark gaze searched her face. "Are you sure?"

No, dammit, she wasn't sure. But she didn't want to admit that to him.

Just then Reid drove into the parking lot. He pulled

up in front of her. "Sorry I'm late. There was an accident on the bridge."

"It's okay. Park that thing and let's go."

Reid glanced between Penny and Cal. Cal moved closer to her.

"I'm going," he said.

"No, he's not. Reid, don't you dare."

Reid shrugged. "It's better this way, Penny. You two need to talk. Besides, he's seen you naked and I haven't. It will be easier."

"No, it won't," she yelled, but it was too late. He'd already driven off. She turned to Cal. "Did you tell him we slept together?"

"Of course not. He was talking about when we were married." He put his hand at the small of her back and urged her toward her Volvo. "Come on. We'll be late. Do you want me to drive?"

She was so upset, she handed him the keys without thinking. It was only after she'd climbed into the passenger side that she realized she'd abdicated authority to Cal. Jeez.

She couldn't believe Reid had turned on her that way. "We're supposed to be friends," she muttered, feeling hurt and abandoned. "I'm going to have to explain that to him later."

"He understands," Cal said as he backed out of the parking space. "He's trying to help."

"Which one of us?" Penny muttered.

"Where are we going?"

She gave him the address, then settled back in her seat. "This is dumb. I would have been fine on my own."

"You still can be. If you don't want me in the room with you, I'll wait outside."

She swallowed. "Maybe that would be better," she said, although she wasn't sure she meant it. While she knew the ultrasound was a perfectly normal procedure, she couldn't help being terrified by the thought of it. That's why she'd asked Reid to come along. So she wouldn't have to face it alone.

"What's wrong?" Cal asked after about ten minutes of silence.

She stared straight ahead. "Nothing."

"Do you have to go to the bathroom? Should I stop somewhere?"

"What?" She sounded deeply insulted. "No."

"You're fidgeting. I wondered why."

She shifted in her seat and didn't answer. Cal considered the possibilities—everything from her hating him so much she couldn't stand to be in the car with him to—

"You're nervous," he said. "Why? Is there something you haven't told Reid? Is there a problem with the baby?"

"No. Not that I know of. I don't know. I'm just scared."

Risking dismemberment, he reached out and took her hand in his. "I know. It's because you lost the baby before and what if something is wrong this time."

She sighed. "Yeah."

"There's no reason to think there's any problem. You'll be fine."

"You don't actually know that."

"You don't actually know I'm not telling the truth."

She squeezed his fingers. "Okay. Maybe."

He sensed her relaxing a little and decided it was a good idea to keep her distracted. "Reid mentioned you didn't want to know the sex of the baby."

"What else did you talk about?" she asked.

"I agree with you," he said, ignoring the question. "There are too few good surprises in life these days."

"Oh, please. You're only saying that because you're assuming I'm having a boy. Typical male. The whole world just lives to be your penis."

He chuckled. "Something like that."

They parked in the multilevel structure by the medical building. He followed her into the office.

The waiting room was uncomfortably cheerful and feminine and he was the only guy in sight. Despite feeling awkward, he was glad he'd come. Especially after Penny gave her name, took a seat and then grabbed his hand in hers.

"You can come in," she said, not looking at him, but instead staring at the floor and speaking very quickly. "Tell me if you hear them talking about anything. I want to know."

He turned and touched her chin so she met his gaze. "I promise." Then he drew their clasped hands to his mouth and kissed her fingers. "Relax. Everything is going to be fine."

"You don't know that. And I'm only letting you be nice to me because I'm scared. Just so we're clear, I'm still furious with you."

He shook his head. "Okay, you can imagine ways to roast me over an open flame after the appointment."

She was quiet for a while, then she said, "I appreciate you doing this."

"Why wouldn't I be willing? It's not that big a deal."

She looked at him. "What do you think is going to happen?"

He didn't like that question. Or the gleam in her eye. "It's an ultrasound. They rub goop on your belly."

The nurse called her name. Penny stood and smiled at Cal.

"Sorry, no. We're not doing it that way."

"What other way is there to see the baby?" He frowned as he followed her.

"From the inside," she said smugly.

The inside? How the hell would they get a probe...

"You're kidding."

"You were going to let Reid see this?" Cal asked fifteen minutes later as Penny lay on a table in a small room filled with equipment.

"He was going to stand by my head, which is where you'll be standing."

"I'm fine with that. Better than fine. Happy, even." He might have recently seen Penny naked and touched every inch of her, but he wasn't excited about watching an intimate medical exam.

"If you start to get queasy, close your eyes and think of England," she said with a grin.

"I'm not British," he muttered as the door opened and the doctor stepped into the room.

"Good morning," she said. "How are you feeling, Penny?"

"Good. Nervous. This is Cal. He's a friend."

"I know you're not the father," the doctor said. "I did the IVF procedure. Hi. I'm Dr. Robins." She shook hands with Cal, then turned her attention to Penny. "Don't be nervous. We're only doing this to check on the baby. There's no reason for any of us to think something's wrong."

"I know. It's just…you know. What happened last time."

"Yes, I know." The doctor checked her folder, then reached for the paper sheet covering Penny's bottom half. "All right. Let's see what your little guy looks like."

Cal did his best to ignore what was happening. He held Penny's hand, only half listened to the conversation and thought about the restaurant. When that didn't work, he considered the yearly question of whether or not the Mariners would make it to the World Series. Now that Reid wasn't playing baseball, he didn't have to worry about divided loyalties.

"There we go," the doctor said.

"Oh, look," Penny whispered.

Cal turned to the screen and saw something moving. It was just a bunch of light and dark patches. Not anything he recognized. Then the picture shifted and sharpened.

"Is that the head?" he asked.

"Uh-huh. There we go. A head, the body. Arms and legs."

"Just two of each, right?" Penny asked anxiously. She tightened her grip on Cal's hand.

"Just two. Everything looks normal." She clicked

a switch and the room filled with the sound of the baby's heartbeat.

Seeing the infant move, hearing its heart, was incredibly profound. Until that moment, Cal hadn't connected Penny's pregnancy with actual life. Her first pregnancy had ended before they got to this stage and he realized now that in some ways, it hadn't been real to him, either.

She was having a baby. A real baby who would grow up to be an actual person.

He stared down at her, seeing her smile, watching tears fill her eyes. How could she be so damn confident that she was willing to take this on by herself?

But he already had the answer. He could see it in the love in her eyes. She'd always wanted children. At first with him, and when he screwed that up, then any way she could.

The magnitude of what he'd lost slammed into him. A wife. A family. They had all been his to lose and he had. She'd truly loved him. Sure, intellectually he'd known but until this exact second, he hadn't gotten it down deep.

Why hadn't he believed? Why hadn't he known how much he'd let drift away? She'd accused him of letting her go, of almost not being surprised that she'd left and she'd been right. He'd been waiting for her to walk out from the first day they met.

CHAPTER THIRTEEN

PENNY FELT A PROFOUND sense of relief. It was as if she hadn't been able to draw in a deep breath for weeks.

"Pretty amazing," she said from the passenger seat of her Volvo.

"The picture was detailed," Cal said. "You could see everything."

"And more than you wanted to," she teased. "Were you completely grossed out?"

"No." He hesitated. "Okay, I didn't need her showing us the hole that was going to be the stomach."

Penny laughed. "That was a little strange," she admitted. "But very cool." All of it had been a miracle. "The baby seems so real now. I knew I was pregnant before, but seeing it like that while hearing the heartbeat…"

"It changed everything," he said.

"Exactly. And I was very tempted to ask about the gender. It would help with getting the nursery ready. The clothes and stuff."

"Do newborns wear clothes?" he asked.

"Oh. Good point. There's not a formal wardrobe, but they do have things to sleep in. I have some books on babies. I guess I should start reading that part."

"The chapter on fashion accessories?" he asked.

She smiled. "Sure. I don't want my baby being out of step with what's in style." She angled toward him. "Thank you for coming with me," she said. "I would have hated to do this alone."

"I'm glad I was there, too," he said. "But Reid would have come."

She nodded. "I know, but he would have freaked out." There'd been something intimate about the experience. While she and Reid were great friends, they'd never shared stuff like that.

She looked at Cal. Happiness, anger and sadness blended uneasily. She'd wanted this experience for *them*. She'd wanted to have children with him.

How involved had he been with Alison's pregnancy? How much of his presence here was to smooth things over? She believed he was genuinely sorry he'd hurt her, and that he hadn't withheld the truth to be vicious, but she suspected he would have been content to keep his daughter a secret forever.

"I'm sorry about our baby," he said.

She stared at him in surprise. "What do you mean?"

"I'm sorry we lost it." He shrugged. "I felt bad before, when it happened, but until today, the experience wasn't real. Intellectually I knew you were pregnant back then, but I didn't think about you having a baby. Sorry. I'm not making sense."

"No, you are." She understood how he could have been more disconnected from the experience. It hadn't been happening to his body. She just wasn't sure she believed him.

"I missed out on a lot," he said, staring straight ahead. "It's sad, for both of us."

Wow. Cal admitting to an emotion. "I'm sad, too," she told him. "But it was for the best."

"You losing the baby?"

She nodded. "There's a reason that sort of thing happens. There was probably something wrong with it and it wouldn't have survived anyway."

"I thought you were going to say it was for the best because we got a divorce."

"That's a factor, but not a big one," she said. "We would have figured out how to be parents without being together."

Not that she'd ever expected to be a single mother. Yet here she was, making it happen.

"You were right before," he said. "About me expecting you to leave. I was. Right from the beginning. Even when we got married, I always thought the relationship was temporary."

"Why? What did I ever say or do to make you think that?"

"It wasn't you." He gave her a smile that didn't reach his eyes. "You were in it for the long haul. It was me. How I was raised. What I believed. There are a lot of reasons that aren't that interesting. But I wanted you to know you were right." He glanced at her again. "It's one of your favorite things."

"Usually," she murmured, stunned by his confession. "This time I would have accepted being wrong." She hesitated, then asked. "If that's how you felt, why did you marry me?"

"I wanted to be wrong."

"But you weren't. I did leave."

"You left to get my attention. I'm the one who let you go. I had a good thing with you, Penny," he said. "When you left, I lost something I'll never be able to replace."

"Thank you for saying that. I always wondered if you'd even noticed I was gone."

"I noticed."

"Just not enough to come after me."

He glanced at her. "You're still mad about Lindsey."

"Mad doesn't cover it, Cal. It's not like you were hiding a tattoo. You kept a huge part of your life separate from me. Not just that you had a daughter, but that you loved her so much, you couldn't love anyone else."

"That's not true."

"Isn't it?"

"Penny, you were my *wife*. I wanted…"

"What? To stay together forever? To have a family?"

"I wanted us to make it."

"I don't believe you. I think you wanted to be alone with your guilt. At least your lack of interest wasn't about me specifically. You would have done this to anyone."

His hands tightened on the steering wheel. "You're not going to give me a break, are you?"

"Do you deserve one? You fundamentally changed everything about our past. I'm still dealing."

"Are you going to be able to work with me?"

"Offering to leave?" she asked.

"If it helps."

Would it? "I meant what I said. I don't hate you."

"Will we ever be friends again?"

Friends? They'd been married before. They now worked together and just about a week ago, they'd been lovers. She wasn't sure they'd ever been friends.

"I don't know," she admitted. "I'm not sure it's…"

Suddenly she felt a fluttering in her stomach. Her breath caught.

"What?" he asked. "Are you okay?"

"I'm great. It's the baby. It's moving."

He smiled at her. "Yeah? What does it feel like?"

Anger and hurt battled with a need to share the wonder. She hesitated a second, then pulled up her sweater and placed his hand on her bare stomach.

"Can you feel it?" she asked. "It's right there."

He glanced at her, his eyes wide, his mouth parted in amazement. "I can feel it. Not a kick. More of a brushing."

"Yes. That's it."

They smiled at each other, then he turned his attention back to the road. Still, he kept his hand on her stomach and she kept her hand on top of his. The moment seemed to stretch on endlessly. Despite everything, they were connected.

He'd been so much a part of her past and now he was in her present. She wanted to hate him and couldn't.

At least she no longer loved him. Only a fool would want her heart broken by the same man twice.

CAL CHECKED over the figures from the previous night. He glanced up as his office door opened and Dani stepped inside.

"Hi," he said before he realized she was crying. He stood and walked around to hug her. "What's wrong?"

Instead of answering, her tears turned into sobs. Her whole body shook as he held her. He felt her pain, even if he didn't know what caused it, and he was more than willing to go do battle on her behalf.

"Whose ass do I have to kick?" he asked, as he rubbed her back and kissed the top of her head.

"I w-wish it was that simple," she said, her voice muffled against his chest. She straightened and looked into his eyes. "It's Hugh."

Cal grimaced. He wasn't comfortable picking a fight with a guy in a wheelchair, but if necessary… "What did he do?"

"He left me."

"What?" Cal had expected to hear anything from a major disagreement to the unlikely statement of an affair. But not this.

"He left me," she repeated.

"Not possible. He loves you." What he was really thinking was that Hugh owed her. After his accident, she'd been the one to stand by him, to insist that they were still getting married, even if he was never going to walk again. She'd loved him and bullied him when necessary, all with the goal of making him want to live, despite being paralyzed from the waist down. She'd stayed at Burger Heaven to keep their insurance so he could continue with his physical therapy.

She'd succeeded. Hugh had slowly returned to the

land of the living and he'd carved out a good life for himself.

"Maybe you misunderstood him."

She gave a strangled laugh and walked to one of the chairs by his desk. He took the other, then leaned toward her and grabbed her hand.

"I don't get it," he said.

"That makes two of us." She wiped her cheeks with her free hand, then fished in her coat pocket for a tissue. "I told him I wanted to talk about in vitro fertilization. We were going to need some help to get pregnant and I thought this was a good time. Okay, I was a little selfish because I knew I wasn't going anywhere at Burger Heaven and I thought maybe this would distract me. Being a mom and all." She sniffed. "It's not that I didn't want kids, it's just that I thought I'd have my career together first."

He tucked her short hair behind her ears. "So what happened when you mentioned getting pregnant?"

"He said he didn't want to." The waterworks started up again. "At first I thought it was about money, because the procedure is really expensive, but it wasn't. He said that he wanted a divorce. He said he'd outgrown m-me."

He shifted his chair closer, then pulled her close. She rested her forehead on his shoulder.

"He said he's been growing and changing and I haven't. He's on the tenure track and I'm just the manager of Burger Heaven." She looked at him. "He threw that in my face. As if I haven't been trying to move up in the company. As if I hadn't stayed there for *him*. I work damn hard. Harder than anyone has in that job."

He cupped her head and kissed her nose. "That's true. Even than me. You've been great and Gloria has never noticed."

"That's what I said. Hugh told me I was getting bitter and he didn't want to live with someone like that. He didn't want to live with me anymore."

She stood up and shrugged off her jacket. "I can't believe it. How dare he? I was there for him. I've *always* been there for him. He got really depressed after the accident. I don't blame him, but he wasn't very fun to be around. And I was there. Even more than his parents. But does he appreciate that? Does it matter now? No. He's grown. La de da. He's so sanctimonious. I really hate him."

Cal thought about pointing out that hating Hugh would make the divorce easier, but something in his male brain told him to keep quiet.

"We're short nearly five pounds of—" Penny looked up from the clipboard she held. "Oh, sorry. I didn't know you had company." She paused, then frowned. "Dani, are you all right?"

Dani sucked in a breath. "Hugh wants a divorce."

"Oh, honey." Penny dropped the clipboard onto the bookcase and held out her arms. Dani walked into them.

"He says he's outgrown me," his sister said.

"Men are such bastards."

Cal wanted to protest, but he kept quiet. This was not the time to defend his gender.

"I was there for him. I loved him. I still love him," Dani said.

Penny stroked her hair. "So do you want to try to work things out?"

"No. If he doesn't want me, then that's fine. I won't be married to him. I don't need him." She started to cry again. "It just hurts. I loved him and he doesn't love me back."

Cal felt his sister's pain and a good-sized serving of guilt. Was this what Penny had gone through when she'd left him and he hadn't come after her?

"What do you want?" Penny asked. "Do you want him to suffer?"

"Yes. Big time. Cal offered to beat him up."

Penny looked at him and smiled. "Your brother is a very good man. But, and no offense, Cal, I think Walker would do a better job."

Dani straightened. "Oh, you're right. The military training."

She was as close to smiling as he'd seen all morning. He rose and moved next to her.

"What do you really want?" he asked.

"A good lawyer."

"I can help you find one."

"Okay." She glanced at both of them and then the tears flowed again. "He wants me to file. Can you believe it? He said he was busy with finals coming up and would I please take care of the paperwork."

He and Penny hugged her. Dani sighed. "I'd tell Walker to break his legs, but that would be redundant, wouldn't it?"

He hugged tighter. Dani clung to him. "What is Gloria going to say? I don't want to tell her."

"Then don't," Penny said.

Dani looked at her. "But I have to."

"Why? She's just your grandmother, not the local oracle. She doesn't see all and know all. Frankly, as mean as she's been to you, I wouldn't say a word. Why give her the satisfaction?"

Dani actually smiled. "I want to be just like you when I grow up."

PENNY HAD JUST FINISHED the tasting for the afternoon, allowing the staff to sample the specials, when Gloria walked in.

"At least she missed Dani by a couple of hours," Penny murmured to Naomi as Gloria walked toward her. Luckily Cal had gone back to The Daily Grind for a big meeting.

"Want a meat cleaver?"

Penny grinned. "Don't tempt me."

She forced herself to smile as the older woman shrugged out of her fur-trimmed coat and slung it over her arm.

"Good afternoon, Penny."

"Gloria. How nice to see you. I'm surprised to see you back here in the kitchen."

Gloria raised her perfectly plucked eyebrows. "You and Cal might think you're in charge, but I still am the majority stockholder in the corporation."

A fact which probably explained the lack of a bonus system.

"So you're here officially?" Penny asked. "Let's adjourn to my office."

While she didn't want to be with Gloria under any circumstances, let alone in the close confines of her office, she wasn't willing to take her on in public. Given what the old bat had dropped the last time she'd been here, who knew what havoc she wanted to wreak today?

"Cal can't join us," Penny said. "He's not here. Should we reschedule?" Unlikely, but a girl had to have dreams.

"No. You're the one I came to see." Gloria paused and looked around at the large space. "Cal's office is much smaller than this."

"Yes, it is."

"Shouldn't he have had the larger office?"

"Nope."

"Are you going to offer me something to drink?"

"Do you want something?"

"Not really."

"Then, no. I'm not." Penny smiled. "Any other questions?"

Gloria frowned. "I'm here because I've received several complaints about the food."

"Really? I'm surprised. We haven't had any."

Which wasn't precisely the truth. There were the usual number of people wanting their fish to taste like something it wasn't or insisting on impossibly overcooked meals that were then not as good as they should have been. But nothing out of the ordinary.

"You seem very proud of your fish and chips and yet I've been told the dish is very substandard. It's really not the sort of thing we should be serving at a restaurant this elegant."

Penny was pretty happy with herself for continuing to see the humor in the situation.

"Interesting point," she said, "but here's the thing. While you might be the major stockholder of the corporation, I don't actually work for you. And even if I did, I have a funky little contract that contains a clause saying that I determine what's served to our customers. Just me. I try to be open-minded and accept other people's input, but it's my name on the top of the menu."

Gloria glared at her. "I don't know why Cal agreed to let you have that much control. It's ridiculous."

"Maybe, but there we are. Now if you're receiving complaints, that worries me. Why don't you give me the names of the people who are unhappy and their phone numbers? I would love to talk to them personally and then invite them back for a free dinner."

She waited, fairly sure that Gloria couldn't give her the information as the complaints weren't real.

Gloria leaned back in her chair. "He's not going to marry you, you know. I don't know if you thought you could appeal to him by being pregnant, but you can't. You already left him once. Callister isn't likely to be fooled again."

Penny bit down on her lower lip. It took all her moral character and inner strength not to tell the old woman that she and Cal had had sex. Not just once, but for a whole night. Over and over again. Like rabbits.

But she held back. This being mature thing was

starting to become a habit. Besides, she wasn't interested in Cal—not in that way.

"If he did show any interest in you," Gloria continued. "I would be forced to cut him off."

"Financially," Penny clarified.

"Yes."

"As he's made millions with The Daily Grind, I don't see that as a big problem." Penny stood. "I don't know what you want, Gloria, but you're not going to get it here. Go torture someone else. I'm not interested in your games."

Gloria rose. "You can't dismiss me."

"Seems that she just did," Naomi said from the doorway. "I couldn't help overhearing some of that. Wow. It's all so ugly." Naomi smiled broadly. "While we're sharing, I've slept with Reid and Walker. Not at the same time, of course, because that would be tacky. But both of them. That should give you something to chew on."

"Slut," Gloria hissed.

Naomi laughed. "If that's the best you can do, I'm not sure why so many people are afraid of you."

Gloria grabbed her coat and walked out. Naomi moved over to the desk and she and Penny gave each other a high five.

"Talk about someone needing an attitude adjustment," Naomi said. "You okay?"

"I'm fine." Penny eyed her friend. "Are you really sleeping with Walker?"

"I just saved your butt. How about thanking me and offering me a big raise?"

"I appreciate the rescue, even if I didn't need it. Are you really sleeping with Walker?"

Naomi shrugged. "Just once. It was nice, but now it's over." She frowned. "We're friends. Weird, because I don't believe in guy friends, but there we are."

Penny didn't know what to say. First of all, Naomi *loved* to talk about her conquests. She always said that was nearly the best part. Second, friends?

"Don't look so confused," Naomi said. "He's different. I like him."

"Like as in romantic affection?"

"No. Just like as in like." Her expression tightened. "This is private information and you are never to talk about it with anyone."

Penny grinned. "Blackmail material. Cool."

CAL RETURNED to the restaurant just before five. As he walked into the kitchen, he smiled at the familiar chaos that preceded the genius that was Penny's menu.

"How's it going?" he asked, raising his voice to be heard over the noise.

"Great," Penny said.

Naomi reached for two salads. "Your grandmother was here and threatened Penny."

He swore. "I warned her if she meddled, I would walk."

Penny shook her head, as if warning him off. Naomi rolled her eyes.

"Oh, right. She acts up and you bail. So we're stuck having to deal with her on our own. Very manly. Remind me to call you first in a crisis."

With that, she picked up a third salad, spun and walked out of the kitchen.

"I haven't even taken my coat off and I've lost a battle with her," he said.

Penny sighed. "With Naomi, it's a real gift. She can make any man think he's incapable of winning. I tried to get you to stop, but no. You had to keep talking."

He eyed her. "You seem plenty cheerful. Obviously Gloria didn't do any serious damage."

"I held my own."

"Did Gloria stop by to see you or me?"

"Me," Penny said.

"What did she want to talk about?"

"The usual. How she was important and I wasn't. Then Naomi popped in to tell her she was sleeping with Reid and Walker. I would say it was a draw."

"Remind me to thank her later."

He dumped his coat in his office, then toured the dining room. They were booked through nine, which wasn't bad for a Wednesday night. The tables were already full and there were several couples waiting in the bar.

He returned to the kitchen. "Looks good out there," he told Penny. "Want to tell me the real reason Gloria stopped by?"

"Not especially."

"Because?"

"Because it doesn't matter. She's a bitter old woman and she wants everyone else in her sphere to be equally unhappy. I refuse."

"Good for you," he told her. He sidestepped a cook

lugging a huge pot of clam chowder. "I should get out of your way."

"Yes, you should," she said, but she was smiling.

There was something about her eyes, he thought. They were so pretty. And her smile. Before he realized what was going on, the wanting had returned. Funny how the past week had sort of sucked it out of him. Her anger, the baby, everything else. But now he could imagine taking her to bed.

Talk about twisted, he told himself and started toward his office.

Naomi stepped into the kitchen. "Cal, there's someone here to see you. Tracy somebody. Are you dating her? Do I need to let the air out of your tires?"

"Tracy?" He only knew one woman by that name. "Lindsey's mom?"

Penny moved to his side. "Does she come to see you often?"

"Almost never. The last time was when Lindsey was sick. She wanted to tell me in person." His insides clutched. Had the cancer returned?

No. He shook off the fear. He'd seen her less than two weeks ago at the school play and she'd looked great. Without thinking, he took Penny's hand.

"Maybe she wants to meet me." After all this time, maybe his daughter had decided she wanted to know about him.

Still holding Penny's hand, he walked out of the kitchen. She shuffled along behind him.

"I shouldn't be here," she said.

"Yes, you should. I was there for you, with the baby."

"This isn't the same."

He glanced at her. "It might be the closest I'm going to get."

He recognized Tracy at once. She stood by the hostess station. But as he got closer, he saw the worry in her eyes and the pain in her expression.

He swore. This was not a happy woman. This was a frightened mother.

"What happened?" he asked.

Tracy glanced from him to Penny. "It's Lindsey. I'm sorry to come here like this. I called your office and they said I could find you here."

Cal gripped Penny's hand harder. He knew. Just looking at Tracy, he knew the truth. "The cancer's back."

Tracy paled. "Yes. There have been signs for a few weeks. Apparently Lindsey did her best to keep them from us. She was determined to star in her school play, but she collapsed after the show that night. They've been doing tests, but we all knew…" She twisted her hands together.

"When it comes back like this," she said, "so aggressively, they want to do more than chemo. They want to try a bone marrow transplant. I came here to find out if you'd be willing to be tested."

"Of course. Right away. I can get in touch with Alison as well." Although he had no idea where the woman was, her parents still lived in Seattle.

"Thank you." Tracy shivered. "We love her so much. She's our baby girl. When she was sick before and then got better, we were all so hopeful." She swallowed. "Cal, you've been so good to us. You've never tried to get involved in her life."

"She didn't want that." It hurt him to speak the words.

"I know, but you didn't have to respect her wishes and you did. You've asked for so little. I...Tom and I have been talking and we think maybe it's time for her to meet you."

CHAPTER FOURTEEN

"I WANT YOU TO KNOW this is the first time I've resented your pregnancy," Naomi said as she reached for a tortilla chip covered in cheese.

"I know," Penny said from her place across the small table. "I understand completely. In your position, I'd feel the same way."

Naomi made an inelegant sound that was halfway between a scoff and a snort. "Oh, please. I'm a much better person than you are. In my position, you'd be making margaritas."

Penny laughed. "You're probably right."

Her friend had arrived less than a hour ago, bearing the fixings for nachos. After announcing she was in the mood to get drunk, she'd handed the food over to Penny and told her to have at it. As Naomi wasn't the type to drink alone, she would accept eating as a poor substitute.

"I did my best with the nachos," she said.

"They're good," Naomi said grudgingly. "But I'm still deeply offended that you're pregnant at a time when I really need alcohol and someone to share it with."

Penny didn't point out that there was a massive list of men who would be oh-so-happy to indulge with

Naomi. Penny had a feeling this was a "girls only" kind of thing.

"Have you heard any more about Lindsey?" her friend asked.

"Just that we're waiting to find out if Cal's a match. It shouldn't be much longer. Another day or so. He's really hoping he is. He wants to be the one to save his daughter."

"What father wouldn't?"

A fact that filled Penny with ambivalence. On the one hand, who could resent a man who loved the child he'd given up for adoption? On the other hand, who could trust a man who couldn't open his heart to anyone else?

If he'd just told her everything all those years ago. She would have understood…eventually. Instead he'd withdrawn until he hadn't wanted her or their baby.

"I hope it works out for Lindsey," Penny said. "The poor kid has been through enough already. Apparently she had chemo when she was first diagnosed. That can't have been fun. With the cancer returning, a bone marrow transplant is her best hope."

"Any news on the Alison front?"

"She's not a good match so everyone is hoping Cal is. If not him, they'll have to look elsewhere, starting with his immediate family. At least if they find a donor, Lindsey will have a real chance of beating this once and for all."

"I know I've had my issues with Cal," Naomi said, reaching for more chips. "But I hope he's a match. He needs to save someone."

Penny looked at her. "Why do you say that?"

"Near as I can figure, it's a Buchanan family trait. Not that any of them have managed it yet. I think it comes from Gloria, the way she emotionally beat up on them when they were kids."

While Penny didn't dispute Naomi's assessment, she wondered about the source of her information. Had it come from Reid or Walker, or both?

The temptation to ask was strong, but she resisted. If Naomi wanted to tell her, she would.

"It's just sad that they lost both their parents within a year of each other," Penny said quietly. "I know Cal always felt he had to be the strong one. I never thought of it in terms of having to save anyone." She remembered how he'd wanted to keep her out of the Buchanan dynasty because he'd been afraid of what Gloria would do. "Or maybe I didn't see it."

"Dani's the only one who keeps trying to please that bitch."

She was fighting a losing battle, Penny thought. Gloria would never accept Dani because she wasn't a Buchanan.

She wondered if Cal had told his sister the truth, then figured he hadn't had the time. But he needed to and soon. If he didn't, Penny had a bad feeling it would come back to bite him in the ass.

"Just talking about Cal and his family makes me realize how normal I am," Penny said. "Who would have thought that was possible?"

"What are you talking about? You're not so bad."

"I'm pregnant through a medical procedure by a man I'll never meet, and working for my ex-husband." Sleeping with him as well, she thought, although she didn't say that. Naomi might have guessed, but she wouldn't ask and Penny wouldn't confirm anything.

But speaking of people sleeping together… "How's the friendship thing working out with you and Walker?" she asked.

"Fine."

"Ha. Like I believe that. There's something you're not telling me."

There had to be. Naomi was actually squirming in her seat. Penny had never seen her act this way about a guy.

"Are you in love with him?" she asked, trying not to sound too incredulous.

"What? No. Of course not." Naomi wrinkled her nose. "It's not like that at all."

"Then what?"

"Nothing. It's nothing." She sighed. "We don't even have sex anymore." She reached for her can of soda. "We're friends, which is strange."

Penny didn't know what to think. "When you say you're not having sex, you mean…"

Naomi shrugged. "No sex. Honestly, I can't imagine us ever doing it again. We don't…we…talk."

"Talking is good."

"No, it's not. This isn't natural. Friends with a man. Oh, please."

Penny did her best to keep from smiling. "So you're having a relationship. That's great."

"No, it's odd. This is nothing romantic and yet I care about him. I don't want to care about anyone."

"You care about me."

Her friend smiled. "Yes, I do, but girl love is different. Caring about a guy…"

Her voice trailed off as sadness filled her eyes. She looked at Penny. "I might have to leave."

Penny had a feeling she didn't just mean that evening. Panic and pain gripped her. She needed Naomi and she would miss her horribly if she went away.

"Want to tell me why?"

Her friend smiled. "Thanks for not instantly saying I can't."

"I want to, but I'm holding back."

Naomi reached for another chip. "I have family back in Ohio. Parents. A couple of brothers and sisters. A husband." She chewed then swallowed. "Actually, I'm not sure about the husband. He might have divorced me. I've been gone a long time."

Penny blinked. "I don't know what to say. You never mentioned anyone."

"I didn't just hatch."

Penny had always figured there had to be someone. But a whole family? A husband?

"Something happened," Naomi continued. "I don't want to get into it, but I did something bad and I couldn't live with myself. Or them. So I left. I just drove and I ended up here. I met you a few weeks later."

Penny felt her heart breaking. She didn't want to lose her friend. "If you think you have to go back, it's fine."

Naomi scowled at her. "You're going to be brave, aren't you? Dammit, I hate that. I don't want to leave, but I think it's time. I have to go mend some fences. I think I'm still in love with him. Talk about insane."

Penny nodded because if she spoke, she would start to cry.

"I wouldn't just leave you," Naomi said. "I'd make sure there were some people in place. To help with the baby and at the restaurant."

"I'll be fine," Penny said. "Don't worry about me."

Naomi gone! It wasn't possible. Who else would she talk to in the middle of the night when she'd just watched a sad movie and couldn't stop crying? Who else would understand the need to never eat blue M&M's on even days of the month? Who else would coach her through delivery and stay with her for the first couple of weeks after the baby was born?

Naomi swore and got to her feet.

"What?" Penny asked.

"You're crying."

Penny sniffed. "It doesn't mean anything. I'm hormonal."

She stood and her friend walked around the table. They held on to each other.

"You're the best friend I've ever had," Naomi whispered. "I won't ever forget that."

"Me, either."

Naomi sighed. "See. This is why love sucks. If I didn't love you, I wouldn't care if I had to leave."

"If you didn't love me after all we've been through, I'd throw a meat cleaver at your head."

DANI GLARED at Cal. "I can't believe you never told me you had a daughter. All this time." Her gaze narrowed. "Walker and Reid know, don't they? You guys always stick together."

Cal put his arm around Dani as they walked from the parking lot on the University of Washington campus. "I didn't know they knew, if that makes you feel any better. I thought it was a secret."

"Oh, right. I swear, it's like living in a soap opera. I keep expecting to hear the smooth-voiced guy murmuring in the background. 'While Dani is unaware of her brother's illegitimate child, Lindsey has dealt with cancer. Of course Dani is an idiot for marrying a jerk like Hugh. More after the commercial break.' It really pisses me off."

"The guy?"

"No. You. What other secrets are there?"

He could think of only one really big one and he wasn't going there today. Dani had enough to deal with.

"Like I said, I didn't know Reid and Walker had heard me fighting with Gloria about Lindsey back when I was in high school. I didn't deliberately keep the information from you."

"But you didn't tell me when you found out the guys knew."

"You had stuff on your mind."

She sighed. "I'm all grown up, Cal. You can stop trying to protect me from the world."

"Sorry, that's part of the job description."

She linked her arm through his and leaned against him. "You're a good big brother."

"Thanks."

While he appreciated the compliment, he wasn't

sure he'd earned it. Penny had told him to come clean with Dani and he planned to. Soon. But not today.

"Are you sure about this?" he asked.

She patted her jacket pocket. "Completely. I'm not paying some guy to serve Hugh the papers when I can do it myself. Plus I want to see the look in his eyes. He won't be expecting me. Some small discomfort on his part isn't a whole lot of reward, I know, but it's all I'm going to get." She glanced at her watch. "He has office hours now. Maybe he'll have students in with him. That would be exciting."

"I'm sorry," he said, not sure how to make things better for her.

"Don't be. I don't like how Hugh handled things with me, but I'm no longer questioning the divorce. Don't get me wrong. I'm still furious. I gave him so much of my life and to have him tell me he outgrew me makes me want to back the car over all of his possessions. He practically sucked the life out of me and now he's acting all noble. But the truth is I don't love him. I haven't for a while."

That was a relief. Bad enough Dani had to go through this. Had she been heartbroken, it would have been so much worse.

"Maybe you'll like being single," he said.

"I'm kind of looking forward to it," she admitted. "I went from a college dorm to married. I've never had my own place."

"Do you know where you're going to move?"

"No. Part of me wants to make Hugh move. After all, this was his idea. But handicap accessible apartments are hard to find." She turned right on the path.

"But it really bugs me that this is all his idea and I'm the only one inconvenienced." She shook her head. "Let's change the subject. The campus looks pretty."

Cal glanced around. Spring had arrived and there were tulips in bloom everywhere. The ground was wet from recent rain, but the sky was a bright blue.

"I have a lot of memories here," he said.

"I can imagine the parties—and the girls—you indulged in," Dani said. "I, of course, only studied."

He chuckled. "Yeah, right. I remember getting more than one call from you because you didn't want to drive back to the dorm after a party."

"Hey, at least I didn't try driving."

"Did I ever complain?"

"There was that one time. I distinctly remember a disgruntled female voice in the background. Hmm, could it have been Penny?"

"Maybe."

"She's great, you know."

"I agree."

"You two are doing a terrific job at The Waterfront."

Cal glanced at her. "I'm sorry about that. Not the success, but that Gloria didn't offer you the restaurant."

"No offense, but me, too. Still, it's done. Once I get Hugh served and move out, I'm going to have a big sit-down with Gloria and lay it on the line. Either she gives me something more to do or I'm quitting."

He didn't know what to say. "You would leave the company?"

"Watch me. Here it is."

She pointed at the flight of stairs, then led the way up to Hugh's office on the second floor. Dani walked down the hall and stopped in front of one of the closed doors.

When she tried the handle, it didn't turn.

"Locked," she said. "But it's his office hours." She glanced at the card by the door to confirm the times Hugh was supposed to be there. "Weird."

She listened for a second, then knocked. "Hugh?"

There was a muffled noise, then a bump. Dani looked at Cal. "Okay, I don't like that."

Cal was with her on that one. He had a bad feeling. "Let's come back."

Her mouth pulled straight as she dug into her purse. "I don't think so. Dammit all to hell, if that bastard…" She pulled out a key chain and searched through the keys. When she inserted one into the lock, Cal nearly pulled her back.

"You don't want to know," he said, putting a hand on her arm. "Let's go."

She shrugged him off. "Don't you think I have a right?"

With that she pushed open the door. Hugh sat in his wheelchair, his shirt open. A young woman, probably a student, stood next to him. Her hair was mussed and she'd nearly finished buttoning her blouse.

"Dani." Hugh sounded surprised and wary. "I didn't know you were going to come by."

"Obviously." She looked between Hugh and the woman. "So, you want a divorce because you've grown as a person? If this is your idea of personal growth, I'm not interested. I would think of it more as being small, petty and a cheater. But hey, I'm just in the restaurant business. I probably wouldn't understand something this complex. I wonder what your department chair is going to say when she finds out you've been getting so *close* to your students?" She held out the papers. "Consider yourself served."

The student shifted uncomfortably. Her face was bright red, and she kept touching her hair. "I, ah—"

"Did you know he was married?" Dani asked, then shook her head. "Never mind. I have a piece of advice for you. I doubt you'll take it, but here it is. If he'll cheat *with* you, he'll cheat *on* you." She turned back to Hugh. "I can't tell you how sorry I am I wasted so much of my life on you. You weren't worth it."

She walked out of the office. "Let's go," she told Cal.

"I want to hit him."

"I appreciate that, but I think I'll clobber him financially, instead. I was going to be fair and kind during the divorce. Not anymore."

He reached for her hand and felt her trembling. "I'm sorry."

"Me, too."

Hugh rolled into the hallway. "Dani, I'm sorry. I didn't want you to find out this way."

She stopped and looked back at him. "How did you want me to find out, Hugh? What's the best way to tell your wife that you want a divorce so you can screw someone else? You should have told me the truth. I would have been angry but I wouldn't have thought you were such an asshole."

She walked away.

"Dani! Come back."

She shook her head and kept walking.

"Just one punch," Cal said.

"Thanks, but no. It's fine." They reached the stairs and she hurried down them. "This is good. I'd actually been wondering what I could have done to make things better between us. I won't be doing that anymore."

They reached the outside. Dani stopped walking and covered her face with her hands. "My whole life totally sucks. I don't have a career or a marriage. I hate this."

He pulled her close and let her cry against him. "Things will get better."

"When? I want a date. Tell me when."

He stroked her hair. "I'm sorry, Dani. I don't know. But soon."

"Promise?"

"Yeah."

"Poor kid," Penny said. "I can't believe Hugh was cheating. I always thought he was a decent guy."

"We all thought that," Cal told her. "Guess we were wrong."

"It's good you didn't hit him. I don't care how strong he is, he's in a wheelchair and you're a big, burly guy. No way you would have won that in court."

Cal shrugged and she could see he didn't much care about the ramifications of his actions. Someone he cared about was hurt and he wanted to lash out.

Funny how she'd never noticed that about him when they'd been married. She'd never seen his protective streak for what it was. Instead of appreciating what he was trying to do and looking for compromise, she'd rebelled against what she'd thought was unreasonable behavior.

She sank lower into the chair and closed her eyes as he continued to push his thumbs into the ball of her right foot.

"You're really good at this," she said, enjoying the massage. "I spend my life standing. Most of the time I don't mind it but lately I've been in some serious pain."

"You're pregnant."

She opened one eye and smiled. "I'd heard that rumor. Where did you learn to do foot massage? One of the many women you dated after our divorce? Or did you know it while we were married and keep the information from me?"

"I took a class on the Internet," he joked. "Just relax and enjoy."

"I might have to make moany noises."

"Have at it."

She gave herself up to the slow, steady massage. There was something erotic about having Cal rub her bare foot. Or maybe it was the fact that when he concentrated on her toes, her heel seemed to end up pressing against his—

Don't go there, she told herself. Not tonight. Maybe not ever. There hadn't been a repeat performance— no surprise, given the emotional roller coaster they'd been on for the past few weeks.

In some ways they were getting along better than ever. In other ways, he was more of a stranger than she could imagine. Neither of which kept her from lying awake in bed at night and wishing he were with her.

"When is Dani moving out?" she asked, as much to distract herself as to get the information.

"As soon as she can find a place. Hugh gets the apartment. It's handicapped accessible."

"She can live here while she's looking."

Cal's hands stopped moving. She opened her eyes again.

"What?" she asked.

"You'd offer that?"

"Sure. I have a second bedroom." She waved at her cozy duplex. "She needs some time to regroup and I don't need the other bedroom until the baby gets here." She smiled. "Plus, she'll probably be so grateful, she'll help me paint when she leaves."

"I think it's a good idea. I offered to let her stay with me, but she didn't want to."

Penny wrinkled her nose. "It would be too much like moving back home. I would move in with a friend way before I would go live with one of my sisters. I would hate the daily reminder I hadn't turned out like them."

He put down her right foot and reached for her left. After pulling off her sock, he rolled up her jeans. "You don't still worry about that, do you?" he asked.

Penny relaxed and gave herself over to the stroking pressure of his fingers on her heel.

"Sometimes. Before I figured out I wanted to be a chef, I was a complete failure. I flunked out of college." She winced at the thought. "I lived two years of my life in Pullman thinking I could become a vet. Like I could ever pass those science classes."

"But you regrouped and moved to Seattle."

"Oh, right. I moved away from Spokane because my parents were done supporting my various screw-ups. For the first month, I was so broke, I slept in my car."

"All the more reason to be proud of what you've become."

"You're right. My parents are excited about my career." If not the baby, she thought. No, that wasn't fair. They were happy to have another grandchild.

"You should invite them out," Cal said.

She opened her eyes and stared at him. "You're kidding, right?"

"Why not? They can see you at the restaurant, see the city."

"Oh, right. Because I need more going on in my life. Don't you dare say anything to them, either."

He grinned. "We don't talk much these days."

"I guess not. As it is, my mother is going to come out when I have the baby." That might be good, what with Naomi talking about leaving. "Families. Who thought up the concept?"

"You love your parents," he said. "You know you do."

She nodded. "They're great. I love my sisters, too. I wish they weren't so perfect, but I can handle it."

Cal moved to the ball of her foot and dug in with his thumbs. "I'm going to have to talk to Dani about her father."

"The whole not being a Buchanan thing?"

"Yes. She told me she wants to have a heart to heart with Gloria and find out the real reason she hasn't been promoted. The conversation isn't going to go well."

"It's better that she hears it from you instead of Gloria. Dani knows how much you care."

He shrugged. "I accept that, but I still don't want to be the one to tell her. It's going to hurt her and she doesn't need any more pain right now. I'm going to try to hold her off a week or so. Let her get settled."

"Don't wait too long."

"I won't."

His cell phone rang. He grabbed for it with an eagerness that told her he'd been waiting. To find out if he was a match, she thought, as he glanced at the display.

"It's Tracy," he said before he pushed the talk button and said, "Hello?"

She looked at him and saw the worry in his dark eyes. Then his mouth curved and she knew even before he hung up.

"I'm a match!" he said with a grin. "Nearly a perfect one. I've got to get through some tests, but I'm healthy, so we're going to assume we can go through with this. I can save her."

And because she knew how much that meant to him, she put her confusion aside.

"I'm glad," she said honestly, then leaned forward and hugged him. "Let's celebrate. We can't go out for a drink, but we can go eat. Or you drink and I'll watch."

"No liquor for me," he said. "I want to be healthy. Let's go get a salad."

She laughed. "I can't believe you actually said that."

"Me, either."

She smiled and squeezed his arms. "Let's call the whole family and have them join us. Everyone will want to know."

"Great idea."

He reached for his cell phone.

As he contacted Reid, Walker and Dani, Penny put on her shoes and socks. Cal was such a good man— caring, determined. He was a good father to Lindsey. But his heart seemed to stop there. No one new got in. Which meant only a fool would expect him to change.

But as he laughed with Reid, she found herself wishing things had been different. That he could have let her in, that they could have stayed together and made a family of their own.

CHAPTER FIFTEEN

THERE WERE A FINITE NUMBER of high schools in the Seattle area and Walker had been lucky enough to find Ben on the first try. His friend had attended West Seattle High School his sophomore year. There had been seven Ashleys in his grade and nearly thirty attending the school that year.

After making a list of them, Walker spent some time on the Internet, tracking down marriages, name changes and locations. Several had moved away. Ben's last physical contact had been right before he'd shipped off to Afghanistan, which meant any Ashleys moving more than eighteen months ago could be eliminated. Anyone married longer than that same period could also be taken off the list. Which still left him with eleven women.

The first, Ashley Beauman, lived in Bellevue, just east of Lake Washington. He turned onto the residential street shortly after ten on Tuesday morning. While he doubted he would find Ashley home, he could at least find her house and come back later.

But when he pulled up there was a car in the driveway and several toys on the front yard. Toys for small children. Either Ashley had been keeping secrets from Ben or this wasn't the right one.

Walker parked and climbed out of his X5. He stepped over a tricycle on his way to the front door.

A tall blond woman answered on the first ring. She looked frazzled and had a toddler on her hip.

"Yes?"

Walker had deliberately dressed casually. He smiled and introduced himself, then quickly explained he was looking for someone who had known a friend of his in the marines.

"I don't remember anyone named Ben in high school," the woman said, shifting her child to her other hip. "Was he in the same grade?"

"One year ahead of you."

He reached into his jacket pocket and brought out the two pictures. The first showed Ben in high school and the second had been taken four months ago at their base camp.

She studied them, then shook her head. "Sorry. I don't know him." Then she frowned. "Why me?"

"His girlfriend's name was Ashley."

She raised her eyebrows. "You're kidding. You're going to talk to every Ashley who went to high school with this guy?"

"Until I find her."

"Good luck with that." She hesitated. "Your friend died, didn't he?"

Walker nodded.

"I'm sorry. I hope you find her."

"I will."

"I'LL BE FINE," CAL said. "I get to sleep through everything. Lindsey's the one with the tough job."

Penny nodded. She'd done a little research on the
Internet and knew he was telling the truth. Cal would
wake up with a few bruises, facing two or three days
of recovery. Lindsey was in for a much rougher time
as her body dealt with the new bone marrow.

"Are you sorry you put off meeting her?" she
asked.

"No. Lindsey has enough to deal with right now.
I want her to focus on getting better. She can meet
me later."

Several members of the hospital staff came into
the room. "It's time," the nurse said.

"Okay." Penny bent down and kissed Cal. "I'll be
here when you wake up."

"You don't have to do that. I'll be fine."

"I know."

He squeezed her hand. "Thanks."

She waited until they wheeled him out, then she
joined Reid in the waiting room.

"Some belly you got there," he said when he saw
her.

She smiled. "Gee, thanks."

He patted the cushion next to him in the colorful,
plant-filled room. "Just trying to distract you. There's
no reason to worry."

"So everyone keeps saying. I'm not worried. Not
exactly."

"Then what?"

"I don't know. This is all so strange. Three months
ago I hadn't spoken with Cal in ages and now…"

"Now you're in a hospital waiting for him to have

a simple procedure that may save the life of a child you never knew about?"

"That's a very nice summary."

Reid leaned back in the sofa and picked up a paper cup of coffee. "Does his willingness to help Lindsey make you mad?"

She considered the question. "Not mad. I want her to be fine. And there was never any choice. Cal's a good man. Of course he would do this."

"But?"

"But...why wasn't he like this with me?"

"When you lost the baby?"

She nodded. Why hadn't he cared more? Why hadn't he been willing to open his heart to their child? "There's so much he didn't tell me, so much he wouldn't say. He's not very forthcoming, emotionally."

"Does that matter?"

It shouldn't. She and Cal weren't together. Not in that way. And yet...

"I don't have an answer," she said. "Let's change the subject."

"Okay. We could talk about how good-looking I am."

"There's a topic that could fill hours."

He smiled smugly. "Yes, it could. It's also one of my favorites. You start."

She laughed. "No, thanks. Have you talked to Naomi lately? She's been off doing stuff. I haven't seen her much."

"She and Walker were in the bar a couple of weeks ago. I haven't seen them since."

"I know she has a lot on her mind. She's mentioned she might be leaving." Penny thought about what Naomi had told her about having a family back in Ohio. "I understand she had a life before she came here, but I don't want her to go. Gee, suddenly everything seems to be about me." She sighed. "I'll miss her."

"She's been a good friend to you."

"I know. You're great, too, but you don't do the girl stuff really well. You never want to talk about pedicures."

"Or body waxing."

Penny smiled. "That, too."

Dani walked into the waiting room. "Has he already gone in?"

"A few minutes ago," Reid said as he stood. "How's my baby sister?"

"I've been better, but I'm surviving." Dani hugged Reid, then smiled at Penny. "So, is that offer still open?"

"Sure. You want to come be my roommate?"

Dani sank down in Reid's seat and nodded. "If you don't mind. I need to get out of the apartment as soon as I can."

"How about right now? We can go get a key made while Cal's still under anesthesia and you can move your stuff this afternoon. I'm going to be staying with him for a couple of days so you'd have the house to yourself while you settle."

"Are you sure?"

"Absolutely. It'll be fun."

"Okay, then I say yes. I appreciate this so much."

Penny stood. "Reid, call me if anything happens. I have my cell on."

He raised his eyebrows. "Moving back in together. That's interesting."

"Oh, please. The man is having bone marrow sucked out of his hip. He's going to have bruises the size of Utah and feel like he was hit by a truck. I don't think you have to worry about anything happening."

Unfortunately.

CAL TRIED to get comfortable on the chair, but it wasn't happening.

"If you'd take the Tylenol, like the doctor said, you wouldn't be suffering," Penny called from down the hall.

He shook his head. How the hell had she known he was in pain? Women were a mystery.

"I'm fine," he yelled back.

"You're lying."

He heard footsteps on the hardwood floor of the hallway, then she stuck her head in the living room. "I'm getting you the pills right now and I'm going to loom over you until you take them. Is that clear?"

"Yes, ma'am."

She grinned. "Respect. I like that. Be right back."

When she returned, she was true to her word, standing over him until he'd dutifully swallowed the two pills.

"I wrote down the time so we'll know when you can take more," she said.

"I'm perfectly fine."

She put her hands on her hips, which tightened

her shirt around her growing belly. "Oh, please. You have massive bruises on your hips, along with what looked like six hundred puncture marks."

"It's not that many. Compared with what Lindsey has to go through, this is nothing."

Penny sank down onto the sofa across from his chair. "I know. I spoke with her mom for a few minutes while you were still recovering. Lindsey's pretty wrecked from the chemo."

Cal didn't doubt it. The kid was in for a brutal process. First chemotherapy destroyed Lindsey's bone marrow, then she received an IV with his. Over the next few weeks, while her immune system was compromised, she would be kept isolated from the world. She would also battle what would feel like the worst flu of her life for that same period of time.

"I've popped onto the Internet and read about the procedure," Penny said. "There's a really good chance your bone marrow will cure her leukemia."

"I hope so."

"I wish there was more I could do," she said.

"You're here. I appreciate that."

"You should. I'll have you know I don't normally make cooking house calls, but I'm making an exception for you. We'll be dining on all your favorites."

His stomach rumbled. "Meat loaf?" He hadn't had Penny's meat loaf since before the divorce.

"Tonight. Then tomorrow, my very twisted Thai lasagna."

"Won't you be at the restaurant? We can't both be gone that long."

"I'll be going back and forth," she said. "Naomi's there, not to worry. Want to watch sports on TV?"

"No thanks."

"Hmm, do you have a fever?"

He smiled. "Reid's the sports guy. Did you unpack?"

"Yes. The guest room is lovely. I'm going out on a limb and saying you didn't decorate it yourself."

"Dani helped. She picked out the colors and the linens and the furniture. I did the labor."

She glanced around the living room. "The house is great."

"Paid for by the coffee drinkers of the Pacific Northwest."

"We do love our coffee."

She looked out the living room windows at the view of downtown. "You did good, Cal. You started with nothing and you created an empire. You should be proud of yourself."

"Thanks."

She turned back to him. "I get it now—the need to go out and make something happen on your own, but when you first left the restaurant business, I thought you were leaving me."

"What are you talking about?" How could she have thought that?

"It's hard to explain. We had a whole life that revolved around being awake when most of the world was asleep. We talked about the same kind of problems with customers and staffs and bosses. Then, suddenly, you wanted out. You became one of them, working nine to five." She shrugged. "I guess that sounds really strange. But at the time, I felt abandoned."

"I'm sorry. I never meant to hurt you. I wanted to get away from Gloria and her constant monitoring of my life. I was tired of the threats, the ugliness."

"I know," Penny said. Funny how with the passage of time a lot of things became more clear. "I wish I'd been more supportive."

Cal shook his head. "Don't. You were great."

"You don't know how angry I was with you."

He looked surprised. "You're right. You hid it from me."

"Not my finest moment. I thought you'd change your mind and come back."

"You thought I'd fail."

Guilt made her uncomfortable. "Maybe."

"I should have explained more to you," he said. "I was embarrassed to. I thought you'd think less of me."

Maybe it was the pain, or knowing his daughter was dangerously ill. Maybe it was the time they'd spent together, but Cal was vulnerable in a way she'd never seen him before.

"I loved you," she said. "I would have done anything for you."

"I know." His dark gaze settled on her face. "You deserved better than the little I had to give. I wish… I wish I'd been honest with you. Lindsey felt like such a big secret. I knew telling you about her would change everything. I should have trusted you to be able to handle it."

Something warm and squishy enveloped her heart. She wanted to be in Cal's arms and have him hold her close. She wanted them to go to bed and make love until the sun came up.

Either he was thinking the same thing or he read the invitation in her eyes. He stood and held out his hand.

She rose and walked to him. As she reached for him, he pulled her close. His arms went around her, she put her hands on his waist and he kissed her.

The contact was as erotic as it was familiar. She closed her eyes as he brushed his lips against hers, generating heat and need and sparks. Within seconds her breasts were swollen and sensitive and her thighs had begun to tremble.

"What is it about you?" he asked before he swept his tongue against her bottom lip.

Rather than answering, she opened to accept him. As he pushed inside and they began an intimate dance, he cupped her head as if to hold her in place.

Had she been able to form coherent thoughts, she would have told him she wasn't going anywhere. She wanted him too much. Wanted this. Funny how in all the time they'd been apart she'd managed to do fairly nicely with only a minimum of sexual contact, but now, with him, she felt weak with desire.

He drew back and nipped on her bottom lip, then kissed her jaw. As he moved to her neck, he shifted and instantly stiffened.

"What's wrong?" she asked.

"Nothing."

Somehow the tightness of his mouth and the shadows of pain in his eyes told her differently.

She stepped back. "What was I thinking? You're

just out of the hospital a couple of hours ago. They used your hips as pincushions and sucked out quarts of bone marrow. Sit down right now."

He shook his head. "No. Let's keep going."

He took her hand and brought it to his groin. He was hard and when she touched him, he flexed against her fingers.

She knew that she was already wet and swollen, but none of that mattered.

"Cal, be serious. You've just had general anesthetic. You're weak, tired and this is the last thing you should be doing."

He stared into her eyes. She looked back, letting him see the need inside of her.

"Rain check," she whispered, as she kissed him. "I promise."

"No. We can do this."

"Right. Because you whimpering in pain is really sexy."

"I don't whimper."

"I know. You're a big strong guy who right now needs a nap. Alone."

He picked up her hand and kissed her palm. "I want you."

Words to make a pregnant woman dance with delight. "I want you, too. We'll do something about it real soon. I promise."

He hesitated, then nodded. "Okay. I think I need to crash for a while."

"The doctor said it would take a couple of days for you to get the anesthesia out of your system. Plus, you have to get your strength back from the whole bone marrow sucking. Go take a nap. I'll run over to the restaurant, then be back to fix meat loaf."

He squeezed her fingers. "Thanks. You don't have to do this."

"I know, but I want to."

Although why, she wouldn't, she couldn't, say.

DANI SEALED the box and put it on top of the others by the front door. She would either have to come back later with a couple of burly guys and a van or work out a financial agreement with Hugh about him buying her out of half the furniture. For now, she only wanted her clothes and some personal items.

She hadn't slept much the previous night. Although Penny's guest bed had been comfortable, Dani had had too much on her mind. So much had happened so quickly. Hugh wanting a divorce, finding out he was cheating on her, moving out. It would be a while before she was finally able to draw in a breath and relax.

She opened the linen closet and pulled out a big box of photos. More things she was going to have to go through. She tossed it into a carton. She would sort them at Penny's and return Hugh's to him. She had no idea what they would do with the pictures they had taken together. Who would want those?

So many things to divide. Their good china and crystal, DVDs, electronic equipment. They'd been together nearly seven years. That made for a lot of baggage.

She heard the garage door open and stiffened. A quick glance at her watch told her Hugh wasn't due home for another two hours. She'd planned to be finished long before that.

She had a brief thought that his chickie had stopped by for something when she heard the soft sound of wheels on hardwood.

"Dani?"

She closed the linen closet door and stepped into the living room. "You weren't supposed to be here," she said.

Hugh looked as he always did—handsome, strong, sexy. The wheelchair did nothing to detract from his appeal. A friend from grad school had once confessed—after too many rum-and-cokes—that the wheelchair only made a woman think about being more creative, where Hugh was concerned. At the time Dani had laughed off the comment. Now she realized she should have paid attention.

He sat straight in his chair, his gold-blond hair a little too long, his blue eyes looking both innocent and soulful. There was something about his mouth, something that made a woman want to kiss him.

He had big hands and, at least for him, the old wives' tale was true. Even with the loss of sensation for Hugh, that part of him could still work, and she'd had plenty of fun riding him to paradise.

As had others, apparently.

"I'm sorry you had to see that," he said. "I didn't mean for you to find out."

She walked into the bedroom and began pulling clothes off hangers. "Interesting. You're not sorry you were cheating on me, you're just sorry you were caught." She heard him move into the room. "With a student, Hugh. That's tacky, even for you."

"It's not what you're thinking."

"You have no idea what I'm thinking." She tossed the clothes into an open box, then glared at him. "You don't know anything about me. I'm furious. You want a divorce. Fine. We'll get one. You've moved on. I can accept that. But what I can't accept is that you're messing around with your students. God knows how many."

"Don't be insulting."

"Oh, right. Because only sleeping with one of them is so noble. What a great man you are. How proud we all are." She moved close and stared down at him. "I was there for you, you bastard. Every day from the second you were hurt. I gave up my life to help you. I encouraged you, I begged you to keep living. I loved you with every fiber of my being. What I expected in return was for you to love me just as much. And if you couldn't do that, I expected you to respect me. But you didn't."

"Sure. Make me the bad guy."

She wanted to scream. "How am I at fault in any of this?"

"I just wanted a divorce. Why is that a crime?"

"It's not, you bastard. You lied and cheated. You betrayed me. That student isn't the first. I'm stunned to find out you're a lousy human being."

He glared at her. "Because I'm in a wheelchair, you expect me to be a saint? I'm not supposed to have flaws like other men, because I'm not really a man?"

She'd never wanted to hit another person before

in her life, but the urge to pick up a lamp and crash it over Hugh's head was incredibly powerful.

"I expect you to be a decent person because we're married," she yelled. "I expected you to honor your wedding vows because I thought you had a sense of morality and because I thought you cared about me and our relationship. Not everything is about you being in a wheelchair. You being an asshole has absolutely nothing to do with you being in a wheelchair. You'd be one even if you could run a marathon. Now get out of here so I can finish getting my things."

"Dani—"

"Get out!"

CHAPTER SIXTEEN

"THE MUSHROOMS SMELL FUNNY," Penny said as she held a clean cloth to her left ring finger.

"They're mushrooms," Naomi told her. "They're supposed to smell funny. Do you need stitches?"

Penny rolled her eyes. "Is my finger still attached to my hand?"

"Yes. Fine. Be that way."

Cal walked into the kitchen. He was moving a little slow, but otherwise was doing fine since his procedure. "How much is she bleeding?" he asked Naomi.

"I'm fine," Penny said.

"It was a gusher," Naomi said. "But I don't think she went down to the bone."

"Good to know," Cal said. "I could forcibly take her to the urgent care center."

"No, you couldn't." Penny moved between them. "I'm right here in the room. Stop ignoring me. I'm fine. Cuts and burns come with the territory. I'm fine. It's barely even bleeding."

Not that she was willing to let up on the pressure just yet, but in a few minutes, she would. Naomi would put on a butterfly bandage and all would be well. If she rushed around screaming for medical care every time someone got cut in the kitchen, no one would ever get fed.

"Hey, it's here," Dani yelled as she walked into the kitchen. "The write-up on new restaurants, and yes, you're mentioned."

She set the newspaper on the stainless-steel counter and flipped through the pages. The two cooks already chopping vegetables there moved in close, as did Edouard. Penny wiggled in front of both Naomi and Cal. If she stayed behind them, she wouldn't see a thing.

Suddenly the sting from her cut faded as an entire squad of butterflies took up residence in her stomach.

"They had to say something good, right?" she whispered, more to herself than anyone else. "Why say something bad?"

"Because it's the newspaper," Naomi grumbled. "What do they know about good food?"

"They are the sort of people who eat fast food," Edouard muttered.

Penny bit her lower lip as Dani continued to flip pages. She stopped on a huge spread featuring new restaurants in the Seattle area.

A friend of a friend had warned her about the write-up and had mentioned there was a bit on The Waterfront. Now Penny scanned the page until she saw a small box.

"There!" she said, as she pointed.

They all leaned forward to read it.

"I'll do it," Dani said, snatching up the paper. "Okay. While we here at the paper were only interested in new restaurants for this feature, The Waterfront has risen like a phoenix from the ashes. A few short months ago one was guaranteed old fish and a tired, uninspiring menu; these days The Waterfront is the place for fabulous dining. It's not just that chef Penny Jackson has redefined delicious with her innovative menus and clever pairings, it's that the dining room, with its wonderful views and good service, provides the perfect backdrop for an exciting and addictive culinary experience."

Penny screamed and jumped up and down. Naomi joined her and they hugged each other while they jumped. Cal put his arms around both of them and suddenly there was a group hug in the kitchen.

"Congratulations," he said to Penny. "I knew we could do it."

"Me, too. Although you're just in charge of the backdrop. I have an addictive menu!" She held up her uninjured hand and hit it against Cal's. "I knew we were good, but I didn't think anyone else was smart enough to figure it out."

"It seems they are."

"Yay, us."

"I've always liked newspaper people," Edouard said.

"We should celebrate," Naomi said. "I vote for liquor."

"Sure. Cheap champagne all around." He handed her the keys to the liquor closet.

Penny laughed and moved to the walk-in refrigerator where she removed a small piece of tuna.

"Hungry?" Cal asked when she returned to the counter and began cutting it up.

"It's for Al. Our cat," she added, when he looked blank. "He's been doing a great job with rodent control. I'm inviting him to the party."

She put the tuna in a dish and walked to the back hallway. After calling for a couple of minutes, she watched the large cat appear. She patted it, then put down the plate of tuna. Al inhaled it in less than thirty seconds.

"I didn't know he was a fish lover," Cal said from the doorway.

"He's a cat with great taste. That was premium tuna."

Al took himself off to clean up after his meal and Penny picked up the plate. She smiled at Cal. "We did good."

"I agree. I thought it would take longer, but I'm not complaining."

"Me, either."

There was something about the way he looked at her. Something that made her insides get all quivery and her mouth go dry.

"About that rain check," he said with a smile.

"Yes?"

"Penny?" Dani called. "You have a call. It's your mom."

"Be right there." She looked at Cal. "Sorry."

"Don't sweat it. I know where you live."

A promise she would hold him to, she thought as she walked toward the phone and checked her cut. The bleeding had stopped. As she picked up the phone, she held out her finger to Naomi.

"Hi, Mom."

"Hi, dear. Your father and I saw the article about you in the paper. It's wonderful. Congratulations."

Naomi appeared with the first aid kit and went to work on trimming several dressings down to the right shape and size.

"Thanks," Penny said, holding the phone between her ear and her shoulder as she ran her finger under water and tried not to wince.

"We've decided we can't wait another minute to see the place. We're driving over."

"That's great. When?"

"In a couple of weeks. I know Saturday is your busiest day, so we'll arrive Sunday and stay until Tuesday."

Naomi fitted the bandage in place and secured it with tape.

"That's great," Penny said. "I'm looking forward to seeing you and Dad."

"Oh, not just us. Your sisters are coming, too. And the kids. Sean and Jack can't take off, which is too bad."

"The whole clan," she said weakly. "My house is kind of small. Oh, and I have a temporary roommate."

"Not to worry," her mother said. "We have hotel rooms. I'll e-mail you the details. We're really looking forward to this, Penny."

"Me, too."

They chatted a few more minutes, then hung up. Naomi sipped from her champagne glass and grinned. "Hell of a time to be pregnant, huh?"

Penny eyed the liquor enviously. "Tell me about it. My parents are coming, along with my sisters and their kids. They're going to want to see the restaurant."

"Yes, they are."

"They're going to poke through my house and want to talk about the future."

"Parents are like that."

"They'll worry about me having a baby on my own."

"Sure."

Edouard swore in French. "The back burners are out. All four of them. I cannot work in conditions like this."

Penny groaned. She couldn't afford to lose half her burners. Not when they were expecting a full house.

"I'll call," she said as she hurried toward her office. Welcome to her world, she thought. Where it was always insane.

"Then we need to talk about the mushrooms," Naomi told her. "They smell funny."

"THANKS FOR COMING," Cal said. "You didn't have to do this."

"I wanted to," Penny told him as they walked through the hospital.

He doubted that visiting his daughter would make the top-five list of ways she wanted to spend her day, but he appreciated her willingness to accompany him.

Penny had really been there for him, he thought. Helping him after he'd donated the bone marrow, feeding him, being a friend. Repaying that kindness by jumping her bones had seemed too slimy, so he'd resisted the urge to suggest they cash in on their rain check. Even though he'd wanted to.

He glanced at her as they waited for the elevator. She was showing more and more. He supposed that some guys would have found her growing size unappealing, but he thought she was sexy as hell, all lush curves and glowing health. He liked the way she moved, the way she smelled, the promise that seemed to be in every smile.

Complications, he thought. Getting involved with Penny would be nothing but complications. Another reason to resist his need for her. But he sure was tempted.

They rode up to their floor, then stepped into the corridor.

"We have to check in," he said. "Tracy, Lindsey's mom, said they'll explain about the mask and gown we have to wear. Her immune system is still recovering. Apparently she's doing much better than anyone expected and she'll be out of the hospital in a few weeks, but until then, we all have to be careful."

Penny touched his arm. "You're nervous. That's normal, but I'm still only going as far as the door. This is a private moment."

"I don't know how to talk to her. I've known about her all her life, but she's never given me any thought. What do I say?"

"I don't know," she sighed. "Speak from your heart. Your goal here is to connect. Just establish some easy conversation, then sort of slide into the fact that you're her father."

Cal tried to imagine himself saying the words, but it was impossible. He'd kept the secret for too long.

"Tracy will be there, right?" Penny asked.

He nodded. "She and I agreed it's important for Lindsey to have her mother around."

Penny smiled. "You always say 'her mother' or 'her father.' Never 'her adoptive mother.'"

"Tracy *is* her mother. Alison's role in Lindsey's life was to provide an egg and rental space for nine months. Nothing else."

And his role had been even less. He'd given his daughter some DNA and then he'd cut her loose.

Penny moved close and stared into his eyes. "Don't go there. You did more than just offer up sperm. Despite wanting to keep her, you made a conscious choice to make her life better. You did everything in your power to make sure she would be happy."

"I didn't want to let her go."

"Knowing what you know now, do you think you made the wrong decision?"

Good question. Could he have raised Lindsey better? Could he have made her more happy? He'd still been a kid himself. What about Gloria and her need to meddle in every aspect of everyone's life? What about Lindsey getting sick?

"This was the right choice," he said slowly. "I know that."

"Then maybe it's time to give yourself a break, Cal. Maybe you should let go of the guilt and be happy your daughter is alive and getting better. How long are you going to punish yourself for giving her the best of everything in the world?"

He stared at Penny. Was it really that simple? Had he been punishing himself for doing what was obviously the best for his daughter?

"You have your moments," he said.

"I know." She smiled. "I can be brilliant on demand. It's a gift."

"Okay. Be brilliant now and tell me what to say to Lindsey."

"How about telling her that you're her father and that you love her very much?"

Before he could answer, Tracy came out of a room at the far end of the hall. She wore a long hospital gown.

"Hi," she said as she approached. "Right on time. Are you ready to get all covered up? Lindsey's doing great. Even better than we'd all hoped. It looks like she'll be able to come home fairly soon. Not that she can go back to school. No crowds for her for a while, but still. We're happy and so very grateful."

She was nervous. Cal could see it in her eyes and hear it in her fast-paced words.

"Tracy," he began.

She shook her head. "It's fine. Really. This is for the best. Lindsey wants to meet the man who saved her life and you want to meet your daughter. I didn't tell her. I…" She swallowed. "I didn't know how," she admitted. "Which is probably a good thing. You've been waiting to tell her for a long time. You've more than earned this, Cal. Really. Tom and I are so grateful."

"Thank you," he said.

He felt Penny take his hand. He laced his fingers

with hers and squeezed. At least he'd been smart enough to bring her along. He had a feeling he was going to need a friend through all this.

Speaking of which… "Tracy, this is Penny Jackson."

Penny leaned forward and shook hands. "It's lovely to meet you. I'm so pleased your daughter is doing well. You've been through such a difficult time and deserve to hear good news."

"Thank you." Tracy stared at Penny's stomach. "Your first?"

Penny hesitated only a second, then nodded. "I'm due in September and getting bigger by the second."

Tracy's smile faded. "We wanted children, but I wasn't able to carry a baby past the twelfth week. There's a complex medical term for it. So we decided to adopt. Cal gave us Lindsey and she's been a blessing to us every day."

"I'm glad," he told her.

Penny's hold on his hand tightened.

"All right, let's go," Tracy said. "Lindsey's doing great. At first she was really sick, but that faded quickly. Now she's just waiting until she's able to go home. Oh, you know she lost her hair in chemo, right?"

Cal hadn't. It made sense, but he hated the thought of her beautiful blond hair falling out.

"She's hoping she'll get some curl when it grows back in," Tracy continued. "Did her biological mother have curly hair?"

"What? No. Alison's hair was straight." And pale

blond. Lindsey's had been golden-blond and long. How much time would it take her to grow it back?

"Welcome to the germ-free zone," Tracy said as they walked through the doorway. "Nothing can go into Lindsey's room without being disinfected."

"I didn't bring her anything," Cal said. He'd wanted to but his reading had warned him that she wouldn't be able to accept anything like flowers or plants. He hadn't known what else to bring.

"Good." She showed him where the gowns and masks were, along with booties and caps for his hair. Penny settled into a chair with a magazine.

"Good luck," she told him.

Five minutes later he was in Lindsey's room. Tracy introduced him. Lindsey smiled and kept her gaze firmly fixed on him.

He looked back. His daughter was tall and slender, with large blue eyes and a smile that could light up Seattle. She wore a scarf on her head that reminded him of Penny's head coverings in the kitchen.

He could see bits of Alison in her—the shape of her eyes, the way she tilted her head.

"I don't know what to say," Lindsey told him with a shy smile. "Thank you."

"You're welcome. I was glad to help."

"Did it hurt when they took your bone marrow?"

"I was asleep. I had a couple of bruises afterwards, but they're no big deal. You're the one going through the worst of it."

Lindsey wrinkled her nose. "I was really sick for a while. Chemo is totally gross. But it's over and now I'm feeling better."

She sat up in her bed, on top of the covers. Brightly colored sweats covered her legs and she had on a blue long-sleeved fuzzy shirt that buttoned in front. There were IV lines coming from her chest and her arm.

"We should all sit," Tracy said as she busied herself pulling up a couple of chairs.

Cal took the one closest to his daughter. She was so beautiful, he thought. He'd seen her before, of course, but always from a distance. Now he was close enough to see the color in her cheeks and the little mole she had on the side of her neck.

"I understand you're a senior in high school," he said.

"Yeah." She sighed. "I'm probably going to miss graduation. Even though I'll be better by then, it's a big crowd and I have to avoid them for the next six months. I'm going to UW. Um, the University of Washington."

He grinned. "I know. I went there."

"Really? What did you study?"

"Business."

"Oh." She wrinkled her nose again. "I'm going pre-law. I want to learn about a lot of different things. Then I'm going to law school to study environmental law. You know, save the planet."

She was young enough to believe that was possible, he thought in wonder. And he was entranced enough to think she could.

"I won't be starting until January, though. The whole crowd thing. But my mom talked to the admissions people and there are some classes I can take online, which is totally great. So I'll have the same number of units as everyone else when I finally get there."

"You'll have to let me know how it all goes," he said.

"Really? You'd be interested?"

Tracy smiled at her daughter. "Honey, he just saved your life. I think he has a little something invested in your future."

"Right. I never thought of it that way. Okay. Sure. I can let you know. Do you do e-mail?"

He nodded.

"Me, too. I love it. And instant messaging. I would just die without that and my cell phone to keep in touch with all my friends." She flashed a smile at Tracy. "Mom's been great about letting me do that. Of course we got unlimited local calling and my friends all have it, too." Her voice trailed off. "You probably don't care about that."

Actually, he did. He wanted to hear about every aspect of her life. He couldn't believe he was here, so close to her. He wanted to hug her and tell her who he was. He wanted to show her New York and Europe and watch her grow into a beautiful woman. Mostly, he wanted to turn back the clock and watch her from the time she'd been born.

The combination of pleasure at her company and pain for all he'd missed immobilized him. He ached in a way he'd never hurt before. She was incredible and no matter what he said or did, he couldn't get those years back.

Lindsey frowned. "You look kinda familiar. It's hard to tell with the mask, but I saw you when you came into the dressing room and I thought…" She looked from him to her mom, then back. "Do I know you?"

He'd been waiting for this moment for seventeen years. Here it was—the perfect invitation. The chance to tell her who he was.

Penny held her breath. Despite being in the waiting room, she could hear their conversation and she could feel Cal's longing to be with his daughter. Love radiated out from him like heat from a stove. He'd done the right thing over and over and this was his reward. Yet she couldn't help wanting to stop him.

The girl was an innocent in all this. She'd never wanted to know her birth parents. Why tell her now? It would change her forever, and possibly not in a good way. But Penny knew that Cal had earned this moment and right or wrong, he would take it.

"You've seen me," Cal said, his voice thick with emotion.

Penny's eyes filled with tears. She glanced at Tracy and saw the woman trembling with emotion. No doubt she was terrified she would lose some part of her daughter. That a piece of her heart would be given to Cal.

"I'm one of the owners of The Daily Grind. My partners and I used to do the commercials on television."

Penny blinked back tears as her heart froze in her chest. Was that it? She braced herself for more and was stunned when after a second Lindsey said, "Oh, yeah. That's it. I knew you looked like somebody I knew."

Then she mentioned how sad she was to miss the

prom, but that her boyfriend had promised her they would go dancing as soon as she could handle the crowds. Cal asked if she had any pets and the conversation continued.

Tracy looked as stunned as she, Penny, felt. What had just happened? Why had Cal passed over the perfect opportunity to tell Lindsey who he was?

Fifteen minutes later the visit ended. Cal promised to answer Lindsey's e-mail and she promised to keep in touch. She turned on the TV before they left the room.

When the door to Lindsey's room was closed, Tracy turned to him. "Why didn't you tell her?" she asked in a low voice.

Cal pulled off his protective gown. "I wanted to, but I couldn't say the words. She's a great kid, Tracy, and that's because of you and Tom. But she's still young and I didn't want to screw with her world."

Tracy threw herself at him. "Thank you," she said as tears poured down her cheeks. "Thank you. I know you could have told her. You had every right. You've given her to us twice now and taken nothing for yourself. I don't know how to repay that kind of sacrifice."

Penny found herself fighting tears of her own. When Cal looked at her and raised his eyebrows, she shrugged. "Hormones," she said with a sniff.

He patted Tracy's back until she straightened. "I should get back to her," she said.

"Thanks for letting me meet her," he told Tracy.

"You're a great man, Cal. Truly." She wiped her face, then entered her daughter's room.

Cal was quiet the whole way to the car. Once they

were on the road, he looked at her. "I know it's only three in the afternoon, but I need a drink. Want to keep me company?"

"Sure. Where do you want to go?"

"Somewhere quiet. How about my place?"

"Okay."

He didn't speak again until they arrived at his house. Penny followed him inside, then watched as he poured himself a Scotch. After he'd taken a long drink, she walked over and touched his arm.

"You did a good thing," she murmured.

He looked at her. "It hurt like hell. All I wanted was for her to be mine. I couldn't stop thinking about everything I'd missed by giving her up. All those years. But look at the life she has with Tracy and Tom. I couldn't have done that. I'd be hard-pressed to do that now, let alone at seventeen."

"What changed your mind?"

He took another drink. "I realized that loving my daughter meant wanting what was best for her. For her, not for me. As much as I might want a place in her life, that's not what she wants. She's looking forward to college and growing up to change the world. She has great parents. She doesn't need me barging in and changing everything."

He put down the drink. "It was the hardest thing I've ever done. Harder than giving her up, even, because now I know what I've lost and back then I could only guess."

She felt his pain as if it were her own. "I can't fix this, but for what it's worth, I'm incredibly proud of you. You did good."

"Yeah?"

She nodded, then moved in front of him and raised herself on tiptoe so she could kiss his mouth. "Lindsey's a very lucky young lady. She has a hell of a father in you."

He wrapped his arms around her and pulled her close. As his mouth claimed hers, she felt his longing for both sex and relief from the pain. He wanted to find solace in her.

She gave in because she couldn't imagine walking away. Not when she wanted him, too. But even as he ran his hands up and down her back and touched her bottom lip with his tongue, she knew she was making a big mistake.

Nothing had changed. If anything, Cal's actions today had only reinforced what she knew to be true. He loved Lindsey enough to make the big and painful sacrifices. He was, at his core, a good man.

But that had never been the issue between them. The problems had been about his inability to love *more* than just his daughter. He hadn't opened his heart to Penny or their child.

Had that changed or was she beating her head against an unmoving emotional wall?

"Earth to Penny," he murmured, kissing the side of her neck. "You're a thousand miles away. Do you want me to stop?"

Heat poured through her body. Every nerve ending begged for his touch. She wrapped her arms around him and surrendered to his sensual caress.

"Of course not," she whispered.

"Good."

He returned his mouth to hers. She parted for him. As he swept inside, she told herself it was a hell of a time to realize she was still in love with him.

CHAPTER SEVENTEEN

LOVE. WAS IT POSSIBLE? Penny told herself it wasn't
and yet she felt the emotion building inside of her.

Not now, she thought as Cal tugged at the hem of
her shirt. Now wasn't for thinking, it was for feeling.

He pulled the shirt over her head and tossed it onto
the table by the sofa. After running his hands across
her shoulders and down her arms, he gently cupped
her breasts.

"They're bigger," he said with a grin, as if he'd just
discovered something naughty.

"Yes, and we've already discussed that fact."

"I like them."

"Typical male."

"That's me." He lightly brushed his thumbs over
her nipples.

Her whole pelvis clenched as he continued to caress her. She felt herself swelling in anticipation.

"That feels great."

"Good."

He continued to touch her breasts as he leaned
in and kissed the side of her neck. Soft, slow, damp
kisses that made her break out in goose bumps all
over.

"You're so beautiful," he murmured. "You always

have been, but with the baby, there's a glow about you."

He nibbled on her jaw before moving to her ear and taking her lobe in his mouth.

"I want you," he breathed.

The erotic words, the feel of his breath on her skin all made her melt. She trembled with need and hunger. She wanted to urge him on, to hurry him to the next step and at the same time, she wanted this to last forever.

"Oh, Cal," she whispered as she leaned into him. "You always did know how to set me on fire."

He raised his head and they kissed. A slow, deep kiss that made her cling to him. Tongues brushed, circled, teased. Lips pressed. He dropped his hands to her hips and urged her closer, only her stomach was in the way.

She broke the kiss, glanced down at her belly and laughed. "Okay. We have a small problem."

"We'll work around it," he said. "Come on."

With that he took her hand and led her toward his bedroom. Once there, he reached for the button on her jeans.

"Why don't you take care of you," she said. "I can undress myself."

"But I like taking your clothes off."

"I like you naked more."

"I can live with that."

He went to work on his shirt, while she removed her shoes and socks. In a matter of thirty or forty seconds, they were both naked.

He pulled back the covers and she slid onto the

cool sheets. It was still the middle of the afternoon. Sunlight poured into the room, leaving her no comfortable shadows in which to hide. For the first time in her pregnancy, she felt large and unwieldy.

She knew that in theory she could make love until the last month, but in practice…

"What?" he asked as he moved next to her. "You're looking scrunchy."

"Scrunchy? What does that mean?"

"You're thinking. Never a good thing."

"I'm worried about this being awkward."

He propped himself up on one elbow, then smiled. "See, that's the difference between men and women. You're concerned that we might have to make some changes and I won't like that. While I've been fantasizing about you on top, my hands on your breasts and you having your way with me."

He painted a very vivid image that she could totally get behind. Her insides tightened at the thought of them making love that way.

"Okay. We'll do it your way."

"Gee, thanks."

He kissed her. She parted for him instantly, wanting to feel the pleasure he could bring her body. Even as his tongue claimed her, he slid his hand along her bare side, over the curve of her hip, to her thigh.

She rolled onto her back and let her legs fall open. He moved between her thighs, lightly brushed her center, then rubbed her other leg.

"You've completely missed the point," she murmured against his mouth.

"No. I get the point." He pressed his erection into

her leg. "I'm taking it slow. Relax. We have all afternoon. Now where was I?"

But instead of picking up where he'd left off, which had been torturing her by not touching her, he shifted his hand to her breasts.

He caressed her curves, moving closer to her nipples without actually touching them. He circled and circled until she thought she might go mad with wanting. Finally he touched the tight tip and she felt ribbons of fire race through her.

"Good?" he asked as he kissed his way down her neck.

"Excellent."

"I aim to please."

He shifted so he could take one nipple in his mouth. She gave herself over to the gentle sucking, the flick of his tongue. Heat poured through her. She felt herself melting. Between her legs, her blood pulsed in time with her heartbeat.

He moved closer, touching, kissing, licking until she could barely catch her breath. Need built inside of her—a restless energy that begged to be released.

He slipped his hand between her legs and this time he slid his fingers through her damp curls and rubbed her hungry flesh. She arched against him and cried out as he found that single point of pleasure.

As he rubbed her, touching her, circling, then brushing right against that spot, she felt him press his hardness into her thigh. His need increased her own. She needed more.

"Faster," she whispered. "Harder."

He obliged with a readiness that earned her gratitude. His fingers moved over her slick, swollen center in a rhythm designed to send her over the edge.

She drew up her knees and parted her legs. Her heels dug into the bed, while her whole body arched in anticipation of her climax. Suddenly her mind filled with the image of her on top of him, feeling him inside of her while she came. Once planted, the idea wouldn't be ignored. She put her hand on his wrist.

"I want to be on top."

His mouth curved into a slow smile of masculine anticipation. "Be my guest. Take me any way you want."

He rolled onto his back, then helped her as she straddled him. She reached between them to guide him inside as she lowered herself onto his arousal.

He filled all of her. She felt her body clench around him as he flexed within her.

"You set the pace," he said with a groan. "I don't need much to make me happy."

She shifted to find the most erotically comfortable position. Her body clenched again.

"This is good," she whispered and closed her eyes.

Slowly, she began to move. The up-and-down rhythm felt awkward at first, but she quickly found a pace that made her nerve endings quiver. She moved a little faster, then faster still.

She opened her eyes and saw him watching her.

"Come for me," he whispered as he slipped his hand between them and rubbed her swollen center.

Every muscle in her body tensed as need built up. He rubbed a little harder, making the circling motion tighter. It was all that she needed to lose herself.

Spasms of pure release claimed her as her orgasm swept through her. She continued to move, riding him, calling out her pleasure.

Up and down, up and down, claiming him, her body contracting again and again.

He grabbed her hips and began to control the rhythm. She stretched out her arms and fell forward so she could keep moving and still support herself.

This angle was even better, she thought in amazement as her release went on. He continued to hold on to her hips until he suddenly squeezed as he held her still. Only he moved. Once, twice and then he groaned.

She opened her eyes and watched as his features tightened. Pleasure pulled his mouth straight. His breath caught. He groaned again and opened his eyes. They both smiled.

"Not bad," she said. "The whole on-top thing was very nice."

"Yes, I liked it, too." His smile widened into a grin, then he laughed. "We should do this again some time."

"I think I'd like that."

He wrapped his arms around her and gently rolled her on to her side. They moved arms and legs so they were facing each other. Cal pulled the covers over them, then touched her face.

"You okay?"

"I feel as if every cell in my body just went to a really great party."

"Good."

"And you?" she asked.

"The same. I was kind of sweating it there at the end. I didn't know how long I could hold out."

"You did great."

"Another two seconds and I would have lost it."

She took his hand in hers and pulled it to her chest. "That would have been okay."

"Not if I'd come first. That would have left you hanging."

"I trust that you would have taken care of things in another way," she told him. "Besides, there's something exciting about a man being so aroused, he loses control. It's very sexy."

"You're very sexy."

She stared into his dark eyes and knew that she hadn't been wrong before. She did love him. Maybe working together had given birth to new feelings, or maybe it had simply stirred up something that had always been there.

Whichever it was, it had taken seeing his emotional sacrifice with Lindsey for her to realize how she really felt.

Now what?

The phone rang. Cal rolled over and grabbed it. "Hello?"

He listened for a second. "Okay. I'll tell her. Yeah. Not long. Okay. Bye."

He hung up and looked at her. "Talk about timing. Your family just arrived at your house. Dani is there, playing hostess."

"What? But they're early by a day! They weren't coming until tomorrow." She sat up and fought panic.

"I'm not ready to see my parents. I was going to use tonight and tomorrow morning to brace myself."

"I don't know what to tell you. They're here now." He leaned over and kissed her bare shoulder. "At least they didn't get here fifteen minutes earlier. That would have been a real drag."

PENNY ARRIVED HOME to complete chaos.

"Penny!" her mother cried as she walked into the house. "I know, I know. We're early. But we were sitting at breakfast this morning thinking there was nothing we would rather do today than drive over to Seattle. The hotel had rooms and your sisters were eager to make the drive, so here we are."

Before Penny could respond, her mother, a petite woman with curly dark red hair and blue eyes, covered her mouth with her hands. "Oh, look at you. You're showing! My baby's having a baby."

Penny stepped into her mother's embrace. "Hi, Mom."

"Joe! Joe, get out here. Penny's home."

Her father walked toward them and swept them up in his arms. "Hey, kid. How's it going?"

"Good, Dad."

Emily and Julie, Penny's sisters, hurried out of the kitchen, their children running after them.

"Penny!"

Dani came out last, holding a bottle of water in one hand and a bowl of pretzels in the other. "I managed to get them fed and watered," she said. "I'll head out now. I have an appointment downtown."

"Don't go," Fay, Penny's mother, said. "We've put

you out enough. We really have to get settled in our hotel." She cupped Penny's face. "It's so good to see you. You're happy. It's right there in your eyes."

Penny held in a wince. Hopefully her mother wouldn't figure out any glow came from her very recent close encounter with Cal.

"I have an idea," Joe said. He wrapped an arm around Penny. "Let's go to the restaurant. We can have a look at that fancy place of hers, then go to the hotel."

"Great idea," Fay said. "We won't keep you too long. We know it's one of your busiest nights."

"Don't be silly." Penny did a quick head count. "Sure. We can go to the restaurant now and look around, then you can come back for dinner at, say, seven." She looked at her sisters. "Is that too late for the kids?"

Emily, her oldest sister, grinned. "No. It's perfect. Sean's mom lives in the area and she's taking all the kids tonight and tomorrow for the day. Isn't that the best? Julie and I will each have a room completely to ourselves. I know that doesn't seem like a big deal to you—you get to be alone whenever you want. But for us, it's heaven."

"Unheard-of heaven," Julie added. "I plan to close the bathroom door and not worry about anyone trying to call me or get in or need something. I may even take a bath."

Penny grinned. "Okay, I'll make sure to cook fast so you can have a maximum of bathroom time."

"You don't have to do that," her mom said as she slipped her arm through Penny's and hugged her close. "Your sisters are exaggerating about wanting to be alone."

From behind Fay's back both Julie and Emily mouthed, "No, we're not!"

BY SEVEN THAT NIGHT, the kitchen was in its usual Saturday night pandemonium.

"Shallots," one of the cooks yelled. "Who the fuck took my shallots?"

Penny grimaced. Stealing setup supplies was a clear invitation to be stabbed in the back. Literally.

Edouard clucked and hurried to the walk-in. He came back with shallots and made sure everyone was supplied before returning to his demiglaze.

"Thanks," Penny told him.

"You are lucky I am in a good mood," he said.

"Things happy at home?"

"Bliss," he told her with a satisfied smile. "George wants to move in. We are talking about getting a cat together."

"You can't have Al. We need him here."

"You'll have to send him somewhere when the health department comes calling," Edouard said.

"I know, but he's worth it." She grabbed a plate of salmon as it came past and slid on a small corn cake topped with crab.

"Order up," she yelled.

Naomi appeared at her side. "Your parents are here. And your sisters. No kids or husbands. Should I be worried?"

"Husbands are at home, kids are with Grandma."

"That's the way to do it." She picked up a second plate. "Should I offer to take them bar hopping?"

Penny didn't want to think about her very married sisters hanging out in Naomi's wild world.

"They're kind of focused on having rooms to themselves and taking baths."

"Well, I wouldn't want to get in the way of that," Naomi said as she hurried out of the kitchen.

Penny glanced around to make sure that everything seemed in order, then she left Edouard in charge as she made her way into the dining room. She smiled at Cal, who stood by the hostess station, then crossed to the table by the water where her family sat.

"Hi," she said as she pulled up an empty chair. "Have you ordered?"

"Not yet," her father said. "We were waiting to get a recommendation from the chef."

Emily leaned close. "This place is terrific. Fabulous view. Did we know you were working with your ex-husband?"

"Oh, you saw Cal?" she asked, hoping to sound friendly and calm, not at all as if she'd spent a fair amount of the afternoon naked and begging for more.

"She told us," her mother said. "I'm sure I mentioned it." Fay glanced at him and waved. "I always thought it was a shame the two of you couldn't work things out. Any sparks?"

"Not really," Penny said, and hoped her mother had lost the ability to tell when she was lying.

Julie shook her head. "Let it go, Mom. Penny's moved on, obviously. She's having a baby on her own. She's the perfect modern woman."

"Oh, I don't know about that," Penny said, although she appreciated the vote of confidence.

"Speaking of the baby," her mother said. "Are you sure you'd still like me to come out for a couple of weeks when it's born? I don't want to intrude or get in the way or—"

"Yes," Penny said, cutting her off in midsentence. "I would love the help. I'm terrified of being on my own with the baby."

Her mother beamed at her. "You'll be fine, but I'm happy to help. We'll work out the details later. Now let's order some food."

Penny made several suggestions, then excused herself to go back to the kitchen. Her mother rose and walked with her.

"You've done a wonderful job here, darling," Fay said. "We're all so proud and happy for you."

"Thanks. It's nice to hear. Especially after all the years I spent screwing up."

Fay frowned. "Don't say that. We never thought of it that way. You were trying to find what was right for you, that's all."

"But I flunked out of college. Twice. And let me tell you, it's hard to flunk out of community college."

"You refused to settle. Your father and I always admired that about you."

"Really?"

"Of course. All I've ever wanted was for my girls to be happy. You've made that happen. Oh, Emily and Julie did, too, but in a more traditional way. They knew what to expect from their lives. You never did. You forged your own path. That takes courage."

Until that moment, Penny had always assumed her parents saw her as a failure. That they'd been disappointed in her stops and starts along the road of figuring out what she wanted to do with her life.

"Thanks, Mom," she said and kissed the other woman on the cheek. "You're the best."

Her mother laughed. "All I ask is a chance to taste your cooking."

"I promise."

Fay returned to the table. Penny continued toward the kitchen, only to be intercepted by Cal.

"Your folks are here."

"I know. Sorry. I forgot to tell you." She stared at his face, liking the way the light played on his features. "Hi."

"Hi, yourself. How are you feeling?"

"As if I could sing opera," she said with a smile. "You?"

"Pretty damned good." He jerked his head toward the table with her family. "Okay for me to go over and say hello? Or would that be too awkward?"

"I think it would be fine. They always liked you."

"Good. Then I'll do that." He brushed his fingertips down her arm. "Maybe we can get together later?"

"I'd like that."

She walked into the kitchen only to find Naomi standing in the middle of the room with her hands on her hips.

"What?" Penny asked.

Naomi grabbed her and pulled her into her office. "I saw that," she said. "The whole thing. The intimate conversation. The private touches. There's something going on with you and Cal."

"No, there isn't. Well, maybe. Something. But it's no big deal." If she didn't count being in love with him. Then it was practically nothing.

"And?" Naomi demanded.

"And, what? I went with him to see his daughter. He decided not to tell Lindsey who he is. It was hard for him. I saw the whole thing and it made me…"

"Yes?"

"It made me like him."

"Ha. As if that's all that's going on between you. I know there's more, but I'm not sure I'm up to the details. Just be sure this time."

"What?"

Naomi sighed. "Be sure. Last time you left. You shouldn't leave. It's wrong and it hurts the people left behind."

The unfair accusation stunned her. "I didn't leave. Okay, technically I did move out, but that was only because Cal didn't care. He's admitted so himself. He didn't love me."

"You didn't fight for him." Naomi held up a hand. "Look, I'm sorry. You don't need this from me and I'm hardly in any position to judge. I'm the queen of running away."

Penny was having a hard time getting her head around the conversation. "I didn't run from Cal."

"Yes, you did. And that's okay. I'm just saying that before you start something up again, you need to know if you're in it for the long haul."

Naomi returned to the kitchen, leaving Penny speechless and annoyed.

She hadn't run. Cal had disappeared emotionally long before she'd moved out. The problems in their marriage weren't about her. Were they?

As she walked to the door a voice in her head pointed out that it took two to make or break any relationship. That no one person was all in the wrong or all in the right. That maybe, just maybe, she had some culpability in what had gone wrong.

DANI HATED EVERYTHING about Gloria's office. The size, the whiteness of it all. Being here always made her feel as if she'd been called to the principal's office, even when she'd been the one to request the meeting.

It was seven-thirty on a Saturday night. Most people were at home with family or out on dates or with friends. Not her grandmother. Gloria was at the office and if Dani wanted to talk to her, that was where she had to be, too.

"You may go in now," her secretary said, holding open the door to the inner sanctum.

Dani smiled at the woman, one of two secretaries Gloria employed. Her hours were such that one assistant simply wasn't enough.

"Dani," Gloria said from behind her very large, very white desk. "How nice of you to ask to see me."

Gloria didn't stand or offer to shake hands or hug. Not at the office. Here things were strictly business. Here they were never family.

"I took the liberty of going over the numbers at Burger Heaven," Gloria continued as she motioned to the chair opposite her desk. "They look good. So I don't think there's a problem there, is there?"

"No."

Dani had dressed carefully in a pantsuit with a silk blouse. She kept her back straight as she perched at the edge of the chair.

"Burger Heaven is doing well," she said. "Which is why I wanted to see you. I've served my time there, Gloria. There's nothing left for me to learn. I'm ready to move up in the company."

Gloria sighed. "You've said that before, Dani. Several times. No matter how I discourage you, you keep insisting on wanting to move up. Why is that?"

"Because I've earned the chance to prove myself somewhere else." She swallowed, then braced herself. "I either want to be promoted within the company or I'm resigning."

Gloria didn't react at all. Not a lash flickered, not a muscle moved. She regarded Dani for several seconds before saying, "I will not tolerate being threatened by you, young lady."

Dani ignored the young lady bit. "I'm not threatening you. I'm stating a fact. I have both the education and experience to take on more responsibility. This is my career and I refuse to spend it managing Burger Heaven. If you don't want to give me a chance, then I'll find a company that does."

"I doubt you'll find many," Gloria said with a sniff.

Dani ignored the hurt that jabbed her. She'd known this was going to go badly. She had to remember why she was here and stay on topic.

"I disagree," she said. "My employment record and

accomplishments speak for themselves. I won't have any trouble finding another job and moving up. We both know that. So why do you have a problem with me? Why are you always treating me as if I'm second best? Is it because I'm a woman? I can't believe that of you. You're a woman and look what you've accomplished."

"You're right," Gloria told her, a flicker of anger in her eyes. "*I* have brought this company to greatness. *I* am responsible for our success. Don't you dare come to me with your stupid request—"

"It's not stupid. It's reasonable. You haven't held anyone back the way you've kept me down. So why?"

Her grandmother leaned toward her. The air seemed to dip ten degrees. "Be very careful before you ask me that," she said, her voice low. "I don't think you're prepared to hear the truth."

"I think I'm up to it, Gloria," she said, suddenly not the least bit afraid. After all, what could the woman say?

"All right. But when I've told you, don't come crying to me, saying it's all too much."

"Sure. Whatever." Talk about a love of melodrama.

Gloria leaned back in her chair. "Many years ago, before you were born, your mother took up with a man. She was unfaithful to my son. My son. Their affair continued for several years and produced a child—you, Danielle. You are your mother's bastard and not a Buchanan at all. I kept quiet to spare my son the shame. But I've never forgotten. Every time I look at you, I see proof that bitch betrayed my son.

You are your mother's daughter and you are nothing to me."

Dani heard the words, but they didn't make sense. They couldn't. Not a Buchanan? But she had always been a Buchanan.

"You're lying," she said.

"I am not, but if it would make you happy, we could have one of those DNA tests done. I'm confident it will show you are not one of us."

Dani didn't remember standing, but suddenly she was by the door.

"Burger Heaven is as much as you deserve," Gloria told her. "Be grateful I let you have that much."

Funny how an hour ago Dani had thought her life couldn't get any worse. Obviously, she'd been wrong.

"You can have it back," she told her grandmother. "I quit."

"You can't."

"Of course I can. If I'm a bitch like my mother, I can do any damn thing I please."

CHAPTER EIGHTEEN

PENNY WALKED OUT OF the kitchen just ahead of the desserts. As she crossed the dining room toward her family's table, they all stood and began to clap.

Stunned, she froze in place.

"My daughter is the chef," her father said loudly to the other patrons. "Wasn't your meal great?"

To her astonishment, everyone else stood and began applauding. She glanced around at the smiling faces and didn't have a clue as to what she should do now.

The door to the kitchen opened. Penny turned toward it, hoping for a rescue or a reason to escape. Instead Naomi appeared with most of the kitchen staff. They started clapping, too. Cal came out last. He walked over to Penny and stood next to her.

"Did I hire the right person or what?" he asked. Everyone laughed.

Servers appeared with glasses of champagne.

"Didn't we recently do the toast thing?" she whispered to him.

"That was about the success of the restaurant," he said. "This is about you. Smile and drink your club soda."

She took the glass he handed to her and waited until everyone had been served.

"To Penny," Cal said.

"To Penny," echoed the crowd.

Fifteen minutes later, when order had been restored to the dining room, Penny went looking for Cal and found him in his office.

"That was surreal," she said. "Did you plan it?"

"No. Naomi came into the kitchen and said that you were getting a standing ovation in the dining room and I said to break out the champagne. You should be proud of what you've accomplished."

"I am," she said. "But I never expected a reaction like that." She sat down. "When I spoke with my mom earlier, I mentioned that she and my dad must be happy that I finally figured out what I want to be when I grow up. I thought they were disappointed that I went from career to career, flunked out of college. All that stuff. But she said she was glad I'd taken the time to really figure out what I wanted to do. She liked that I didn't settle."

"So they surprised you in a good way."

"It's more than that. Their opinion of me was never what I thought it was and it never occurred to me to ask. I guess I didn't want my worst fears confirmed. I made a lot of assumptions."

"You know what they say about that."

She wrinkled her nose. "I'm going to pretend you didn't say that. My point is, what else was I wrong about?"

"Maybe nothing."

Or maybe everything. She'd been so sure that leaving Cal had been the right thing to do. She'd been so sure she knew everything about him. Now she was beginning to feel she knew nothing about anyone.

"Did I run away from our marriage?" she asked.

He shrugged. "A case could be made for that, but I sure as hell didn't come after you. There was so much crap going on back then, Penny. We were both struggling to make sense of things. I should have told you about Lindsey."

She considered that. "The information would have made a big difference."

"But would it have changed the outcome? Back then I couldn't imagine ever being ready to have another child."

And now? On the one hand she knew that he was a different man—that he'd changed and grown. On the other, he'd admitted to never really loving her during their marriage.

"We couldn't seem to find common ground," he said. "I wanted to protect you. You didn't think you needed it and saw my actions as walking all over your dreams."

"Because you didn't help me get the job at Buchanan's."

"I'm sorry about that," he said.

"It's okay. I understand now what you were doing."

"But you didn't back then. I hurt you and I never wanted to do that. I'm sorry." He'd obviously cared. So why not love? Had he been afraid?

Her heart swelled, making her chest ache. "I'm sorry, too," she whispered.

They'd had so much and then they'd lost it. If only they could have talked back then.

Or was this the way it was supposed to be? Did they need a chance to grow and change to find themselves at this point in time?

Naomi stuck her head in the office. "Sorry to interrupt, but the kitchen's on fire."

Penny scrambled to her feet. "You're kidding, right?"

"Not really."

Cal followed her. They walked into a smoke-filled kitchen.

"Just some grease," Edouard said, fanning the air. "It's out now."

The printer kicked to life, spitting out several more orders.

"Can we get back to business?" she asked. "Is it manageable or do I need to kick someone's ass?"

"We're good," Edouard said.

Cal's cell phone rang. He flipped it open and said, "Hello."

Penny went around the counter to deal with the residual cleanup from the fire. One of their pans was misshapen and two dinners had been ruined, but the flames were out and the vent system made short work of the smoke.

"Are these dinners at different tables?"

They would be. That was always the way, but a girl could hope.

Naomi confirmed the bad news.

"Get them up and cooking," Penny called. "These

are our priority, people." She turned to say something to Edouard when she noticed Cal hanging up.

"What happened?" she asked as she took in his worried expression. "Is Lindsey okay?"

"What? Oh, she's fine. That was Dani. She needs me to come by after work. Something happened. She sounded upset, but she won't say what."

One of the servers came into the kitchen. "Um, Penny? Your family is leaving. They'd like a chance to say goodbye."

Cal touched her arm. "There's nothing we can do now. I'll come get you before I leave, then we'll go over to your place together."

"No. I think this is a family matter. I'll stay here until you've talked to her. Then you can call and give me the all clear."

"It's not that big a deal."

"You don't know that, Cal. If Dani had wanted me there, she would have asked. I'll stay here."

While part of her brain processed details like the number of customers and orders yet to be filled, the rest of her mind turned over the problem of Cal.

Had she left their marriage too soon? If she'd stayed, could they have learned their lessons—him to give with his whole heart, her to believe he wanted her to succeed? They'd come a long way. If only he would love her—really love her.

Was it possible, or was she just wishing for the moon?

CAL PARKED behind Reid's car and an unfamiliar truck he figured had to belong to Walker. Which meant

Dani had called a family meeting. Maybe Penny had been right—this looked serious.

As he climbed out of the car, he wondered if Hugh had dropped another bombshell. If so, wheelchair or not, Cal was going to have to beat the crap out of the man.

He walked up to Penny's front door, which opened before he could knock.

Reid greeted him. "Good. She wouldn't say anything until we were all together. Why do I know Hugh just won bastard of the year?"

"That's what I'm thinking, too. If so, we'll take care of it."

"You got that right."

They walked into the living room, where Walker sat on the sofa. Dani stood by the small fireplace. She had a drink in her hand and a look of stark pain in her eyes.

He crossed to her. "Dani, what's wrong?"

When he went to hold her, she sidestepped his embrace.

"Get yourself something to drink and have a seat," she said.

"Dani?"

She shook her head. "You can't fix this with a hug, Cal. Just get a drink. Please."

Reid walked into the living room and handed him a beer. The two of them joined Walker on the sofa.

Dani faced them. "I went to see Gloria. I wanted to talk to her about my career with the company. I told her I was done with Burger Heaven and either she moved me up the food chain or I was quitting."

Cal was getting a bad feeling in his gut. Nothing good could have come from the conversation.

"She's a bitch, Dani," Reid said. "Consider the source."

His sister clutched her glass in both hands. She looked each of them in the face, then spoke. "She told me I would never move up in the company. When I pointed out that I had the most education in the business of any of her grandchildren and that I wanted it more, she explained why neither of those things was an issue. Can you guess why?"

Cal kept his gaze firmly locked on Dani. He watched pain fill her eyes and then he knew Gloria had finally made good on her threat to tell Dani about her father.

He stood. "Dani, it's not—"

She turned on him. "Don't you *dare* try to tell me this doesn't matter. Of course it matters. It's my life. It's who I am."

She glared at him as she spoke, then she set her glass down on the mantel and folded her arms over her chest.

"Oh, God. You know."

He didn't know what to say or do. Penny had warned him to come clean with Dani more than once. She'd said it would be a disaster if Dani found out on her own and she'd been right.

Walker and Reid stood. They looked at each other, then at Dani.

"Listen," Reid began.

"No!" Dani took two steps back.

Cal moved toward her. "I'm sorry," he said. "I'm so sorry."

Tears filled her eyes. "I thought the worst of it was finding out I wasn't who I thought I was. I thought the worst was knowing I wasn't really one of you, but that's not the worst, is it?"

"You're one of us," Cal told her. "You're my baby sister. I love you, Dani."

"How long?" she demanded. "How long have you known?"

Walker looked at him, then turned to Dani. "Since high school. That's when Gloria told me. She said that she would tell you the truth if I went into the marines. I talked to Cal and Reid and found out she'd threatened them, as well. It was information she used to keep us in line. But I knew that if she hadn't already told you the truth, for some reason she didn't want to."

Cal hadn't thought of the situation that way, but Walker was right. Gloria had used whatever threat she thought would work best. He'd never considered that it was all just a game to her. He'd always been willing to do anything to protect Dani.

"I love you so much," he told her. "I didn't want to hurt you."

She dismissed his statement with a frown. "Oh, please. You've been keeping secrets from me all my life."

A single tear rolled down her cheek. She brushed it away impatiently. "What else did you know? What else did you keep from me? Hugh's affair? Did he tell you all about it?"

Reid grabbed her by the upper arms, and stared

into her face. "Dammit, Dani, stop it. I'm sorry. We're all sorry. No, we didn't know about your bastard husband. Yes, we've kept secrets, but only because we didn't want to hurt you."

"Don't you think it hurts to never fit in? Don't you think it hurts to not be one of the guys? To know you three have a bond I'll never have?"

Cal reached for her. She jerked away from him, but he pulled her close and held her against him.

"You mean the world to us."

"Bullshit. You treat me like a child. Do you know what it was like to keep trying and trying? Year after year I worked my butt off trying to please Gloria and no matter what I did it wasn't enough. You all stood there, watching me fail and you never once thought to tell me why? To spare me that?"

She was right, he thought. This time when she tried to pull away, he let her.

She glared at them. "This was not your decision to make."

Reid shook his head. "How do you say something like that to your only sister?"

"You find the words and if they don't come easily, you keep looking for them. And I'm not your sister."

Cal stared at her. "You will always be my sister. I don't give a damn about who your father is. You're my sister."

"Half, technically," she told him. "Get out."

"What?"

She sucked in a breath. "Just go. I don't want to talk to any of you. Go!"

The last word came out as a scream. Cal looked at his brothers, then back at her. Was it better to give her time, or should he try to get her to understand that he'd only been trying to protect her?

As soon as he thought the words, he realized that he'd screwed up trying to protect Penny all those years ago and he'd just made things even worse with Dani. It seemed as if he wasn't very good at taking care of those he loved.

"Dani," Reid began.

She took a step back. "Just get out of here. I don't want to see you or talk to you."

Walker nodded. "We'll be in touch tomorrow."

Instead of responding, she walked out of the living room. A few seconds later, a door slammed.

"Shit," Cal said as he rubbed his jaw. "What the hell was Gloria thinking? I never thought she'd really tell Dani."

"We should have been the ones," Reid said.

"Ya think?"

Walker stepped between them. "We need to give her time. Some wounds need to bleed for a while."

Cal knew Walker was right but he didn't want to think of his sister bleeding. He didn't want her hurt ever and he hated knowing he could have helped ease this one.

"I don't think she should be alone," Reid said.

"Penny will be home soon," Cal told him.

Walker looked between them. "Should we give her a heads-up?"

Cal wasn't sure how to answer. In truth, Penny already knew about Dani, so she wouldn't be surprised.

"I'll call her," he said at last. "She'll get here as soon as she can."

PENNY HESITATED a second before turning in to her driveway. She was still trying to figure out what she was going to say to Dani.

A fight with family was one thing. Finding out you weren't family was something else.

Of all the siblings, Dani was the one most interested in being a Buchanan. She had always defined herself that way—by her name and her connection to the business. Even when she'd married Hugh, she'd refused to change her name.

Penny parked, then climbed out of her car. She cupped her belly, hoping her concerns weren't upsetting the baby.

"There's going to be a lot of emotion, little one. Some crying and maybe even some bad language. None of this is about you. I love you very much and we're going to be fine."

With that she drew in a breath and walked into the house.

She found Dani curled up on the sofa in the living room. There was an open bottle of Merlot in front of her. Her eyes were swollen and bloodshot, her face blotchy. She was misery personified.

"Oh, Dani," Penny breathed.

Her new roommate looked up. "Tell me Cal already told you so that I don't have to repeat myself."

"He did. I'm so sorry."

"Yeah. Me, too." She picked up her wine and took a drink. "Screw 'em all. What do I care about being a Buchanan? They're all a bunch of losers. Good riddance. The same with Gloria."

But as she spoke tears spilled onto her cheeks.

Penny dropped her coat and her purse on the floor, then hurried to her friend's side.

"I don't know what to say," she admitted as she sat on the sofa and touched Dani's arm. "I wish I did."

"Me, too," Dani admitted. "Oh, God, Penny, this hurts so much. Way more than finding out Hugh was having an affair. That was a betrayal of trust. I wasn't happy, but I knew I'd recover. This is different. I don't even know who I am anymore."

"Yes, you do. You're a bright, ambitious, hard-working, wonderful woman. You're caring and loyal. Plus you got the looks in the family."

Dani gave a faint smile as she brushed away her tears. "So you're saying I'm prettier than my brothers?"

"Absolutely. Although Reid comes fairly close."

"I agree. It's the eyes." Her mouth began to quiver as her smile faded. Her whole body trembled. "I can't do this. I can't survive."

"Yes, you can," Penny told her. "You may not like it and you're going to hate how much it hurts, but you will survive. You know why?"

Dani shook her head.

"Because you're tough. That's the main reason. The other is you're not going to give that bitch Gloria the satisfaction of winning."

Once again Dani smiled through her tears. "You're right about that. I'm so angry at her. Furious. I always knew she had a thing for power and running our lives, but I refused to believe she was deliberately cruel. But she is."

"She's horrible," Penny said. "You're doing such a great job for her, but she can't see that."

"I know." Dani sighed. "And to tell me that way. I think she was almost happy to be able to ruin my life."

"No," Penny said. "Don't say that. She didn't ruin anything. Not if you don't let her."

"She sure didn't make things better," Dani said. "I don't know who I am anymore."

"That's bullshit," Penny said.

Dani blinked at her. "Excuse me?"

She stood and then motioned for Dani to rise. "Come here."

Penny led the way into the hall bathroom. After turning on the light, she pulled Dani in next to her and had her face the mirror.

"What's different?" she asked. "Look and tell me what's different."

Dani glanced at her reflection and grimaced. "I'm really puffy."

"Ignore that. I mean what's different about you? What has changed in the past twenty-four hours?"

"I don't know who my father is. I'm not a Buchanan."

"I know that. But your experiences are still your experiences. Your body is still your body. You're talking about context, and yes, I'll agree that can change everything, but it doesn't have to. Not if you don't let it."

"But…"

Penny shook her head. "No buts, young lady. Yes, things are crappy now. Really crappy. This may be the worst moment of your life. But you will come out of it and you will be fine. Because the wonderful, empowered person you are hasn't changed."

Dani leaned over and hugged her. "Thanks for trying to help."

"Hey, I'm not just trying here."

Dani managed a weak smile. "Okay. Thanks for helping."

"Better."

She dropped her hand to Penny's stomach. "You must be so happy about the baby."

"I am."

"I'll get there someday. You're right. This hurts so much and I don't know how I'm going to survive it. But I will survive and I'll go on and one day I'll have everything I want."

"Yes, you will. And when that happens, I'm going to be standing right next to you saying 'I told you so.'"

THE NEXT WEEK PASSED in relative quiet. Penny figured they'd all earned the break.

The restaurant did well, Lindsey was released from the hospital, and while Dani was still emotionally devastated, she was making forward progress. Even the rats were gone, thanks to a very efficient Al.

Penny sat at her desk playing with different combinations for specials for the following week. The Alaskan fishing season was well underway, giving her access to some wonderful seafood. She was already receiving produce from the Walla Walla area and parts of Oregon. When the Walla Walla onions made their appearance, she had some great ideas in mind.

"Maybe a special tasting dinner," she murmured. "One that features whatever is fresh and special."

She made a note. That was something she would discuss with Cal later. Right now she needed to be brilliant.

"Salmon?" She loved salmon. It was about her favorite fish. But maybe something else. Something…

"Am I interrupting?"

Penny glanced up and saw Gloria standing in the doorway to her office. Great. The rats might be gone, but now there was a snake in the kitchen.

She wanted to tell the older woman to get her ass out, but technically, she did own The Waterfront and was Penny's boss's boss.

"I'm working on specials for next week," Penny said. "I'll be putting in my fish order fairly soon."

"Ah, how interesting. I don't suppose there's any chance you'll be taking the fish and chips off the menu."

Penny forced herself to smile. "It's our best seller."

"How unfortunate. I always thought the people of Seattle had better taste than that."

Penny ground her teeth together. "Did you stop by just to insult me, Gloria, or is there another reason?"

Gloria moved into her office and took a seat. "Insult you? I most certainly did not. Really, Penny, what a thing to say. I was saying that I didn't like the fish and chips and wished they weren't on the menu. How is that an insult?" She sighed. "You're the executive chef. I suppose it's reasonable for you to have a sense of ownership where the menu is concerned. That's quite commendable."

Penny frowned. Gloria sounded so reasonable, yet she was sure there was plenty more to come.

But before she could ask Gloria why she'd stopped by, the other woman glanced at her stomach and said, "You're showing, dear. When is the baby due?"

"September."

"A lovely time of year. I was told you don't know who the father is. Is that true?"

"I had in vitro fertilization using a sperm donor, if that's what you mean."

"Uh-huh. So you know nothing about the man."

"I have general information on him and his medical history."

"But not his character." She leaned forward. "It's very much like buying those unmarked cans at the grocery store. It's so very easy to get a bad batch of peas or carrots and not know until you've already brought them home."

"Thanks for the warning."

"I did want to warn you, dear," Gloria continued. "I know you have your heart set on Cal, but it's not going to happen. He's never forgiven you for walking out on him. He's not interested in you or your bastard. I know. He told me."

Penny didn't care that this woman was in charge or that she was elderly. She stood and pointed to the door. "Get out."

Gloria rose. "He won't marry you, if that's what you're hoping. You may think he's changed, but who really does? In truth, he gave up Lindsey and he gave you up once already. Why would he keep you now?"

"If you don't leave, I'm going to call for the guys in the kitchen to haul you out," Penny said, trying not to give in to the anger rising inside of her.

"We both know you won't do that," Gloria told her. "My words may sound cruel, but I'm telling you this for your own good. Cal's contract with the restaurant is only for four months. He's leaving."

She spoke so triumphantly that Penny didn't feel bad about bursting her bubble.

"You love to get in between people and mess around. I think it's your idea of a good time. But here's the thing. I already know Cal's leaving. He told me the first day he tried to hire me."

Gloria smiled. "Of course he did. Did he also mention that his little coffee company is expanding? They're going to be opening stores back east. A complete waste of Cal's talent if you ask me, but there we are. He's heading the team. As soon as his job here is finished, he's moving to New York. Did he happen to mention that?"

Penny didn't want to believe her. It couldn't be true. Cal moving? He hadn't said a word.

"You're a cold, calculating lying bitch," she told Gloria. "I don't know why you find such pleasure in hurting people, but you do. Dani only ever wanted to make you proud of her, but you couldn't accept that. You had to run her off."

Gloria sniffed. "Dani is hardly my granddaughter. We're no blood relation at all."

"Funny how worried you are that Dani's not a Buchanan when you're not one yourself. If I remember my history correctly, you married into this family. You were a poor nobody. What? A hotel chambermaid?"

Gloria stiffened.

Penny allowed herself a slight smile. "Oh, yeah. I did my research on you years ago. I know all about your affair with Ian Buchanan and how when that ended, you married his son. Tell me, Gloria. Were you still banging Daddy when you walked down the aisle with the son?"

"You slut," Gloria hissed.

"You should know."

"I'll destroy you."

"You can try. I'm up to the fight. But before you waste your effort on that, let me share one thing with you. You're an old woman. You'll be dead soon. But first you're going to be alone because you've driven anyone interested in loving you away. Now get the hell out of my kitchen."

CHAPTER NINETEEN

PENNY SAT IN HER OFFICE long after Gloria had left. She had to wait for the shaking to stop before she could catch her breath. That hadn't just happened, she told herself, even though she knew it had. No one could imagine an encounter like that. At least not on purpose.

"A nightmare," she murmured. "That woman is a nightmare."

She put her arms on her desk and rested her head on them. It was fine, she told herself. She was fine. Gloria could scream and yell and tell all the lies she wanted, but Penny refused to believe them. There was no way that old bitch was going to drive a wedge between her and Cal.

Of course she knew he was only working at the restaurant for four months. He'd told her that from the beginning. He wasn't the man he had been three years ago. He didn't keep secrets anymore. She knew about Lindsey and Dani and why he'd tried to keep her out of the family business. Honestly, after Gloria's last visit, his motivation seemed more noble than ever.

But he hadn't mentioned anything about expanding The Daily Grind back east.

"No," she said as she sat up. "No, no, no. I won't let her get away with this."

Cal wasn't leaving. He would have told her. They'd become friends. They were lovers. Their lives were entwined in a way they hadn't been since they were married. She mattered to him. She had to because she was totally in love with him.

"Everything is fine," she said aloud. But the words didn't sound right and she didn't believe them.

Hating herself for letting Gloria get to her, she found an old phone book in her bottom desk draw and looked up the corporate headquarters for The Daily Grind. After a receptionist answered, she asked for someone in charge of their corporate expansion.

CAL SAT in his office at The Daily Grind and considered his life. After tallying up the wins and losses, he knew he'd come up short of even, which meant he needed a new game plan.

Dani was furious at him, and rightfully so. He should have told her a long time ago. He should have known she was tough enough to hear the truth and that however it hurt her, better that she hear it from someone who loved her rather than from Gloria whose agenda was her own twisted secret. Dani would survive, but the timing sucked, coming on the heels of Hugh's shitty behavior.

He should have listened to Penny.

Shaking his head, he turned to his computer, but instead of the screen, he saw Penny's smiling face. So much had happened so quickly, he thought. So much had changed. After the divorce he'd assumed she was out of his life forever. He'd resisted taking the job at The Waterfront because he didn't want to deal with Gloria. But she'd guilted him into it and because of that, he and Penny were...

Were what? Back together? He wouldn't go that far, but they mattered to each other. Once again he'd fallen for her smile, her brain, her talent. She was funny and beautiful and fearless.

She was strong. Having a baby on her own. He never would have guessed that one, even knowing how much she wanted children. She would be a great mom.

He stood and walked to the window. His side of the building looked toward Lake Union. As he stared out on the cloudy sky, he thought about her growing bigger with her baby. About her giving birth...by herself.

No, not by herself. Naomi would be there. And Dani. Reid. Would he? Would he want to be in the room with her, holding her hand, telling her to breathe?

The question immobilized him. What did he want with Penny?

Instantly Lindsey came to mind, but for once he didn't think about all he'd lost by giving her up. Instead he thought about her life. How much her parents loved her. How much she was their world. They didn't care that they hadn't created her themselves.

It could be like that, he thought. For him and Penny's baby. Loving a child wasn't about biology. It was about the heart.

Seventeen years ago, he'd made the only choice that made sense. Now, with hindsight, he knew it was the right choice. He'd allowed guilt and anger to blind him to that. He'd punished himself by refusing to be happy.

He swore under his breath. That blindness had cost him his marriage, he realized.

How long had he been holding his heart in check so he didn't get hurt? All his life? Maybe since his parents had died. Maybe since Gloria had started running his world with her twisted rules and cruel threats.

"Damn," he muttered. "Get some therapy and move on, guy."

He would move on, but not by himself. He loved Penny and he'd learned enough to make things work with her, if she would give him a chance.

Talk about an uphill battle, he thought grimly. If she knew he hadn't wanted children before, children who were his, why would she believe he was willing to accept someone else's baby?

He would convince her, he told himself. He would make her understand what was in his heart. He would tell her he'd finally learned what it meant to love someone. To love her.

He walked back to his desk and started to shut down his computer. Before it had finished, his assistant buzzed him.

"Yes," he said.

"There's someone to see you. Penny Jackson."

Penny? "Send her in."

He'd hoped to have a little time to figure out what he was going to say, but maybe it would be better to simply tell her now. The sooner he started convincing her, the sooner they could begin their life together.

The door opened. He stepped toward her, then stopped when he saw the fury in her eyes.

"You snake," she said, her voice low and angry. "You lying, scummy, slithery snake. I consider myself a reasonable person. I'm willing to overlook a lot. I give second chances, but you are disgusting."

He crossed to her and reached for her shoulders. She quickly stepped back.

"Don't you dare touch me. Don't ever touch me again."

Cold panic slipped through him. "What the hell happened?"

She glared at him. "I defended you. I can't believe it, but I did. Gloria came by for one of her emotional hit-and-runs. I defended you and all the time it was true."

He opened his mouth to ask what she was talking about when he suddenly knew. He groaned.

"You're leaving," she said. "In less than a month you're packing it all up and leaving Seattle. I understand everyone is very excited about The Daily Grind expanding back east. Too bad I don't have stock in the damn company."

"Penny, no."

Her eyes narrowed. "Don't try to tell me it's not true, Cal. I've already spoken to someone at your company. He was very friendly and explained the whole damn plan."

Tears filled her eyes. She brushed them away with her hand. "I believed you," she said. "I trusted you."

"I'm sorry," he said as sincerely as he knew how. "I should have told you."

"Oh, right, but it just slipped your mind."

"Yes," he yelled. "I forgot! With all the crap going on lately, is that so much of a surprise? When I first hired you I told you I was the GM for four months. I didn't think you cared what I did after that. Later, when we got involved, I planned to tell you but it wasn't foremost on my mind. I didn't keep this from you deliberately. It just happened. Besides, I've been talking to my partners. I've been rethinking my plans. It might be better if I stayed here."

"Might be better?" she screamed. "That's the best you can do? But it might not? Tell me, when do you plan to make up your mind?" She raised her hand. "On second thought, forget it. I don't care anymore."

She closed her eyes, then opened them. "I am such a fool," she said, her voice back to normal, but so thick with sadness that he ached to hear her.

"You're not," he told her.

"A lot you know. You're the reason. You'd think I'd learn. What's that old saying? Fool me once, shame on you. Fool me twice, shame on me. Well, shame on me."

What did that mean? He knew he was in deep shit with Penny, but he couldn't help a flicker of hope deep inside.

"Penny?"

"Don't even go there," she told him. "Not anymore. I loved you, Cal. Maybe for the second time, maybe I never stopped. I don't know and now I don't care. Because the truth is, you're no different than you ever were. You still keep secrets. You're still holding back, playing it safe, making sure you don't get hurt. You're still not willing to put your heart on the line. I'm not interested in a man like that. I'm not interested in someone I can't trust."

"But you love me."

She grimaced. "I'll get over it. And you."

"But I love you, too."

She stared at him for a long time, then turned toward the door. "I've heard that before and I know how little those words are worth."

"IF THIS IS GOING TO become a regular occurrence," Naomi said from her place next to Penny on the sofa, "then we're going to need to establish some ground rules."

Penny used the tissue to wipe her face, although she wasn't sure why she bothered. No mattered how quickly she mopped up her tears, there were plenty of new ones to take their place.

"A code so we can call each other on the phone," Naomi said as she continued to rub Penny's back.

"A schedule so we don't all break down at the same time," Dani said from Penny's other side.

"T-that would be good," Penny said as she tried to fight the sobs building up inside of her.

She'd been hurt before—mostly by Cal—but somehow this felt worse. Maybe because she'd thought she'd figured everything out. She thought she'd found the solution, only to realize she'd been wrong about everything.

Despite the ache around her heart and the sense

that she would never again draw breath without wanting to scream, she knew she had to do her best to get past what had happened. At least the physical part. Her trembling, sobbing, angry state couldn't be good for the baby.

"You guys are great," she said, trying to focus on them instead of herself. "For being here with me."

"Hey, I don't have a job," Dani said with a sigh. "Where else would I be?"

Penny did her best to smile. "Good point."

"I work for you," Naomi said. "You're the boss. You say jump, I say how high."

"Also good."

"So we're not here because we care," Dani said.

Penny sniffed. "That'll put me in my place."

The two women leaned in and hugged her.

"I'm sorry," Dani whispered in her ear. "I never knew my brother was such a big butthead."

"Yeah," Naomi said. "I'd nearly forgiven him for being a bastard the last time. I'll never forgive him for this."

"That'll show him," Penny said, then choked on a sob. "Oh, God. I don't think I can get through this. I know wounds heal and time helps and all that crap, but right now, I don't think I can do it."

"We're here," Naomi told her.

"Not going anywhere," Dani added.

"I just thought this time was different," Penny said as she wiped her face with another tissue. "I thought he was different. I thought I mattered. I fell back in love with him."

"Men'll get you every time," Dani said as she

leaned against Penny's shoulder. "I just didn't think Cal…" She paused, then said. "I'm sorry. I'm fighting the urge to defend him. I want to tell you that he had a hard time, being the oldest. Gloria, trying to protect us. The usual. But I won't."

"You can," Penny said. "How sick is that? I wouldn't mind listening to you defend him."

"Typical," Naomi murmured. "I forgive you."

"Thanks." She drew in a deep breath and did her best to absorb the support from her friends. "I thought he was different. I thought he would be willing to take a chance on us. I was so stupid."

"Loving someone is never stupid," Naomi said. "It can hurt like hell, but it's never stupid."

"I agree," Dani said. "I say that even as I feel like the world's biggest idiot. I mean, my soon-to-be ex-husband is currently sleeping with one of his students. So I'm not just stupid, I'm a bad cliché. But there's hope. I can still laugh at things and I have you guys."

"I'm glad we're together," Penny said, putting her arms around both of them. "You're right. This will get better. I have so much in my life. The restaurant, the baby. My family. And the good news is with Cal leaving, I don't have to worry about running into him anywhere. I would really hate that."

More tears filled her eyes. "I seem to be leaking again."

"That's okay. Things could be worse," Naomi told her. "I'm not sure how, but they could."

Penny laughed. "You are always a ray of sunshine."

"That's me."

Penny looked at her friend. "I'm going to miss you so much."

Naomi straightened. "What are you talking about? I'm not going anywhere."

"Of course you are. I've known you a long time and I know you're not the type of person who runs away from things. You've always lived on your own terms."

Naomi snorted. "I'm the queen of running away. I've been on the run nearly eight years."

"It's time to go back."

Naomi shook her head. "I haven't decided."

"Of course you have. You wouldn't have told me about your son if you weren't already halfway out the door." She glanced at Dani. "Do you know what we're talking about?"

Dani nodded. "We've been talking."

Penny glanced between them. "About what?"

"About nothing," Naomi said firmly. "I'm not going to leave. You need me."

Penny did. She couldn't imagine having to go through all this without her friend, but it was wrong to expect Naomi to put her life on hold because she, Penny, had been stupid enough to get her heart broken twice by the same man.

"Of course you're going," Penny said briskly. "Like you said, you've been the queen of running away for eight years. It's time to go connect with your family. To find out what you still have there in the way of a life."

"You might still be married," Dani said. "Given

what you've been doing, wouldn't that be interesting?"

Naomi shook her head. "Sam wouldn't have waited. Not his style. I'm sure he's divorced me by now," she said, but her tone was wistful, as if she wanted to believe in the possibilities.

"See? You have to go," Penny said quietly.

"I can't leave you now. Not with everything going on and the baby coming. What about the restaurant? You need me."

Dani looked at Penny. "I could do that."

Penny stared at her. "But it's The Waterfront. Why would you go work for your grandmother again?"

"I wouldn't be. Your contract allows you to bring in your own crew, doesn't it?"

"Hello," Naomi said. "Still in the room. There's no need to have this conversation right now."

Penny ignored her. "Three people. I only brought in Naomi and Edouard because the rest of the crew is so great. So adding you wouldn't be a problem."

It could work, she thought. She and Dani hadn't worked together, but they knew each other and she knew Dani put in long hours. She'd survived Burger Heaven nearly five years. She was tough and smart.

"The job is yours if you want it," Penny told Dani.

Naomi stood. "You're giving away my job? Just like that? What about the baby? You're going to need help as you get closer to your due date."

"I'll be here," Dani said. "I can help."

"There," Penny said. "You don't have any more excuses."

Maybe it wasn't fair to push her friend, but thinking about Naomi's life kept her from dwelling on the disaster hers had become. A disaster that would get a whole lot more lonely once Naomi left.

Penny stood and hugged Naomi. "I'll miss you so much."

Naomi squeezed her. "I won't be gone that long. Just a few weeks."

Or forever, Penny thought. Maybe Naomi would be lucky enough to find there was still a whole life waiting for her back in Ohio.

"Is this a chick thing or can anyone join in?"

Penny turned at the sound of Reid's voice. "What are you doing here?"

"Hell of a way to greet me," he said as he walked over and pulled her close. "Dani called me."

"I thought you'd want him here," Dani said. "Is that okay?"

Penny was too busy crying to do much more than nod.

Reid wrapped his arms around her. He was tall and strong and she felt as if she could lean on him forever.

"Go ahead and cry," he said, smoothing her hair and rocking her gently. "My brother is a lying bastard and his days are numbered."

"You can't kill him," Dani said. "Not even for Penny."

Penny raised her head and sniffed. "I don't want him dead."

"Fine. I'll just teach him a lesson. How's that?"

Penny shook her head. "No fighting."

Reid grunted. "I'm sorry," he said.

That was enough to set her off again. She pressed her face into his chest. "It hurts so much. He doesn't love me. He's moving away and so's Naomi and Dani's going to help me but nothing is ever going to be the same."

"I'm here and I love you," Reid said.

"I know. That's good."

She raised her head again and looked at him. "Why couldn't I fall in love with you?"

He smiled, then kissed her cheek. "Not a good idea, kid. I'm not one of the good guys. You're better off with Cal or Walker."

Penny didn't think so but it didn't matter. She and Reid could only ever be friends. The heart, ever a contrary organ, had apparently decided she could only love one man. Even if that man was destined to forever be breaking her heart.

CAL DROVE AROUND until sunset, then returned to his house. He wanted to go see Penny, but first he had to figure out what he wanted to say to her. Until then, he had a feeling showing up there would only make things worse.

She was right about him, he thought as he turned onto his street. She always had been. In the past, he'd been okay with that but this time he wanted things to be different. He wanted to *be* different.

He headed into his driveway and saw two other cars there. As he glanced toward the front door. He saw Reid and Walker on the porch, having what looked like a heated conversation.

"What's up?" he asked as he climbed out of his car and walked toward them.

Reid glared at him. "You made Penny cry," he said, his voice a low growl. "Nobody makes Penny cry."

"So what does that mean?" Cal asked. "You're here to make me pay?"

"You got that right."

Cal shrugged, not the least bit worried about taking Reid on in a fight. His brother might be the same size and in great shape, but Cal had some repressed anger on his side.

He turned to Walker. "You gonna help him?"

Walker shrugged. "No. I'm here to make sure you don't both kill yourselves."

Cal knew fighting wouldn't change anything one way or the other, but in that moment, he didn't care. He wanted to lash out at someone and if his brother was willing to be a target, then that was good enough for Cal.

He stepped onto the lawn and beckoned Reid. "Bring it on, little brother."

For a second he thought Reid wouldn't react. Then his brother came flying at him.

Their bodies collided with a force that rattled every bone in his body. They both went down. Cal got to his feet first and was ready to defend himself when Reid came out swinging.

Cal ducked, got in a good punch to the gut that reverberated back to his elbow. Reid clipped his jaw, which made Cal stagger back a step. A couple more hits by each of them and he was rethinking his plan.

He hadn't been in a fight since he was thirteen years old and he'd forgotten how much they hurt.

Still, he liked the raw emotion pouring through him, the need to destroy that blocked out every other thought. He got in a one-two punch before Reid nailed him with a shot that reminded him his brother had a thunderbolt for a right arm.

Lazily, Walker strolled over and stepped between them.

"That's enough," he said calmly. "You're both going to be regretting this in the morning."

Cal touched his mouth and winced as he felt blood and rapidly swelling flesh.

The anger had drained out of him until he was left only with pain and a sense of loss so strong, it nearly drove him to his knees.

Penny. He'd screwed things up so badly with her, he didn't know how to recover.

"I've lost her," he said as he sank onto the damp lawn. "Haven't I?"

Reid sprawled next to him. "You screwed up on a massive scale," he said. "Naomi wants your balls."

The part of him in question tightened into his body.

"What does Penny want?" he asked hoarsely.

"To not love you anymore."

Reid couldn't have hurt him more if he'd shot him. "She has to love me," Cal whispered. She was all he had.

Walker crouched in front of him and touched a sore spot just above his eyebrow. "You're going to need stitches for that." He looked at Reid. "Your knuckles are pretty bad, too. Let's go inside and I'll patch up the two of you."

Cal looked at Reid. "I'm sorry."

His brother grimaced. "I'm not the one you should apologize to."

"I know. But I'm still sorry."

Reid shrugged, then stood. But instead of turning to the house, he held out his hand to Cal.

"You might be an asshole," he said as he pulled Cal to his feet. "But you're still my brother."

They looked at each other and Cal knew that things were right between them. If only the situation with Penny were so easily resolved.

He took a step and had to hold in a groan. Blood dripped down from the cut beside his eyes and from his lip. His body ached and he felt about a hundred and fifty years old.

But before he could make it to the porch, a car pulled up. Cal glanced over to see if by some miracle, Penny had come to see him. Right now he would be happy if she were simply willing to yell at him some more.

But she wasn't the one who stepped out of the vehicle. Instead Lindsey opened the passenger's door and got out.

She was too thin and wearing a scarf over her head, but he'd never seen anything so beautiful in his life.

"Lindsey," he called. "What are you doing here?"

She glanced from him to Reid and Walker. "Um, is this a bad time?"

"No."

"But you're…" She squinted. "Have you been fighting?"

He groaned. Talk about perfect timing. "Yeah, well, my brother and I had something we had to work out."

Lindsey's eyes lit up. "Brothers. Both of them?"

He nodded. "This is Reid and this is Walker."

"Wow," she breathed. "Uncles."

His heart stood still. "What did you say?"

She looked at him and her smile quivered a little at the corners. "Um, I said uncles. That's why I'm here. I just found out you're my dad."

CHAPTER TWENTY

LINDSEY WATCHED AS WALKER set out first aid supplies on the dining room table. Cal wanted to reassure her, but he was busy trying to stop the blood from dripping down the side of his face.

"We're, ah, not usually like this," he said, wishing he sounded less lame and slightly more smooth. "Reid and I haven't had a fight in ten or fifteen years."

Lindsey's blue eyes widened slightly. "So why were you fighting now?"

Reid glanced at Cal, then at Cal's daughter. "Long story."

She sighed. "That's what adults always say when they don't want to tell you the truth."

"Bummer, huh?" Reid said.

Lindsey smiled, then turned her attention to Walker. "Are you a doctor or something?"

"I used to be a marine and I know basic first aid."

She looked him up and down. "That's cool. Were you overseas?"

He nodded without looking up.

There was an awkward silence which Cal broke by saying, "You have an aunt, too. Our youngest sister. Dani—short for Danielle."

"Big family," Lindsey said. "It's just my mom and

dad and me. We're—" She paused and pressed her lips together. "Can I still call them that? Are you going to get mad?"

"What? Of course not. Lindsey, Tracy and Tom *are* your parents."

"Yeah," Reid said. "He's just some guy who donated— What?" he asked as Walker cuffed him on the arm. "What'd I say?"

"We have a young lady present," Walker reminded him. "Not one of your women."

Lindsey looked instantly intrigued. "You have women? A lot of them? Like more than one girlfriend at a time? Are you—" Her mouth dropped open. "Ohmygod! You're Reid Buchanan. You're a baseball pitcher."

"Used to be," Reid said curtly. "Now I run a bar."

"Okay, but you're famous." She turned to Cal. "He's your brother?"

"Uh-huh. And your uncle."

"My uncle is Reid Buchanan? My friends are going to *die* when I tell them."

Reid looked more uncomfortable than excited. Cal changed the subject by asking, "How did you find out about me?"

"What? Oh, my mom told me. We were talking about the transplant and how well it went and I was really surprised because there can be problems with blood from an unrelated donor. And when I said that she got this really weird look on her face."

Walker motioned for Cal to take a seat by the dining room table. Cal settled down, then removed the washcloth from his temple. Instantly blood began to trickle down his face.

"Are you sure you're not going to need stitches?" Lindsey asked.

"That's what I'm thinking," Walker said.

"I'll be fine. Try the bandage," Cal told him. "Go on, Lindsey."

"Oh. Okay. Well, she, um, got this weird look on her face and then she just blurted it all out. She told me who you were and that you'd always wanted to be a part of my life, but you didn't want to push and that you were my biological dad and stuff. So I wanted to come see you."

Cal groaned. "Did we just walk in the house and leave your mom parked out there?"

Lindsey laughed. "No. She went to get coffee. I'm going to call her when it's time to come get me."

Walker tugged on his skin. Cal did his best not to react to the pain. The bandages were put in place, but Walker didn't look pleased. "These aren't going to hold."

Lindsey moved close and wrinkled her nose. "He's right. You really need to go to the hospital."

"In a minute." He smiled at her. "I'm glad you're here."

"Me, too. I thought, you know, maybe we could be friends."

"I'd like that."

She glanced at Reid and Walker. "It's nice to have more family. I've always wanted that. Are any of you guys married?"

Walker snorted. "Reid settle down with one

woman? Not likely. I've been out of the country and Cal… You're going to have to talk to him about that."

Lindsey glanced at him expectantly.

Cal shook his head. "Another long story," he said, knowing there was no way he could explain about Penny.

"That's too bad. I'd like some cousins or even half brothers and sisters. I wouldn't even mind babysitting. Well, at least until I go to college. Then I'll be really busy."

Impulsively, Cal grabbed Lindsey's hand. "Thanks for coming to see me. I know you're all grown up and have a life, but maybe we could get together for lunch sometime."

She ducked her head, but squeezed his fingers. "That would be nice. I can give you my cell number. We can talk and stuff. And e-mail, too." She grinned. "I love e-mail."

"Me, too."

Reid pulled the towel away from the cut on his jaw and showed it to Walker. Just then a fresh gush of blood dripped down the front of his shirt.

"That's it," Lindsey said forcefully. "I can see I'm going to have to take charge here. You're both going to the emergency room. You need stitches. There's no discussion about this. I just went through chemo and a bone marrow transplant. I think you tough guys can survive a couple of stitches."

"What were you thinking?" Dani asked as she sat next to Cal in the emergency room. "You're too old to be fighting each other."

"We weren't thinking," Cal told her. "That's how fights usually start. No one plans them. Well, Reid kind of planned this one."

"But you're mature adults. At least you were. And on the front lawn."

He winced. "How'd you hear that?"

"I had a fascinating talk with your daughter before she had to leave. This was while you were being stitched up." Her stern expression softened. "She's great."

"I know." He still couldn't believe she knew about him and wanted them to be friends.

"And her first impression of her father is he and his brother fighting. I should slap you myself."

"Please don't."

"Are you in pain?" Dani asked.

"Yes."

"Good. I hope Reid is suffering. Maybe that will teach you two." She studied the bandages on his face. "What were you fighting about?"

"I made Penny cry."

Dani's eyes narrowed. "You sure did."

"I don't need you taking me on, too," he told her. "I feel like shit."

She socked his arm anyway, which, fortunately, was one of the only spots that didn't hurt. "Why didn't you tell her you were moving back east? What kind of moron has a relationship with a woman and doesn't mention that at least once?"

"At first I didn't think it mattered. Then I didn't think about leaving at all. Over the past couple of weeks, I've been thinking that maybe I wouldn't now."

"Maybe?" She socked him again.

"I won't go," he said as he rubbed his arm. "I know I should have told her. I never meant to hurt her."

"Too bad. If you had meant to, you could be happy you'd accomplished your goal. As it is, her heart is broken and you're an ass."

"Gee, thanks."

"I mean it, Cal. You're better than this. You don't play with other people's feelings. You've never been mean."

He went from feeling like slime to feeling like slime was only something he could aspire to.

"What do you want me to say?" he asked.

"To me? Nothing. I'm not the problem."

He knew that. But Penny had been so angry—not without cause, he admitted. "I should have told her," he muttered. "I should have made it clear."

"Not many people get a second chance," Dani told him.

"I know. I lost Penny before. I'm not going to lose her again." He couldn't. She'd come to matter too much to him.

Three months ago, he'd been eager to leave Seattle, to try something new, but now...

"Is she all right?" he asked. "She was upset, and with the baby and all."

"Upset? You call that upset?"

His insides clenched as he swore. "I should let Reid beat on me some more."

"That will only help you. There's someone more important to worry about."

"How much have I blown it?" he asked.

"A lot, but Penny isn't unreasonable. Lucky for you, she's especially vulnerable right now. Naomi's leaving."

"What? Leaving for where?"

"Ohio. But that's not important. What are you going to do?"

Beg and crawl, he thought. Hope the words came to him and if they didn't, he was going to camp out on her doorstep until she finally agreed they belonged together.

He stood. Every muscle in his body complained loudly. "I'm too old for this crap," he muttered. "Tell Reid and Walker I went to see Penny."

Dani glanced at her watch. "She'll be there the rest of the night."

"Good. Don't let her know I'm coming. I have another stop to make first, and I don't know how long it's going to take me."

Dani glared at him. "You're not going directly there?"

"No, and get off of me. I know what I'm doing."

"Oh, that's clear. We should all allow you to run our lives. You're doing such a great job of your own."

He bent down and kissed Dani's cheek. "I love you, too."

THIRTY MINUTES LATER Cal walked into Gloria's office. His grandmother took one look at him and jumped out of her chair.

"What on earth happened?" she asked. "My God, you have stitches and a black eye. Is your lip cut?"

He waved away her questions. "Not important," he said. "That's not what I'm here about."

"All right." Gloria sank back in her chair. "Then why are you here? Not that I'm not delighted to see my oldest grandson."

She even smiled, he thought in amazement. As if nothing had happened. As if she hadn't tried to destroy Penny and any chance he had with her.

"You crossed the line," he said, doing his best to stay calm. Gloria might be the devil, but she was still old and female. He had to respect that, if not her.

"I have no idea what you're talking about," she said easily.

"Bullshit. You know exactly what's going on and don't pretend you don't."

"Callister, I will not allow you to speak to me that way."

He leaned forward and braced his hands on her desk. "I don't give a good goddamn what you will or will not allow. You've had more chances than you've deserved and I'm through with you. You screwed up, Gloria. You messed with Penny and I won't have anyone doing that."

She sniffed. "Is this all about that woman? She left you, Callister, a fact I remember, even if you don't."

"This is about me protecting the ones I love. I'm through with you." He straightened.

She stared at him. "What are you talking about? You can't be through with me. I'm your grandmother. Your family."

"We might be related by blood, but you're not family. You don't know how to be. You don't know how to be anything other than an emotional vampire. You take and you take. You always have to be in control." He shook his head. "We're not kids anymore. You can't make us do anything. You have officially meddled and per the contract I'm out of The Waterfront."

She stood. "You can't leave. The restaurant needs you."

As always, business came first, he thought grimly. "The restaurant will be fine. Randy will take over and you'll still have Penny as the chef. But don't screw with her too much. I put an escape clause in her contract, too. If you start micromanaging, not only does she get to walk, but she takes all her recipes with her. You wouldn't want that."

"How dare you?"

"I dare because you don't give me a choice. I wanted to care about you, Gloria. But you make it impossible. You want to own us and we weren't about to let that happen. One by one, you've driven off your grandchildren until only Dani was left. But you refused to accept her and now she's gone as well."

"You can't leave," Gloria insisted. "This is who you are. This is your heritage."

"This is not who I am. This is never who I've been." He looked at her for a long time. "I thought I'd hate you, but I don't. I feel sorry for you."

He walked to the door.

"I'll bring you back," she called after him. "All of you."

"Not in this lifetime," he said and left.

PENNY LAY CURLED UP on the sofa, wishing she could find a way to put the pain in a box. If only she didn't have to deal with it right now. In a few weeks or months, she could take it out and feel it for a while, then put it away until she was strong again.

Unfortunately, that wasn't an option. So all she could do was endure the pain that filled her and wait for the horror to ease just enough for her to function.

She ached—every part of her felt as if she'd been run over by a car. Even her bones were sore. Every time she figured she'd finally cried herself out, new tears spilled down her cheeks. At some point would she simply run out of bodily fluids? Dani would come home and find her flat, cracked body on the floor.

She gave a half laugh, half sob and wondered if she was slipping over to the dark side.

Someone knocked on her front door. It could be anyone, she thought. Reid, even Walker. Dani had a key and Naomi was gone.

Penny struggled to her feet. Bad enough that Cal had turned out to be a major candidate for jerk of the month, but Naomi had left.

"Because I insisted," she reminded herself aloud. Keeping Naomi in Seattle to watch Penny suffer had seemed selfish and wrong. So she'd urged her friend to start the drive back to Ohio and had made her promise to check in when she got there.

She pulled open the door and stared. Cal stood in front of her, but not the same man she'd seen earlier that afternoon. He had a black eye, a bandage by his temple and a split lip.

"What happened to you?" she asked, not able to believe his injuries.

"Nothing important." He stepped past her into the house, then closed the door behind him. "Penny, I'm sorry. I can't tell you how sorry I am. I don't know the words. I never meant to hurt you or not tell you about moving. I never thought about it. With everything else going on, the move wasn't important."

She started to speak, to protest that it was very important, but he touched his finger to her lips.

"Please," he said. "Hear me out. I know the information itself is important, but I never actually thought about leaving. I didn't get involved with you thinking that I was going to cut and run. I didn't think much at all. You were there and so incredible and I found myself falling for you. Then Lindsey got sick and there was that, and the restaurant and you again. I'll accept that I was stupid and thoughtless, but I never, ever kept the information from you as a way to trick you."

Part of her thought he actually spoke the truth, but he'd hurt her so much she wasn't sure that mattered.

"Okay," she said quietly. "Thanks for telling me."

He moved closer and touched her chin. "I'm not done. Not even close. You were right, what you said about me. That I never risked my heart. I was never willing to go all out because that meant there was a risk of losing everything. I couldn't face that. I loved Lindsey and I felt guilty. It was a bad combination. I wanted our marriage to work, but I wasn't willing to be there. I let you down again and again. Holding back, about the baby."

He swallowed. "I swear, Penny, I was never glad

you lost the baby. It hurt, but I was afraid to admit that. I was afraid it would mean I didn't love Lindsey enough. You were right. I let you go. I should have come after you. I should have begged."

"The news flash doesn't change anything," she told him. No way was he going to sweet-talk her into believing him when he'd already broken her heart twice. Although it was nice of him to finally admit he'd been wrong in letting her go.

"I get it," he told her. "I get that I can love you and Lindsey and your baby and my brothers and Dani. I don't have to just love one person. I don't have to pick. I want to be the kind of man who loves with every fiber of his being." He took her hand in his and held on, even when she tried to pull away. "I know we could be great together, Penny, and I think you know it, too. We're good for each other. I always thought the best families were born and I was just screwed on that front. But it's not true. Families can be created consciously. It's not about bonds of blood, but bonds of the heart. I want to build a family with you."

Her breath caught. "What are you saying?"

"That I love you. I want us to be a family together. You, me, the baby, Lindsey, my brothers, Dani. All of us." He shrugged, then said, "Not Gloria."

"Good. She wouldn't exactly be welcome in my world right now."

"Please," he said softly, staring into her eyes. "Give me a chance. I'm willing to work to prove myself. I'm willing to pay. Whatever it takes to make you believe I love you and that I'm not going anywhere." He kissed her fingers and smiled. "Except I quit my job earlier. Which you can do, if you want. I wrote an escape clause into your contract with the restaurant."

There was too much information, she thought as the room began to spin.

"I need to sit down," she said.

He led her over to the sofa.

She drew in deep, steady breaths and tried to clear her head. This wasn't happening, she thought. He couldn't be saying all those things to her. Love her?

Before she could ask him to clarify, he went down on one knee. Just like that. In her living room.

"Penny Jackson, you are the brightest light in my life," Cal said. "I love you and need you with a desperation that defies words. Give me another chance. Marry me again."

She felt her mouth drop open.

"I don't expect you to answer me right now," he told her. "I suspect I'll have to do some crawling first, but that's okay. I'm not afraid of proving myself to you. In fact, I look forward to it. I want you to know without a doubt how much you mean to me."

She didn't know what to say.

"I can keep saying it," he told her with a smile. "I love you. Remember, before when we were married, you complained that I never said it enough? That's because I was holding back. I was afraid of opening up to you. Not anymore. I'm never holding back. You're my world and I love you."

The pain faded as if it had never been. Penny stared into his eyes and saw down to his soul. The truth was there—shining so bright it nearly blinded her.

"Say yes," he pleaded. "Marry me and have babies with me. You know we're great together."

She felt tears fill her eyes, but these had nothing to do with being alone and everything to do with finally finding her heart's desire.

"I'll still want to open my own place," she said.

"Of course you will. You're a great chef. But you're more than that. You're the woman I love."

She threw herself at him and let the tears escape. "Yes," she whispered. "Always yes. I never stopped loving you."

He held her tight. "You're the best thing that ever happened to me."

She sniffed and straightened. "I could say the same about you."

He touched her cheeks. "Hormones?"

She nodded. "And I'm happy."

"Good. So you want to get married?"

She laughed. "I do."

* * * * *

Read on for a delicious recipe from
SUSAN MALLERY'S FOOL'S GOLD COOKBOOK
and a sneak peek of the next,
new FOOL'S GOLD *romance,*
UNTIL WE TOUCH.

Chewy Chocolate Chip Cookies

Do you really need another chocolate chip cookie recipe? You do if you've been searching for a cookie that's perfectly crisp around the edges, yet rich and chewy in the middle.

Makes about 32

4   cups all-purpose flour
1   teaspoon baking soda
1   teaspoon baking powder
1   teaspoon salt
1   cup (2 sticks) unsalted butter, at room temperature
1   cup light-brown sugar
1   cup granulated sugar
2   large eggs
1   tablespoon pure vanilla extract
3   cups (18 ounces) semisweet chocolate chips

1. In a bowl, whisk flour, baking soda, baking powder and salt until blended.
2. In a large bowl with an electric mixer on high speed, cream butter and both sugars until light and fluffy. Add eggs, one at a time, beating well after each addition. Beat in vanilla. Reduce mixer speed to low, add dry ingredients

and beat just until blended. Remove from mixer; fold in chips. Cover bowl and refrigerate 24 hours, or up to 72 hours.

3. Preheat oven to 350°F. Line 2 baking sheets with parchment paper or nonstick baking pads. Drop dough in golf ball-sized mounds onto prepared sheets. Press down on balls with your palm to flatten slightly. Bake, 1 sheet at a time, for 12 minutes, or until golden around the edges but still slightly wet in the middle. Let cool 5 minutes on the pan. Transfer cookies to a wire rack to cool completely.

Tip: Refrigerating the dough for at least 24 hours helps to make the cookie extra-chewy. The dough will feel dry, but that lack of moisture improves the baked texture.

CHAPTER ONE

"YOU KNOW WHY I'm here."

Mrs. Nancy Owens made the statement with a firm voice and an unyielding stare. All of which were impressive.

Unfortunately for Jack McGarry, he didn't have a clue as to what she was talking about.

He knew a lot of things. He knew the L.A. Stallions wouldn't get to the Super Bowl this year, that his right shoulder ached when it was going to rain, that there was a saucy merlot waiting in his kitchen and that while every part of his being wanted to bolt right now rather than have this conversation, he couldn't. Because Mrs. Owens was Larissa's mother and even if she wasn't, she was old enough to be *his* mother and he'd been raised better.

"Ma'am?"

Mrs. Owens sighed. "I'm talking about my daughter."

Right. But the woman had three. "Larissa?"

"Of course Larissa. Who else? You moved your business to this godforsaken town and my daughter moved with you and now she's here."

An excellent recap, he thought, struggling to find the point.

"You don't like Fool's Gold," he said, stating what was probably the obvious.

"I neither like nor dislike the town." Her tone implied he was an idiot. "That's not the point. Larissa is *here*."

He knew that, what with signing her paycheck—figuratively rather than literally—and seeing her every day. But Mrs. Owens already knew that, too.

"She is here...with you." Mrs. Owens sighed heavily. "She loves her job."

Okay, fine. He was willing to admit it. He was just an average guy. Maybe a little taller, with a used-to-be-better throwing arm and a strong desire to win, but at his heart, he was pretty much like every other beer-drinking, truck-driving man in America. Ignoring, of course, the merlot in his refrigerator and the Mercedes in his garage.

Nancy Owens, an attractive woman in her early fifties, smacked her hands palm down on the table and groaned. "Do I have to spell it out for you?"

"Apparently so, ma'am."

"Larissa is twenty-eight years old, you moron. I want her to get married and give me grandchildren. That is never going to happen while she's working for you. Especially not after moving here. I want you to fire her. That way she'll move back to Los Angeles, find someone decent to marry and settle down."

"Why can't she do that here?"

Mrs. Owens sighed the sigh of those blessed with intelligence and insight most could only aspire to.

"Because, Mr. McGarry, I'm reasonably confident my daughter is in love with you."

Larissa Owens stared at the blue-eyed cat standing in the center of her small apartment. Dyna was an eight-year-old Ragdoll, with big, beautiful eyes, a sweet face and a thick coat. She had white fur on her chest and front paws and bits of gray on her face. She was the cat equivalent of a supermodel. It was kind of intimidating.

Larissa's instinct was always to rescue. Cats, dogs, butterflies, people. It didn't matter which. She knew her friends would claim she jumped in without thinking, but she wasn't willing to admit that. At least not without prompting. So when she'd heard about a cat in need of a home, she'd offered to take her in. She just hadn't thought she would be so gorgeous.

"You're a little overwhelming," Larissa admitted as she crossed to the small kitchen and put water into a bowl. "Should I dress better now that we're roommates?"

Dyna glanced at her, as if taking in the yoga pants and T-shirt that were Larissa's work wardrobe, then continued to explore the small apartment. She sniffed the sofa, checked out corners, studied the full-size mattress in the bedroom and totally ignored the small bathroom.

"Yeah, I know," Larissa said, putting the water on a place mat by the back door and then trailing after her. "The bathroom is really tiny."

There wasn't a counter—just a pedestal sink, a toilet and a stall shower.

Okay, so the apartment wasn't grand. Larissa didn't need much. Besides, the place was clean and the rent was cheap. That left her with more of her paycheck to give to her causes. Because there was always a cause.

"The windowsills are wide and you'll get a lot of light," Larissa told the cat. "The morning sun is really nice."

The small apartment came with one unexpected feature—a laundry room. She'd tucked Dyna's litter box next to the dryer. The cat perused the facilities, then jumped lightly onto the kitchen counter and walked to the sink. She glanced at Larissa, her gaze expectant.

Larissa knew this was why she'd always resisted actually adopting an animal before. She'd told herself it was her lifestyle—that she was so focused on saving them all that she couldn't be with just one. But in her heart, she'd been afraid she simply didn't have it in her. Now, as she stared into big blue eyes, she knew she'd been right.

"What?" she asked softly. "If you just tell me what you want, I'll do it."

Dyna looked at the faucet and back at her.

"From the tap?" Larissa asked, then turned on the cold water.

The cat leaned in and delicately lapped at the water. Larissa grinned in triumph. Maybe she could conquer this pet thing after all.

She waited until Dyna was done, then picked her up. The cat relaxed in her arms, gazing at her for a second, before letting her eyes slowly close. From deep inside came a soft, rumbling purr.

"I like you, too," Larissa told her new roommate. "This is going to be great."

She settled Dyna on the sofa, then glanced at the clock. "I hate to bring you home and run," she said, "but I have to get to work. It's only for a couple of hours and then I'll be home." She grabbed her battered handbag and headed for the front door. "Think about what you want to watch on TV tonight. You get to pick."

With that, she closed the door and raced down the stairs to the ground level of her apartment building, then out onto the street.

She'd only been in Fool's Gold a few months, but she loved everything about the town. It was big enough to be thriving, and small enough that everybody knew her name. Or at least enough people to make her feel as if she belonged. She had a great job, friends and she was a comfortable 425 miles from her family.

Not that she didn't love her parents, her stepparents, her sisters, their spouses and kids, but sometimes she felt a little overwhelmed by so much family. She hadn't been sure about leaving Los Angeles, but now she knew it had been the right thing to do. Her mother's two-day visit, while enjoyable, had been an intense campaign to get her to move back home.

"Not happening," Larissa told herself cheerfully.

Ten minutes later she walked into the offices of Score, the PR firm where she worked. The foyer was huge, with high ceilings and plenty of life-size pictures on the wall. There was a photo of the four principles of the firm, but the rest of the wall space was devoted to all things Jack, Kenny and Sam.

The three guys had been NFL stars. Sam had been

a winning kicker, Kenny a record-breaking receiver and Jack was the brilliant and gifted quarterback.

There were pictures of them in action on game day and others of them at various star-studded events. They were smart, successful, good-looking guys, who didn't mind exploiting themselves for the betterment of their company. Taryn, their lone female partner, kept them in line—something of a challenge, considering the egos she was dealing with. Larissa was Jack's personal assistant. She was also the guys' private masseuse.

She enjoyed both aspects of her job. Jack was easy to work for and not overly demanding. Best of all, he supported her causes and let her manage all his charitable giving. As for being the company masseuse—each of the men had played a rough sport professionally. They all had injuries and ongoing pain. She knew where they hurt and why and when she got it right, she made them feel better.

Now she headed directly for her office. She had phone calls to return. There would be a Pro-am golf tournament in Fool's Gold in a few weeks. She had to coordinate Jack's schedule with the publicity folks from the tournament. Later she would go over requests from a charity that helped families with a member in need of an organ donation—the cause Jack supported the most. Sometimes he was asked to reach out to a family personally. Other times he provided direct funding for the family to stay near a child in the hospital. He'd done PSAs and been in several print and internet campaigns. Larissa was his point of contact. She could gauge how much he was willing to do at any given time and when it was better for him to simply write a check.

Her other duties were of a more personal nature. He was between girlfriends, so there were no gifts to buy or flowers to send. Because, in that respect, Jack was a fairly typical guy. He liked women and they liked him back. Which meant there was a steady stream of them through his life. Lucky for him, his parents lived on the other side of the world. So he didn't have a mother demanding that he settle down and produce grandchildren.

She'd barely taken her seat when Jack walked into her office.

"You're late," he told her, sitting across from her and stretching out his long legs. His words sounded more like a statement than a complaint.

"I told you I would be. I had to see my mother off and then go pick up Dyna."

One dark eyebrow rose. "Dyna?"

"My new cat." She rested her elbows on her desk. "I told you about her, remember?"

"No."

Which was so like Jack. "That's because you weren't listening."

"Very possibly."

"She's a rescue."

"What else would she be?"

She waited for him to say more or tell her why he was here. There was only silence. The kind of silence that she understood as clearly as words.

She'd first been hired in 2010 when Jack had left the L.A. Stallions and joined Score. He'd been a silent partner since the firm's inception and Larissa would love to know how Taryn had reacted to Jack changing from the guy who had fronted her the cash to an actual working member of the team. She would guess there had been fireworks. Or maybe not. Jack and Taryn had a past.

Larissa had graduated from college with plans to work for a nonprofit. Paying jobs in her chosen field had been impossible to find and she'd quickly learned she couldn't support herself on volunteer work. So she'd gone looking for another job.

She wasn't the type of person who enjoyed faceless corporations and had settled into waitressing while putting herself through massage school. Then a friend had told her about a job as a personal assistant at a PR firm. That had sounded like a better paying option than her shifts at the diner.

Her interview had been with Taryn. It had lasted two hours and had ended with words that Larissa had never forgotten.

"Jack is a good-looking guy with beautiful eyes and a great ass. But make no mistake. He's not interested in more than a couple of nights with any given woman. If you fall for him, you're an idiot. Still interested?"

Larissa had been intrigued. Then she'd met Jack and she'd been forced to admit Taryn hadn't been lying about Jack's appeal. She'd taken one look at his studly manliness and had felt the shivers clear down to her toes. But instead of flirting with her, the former quarterback had rubbed his shoulder and sworn.

She'd recognized the pain and reacted instinctively. She'd dug her fingers into the scarred and tense muscles, all the while explaining that she was only a few weeks away from graduating from massage school. She'd gotten a job offer thirty seconds later.

In the past four years Larissa had become a part of the Score family. By the end of the second week, she'd ceased to see Jack as anything but her boss. Six months later, they were a good team and close friends. She regularly chided him about his choices in women, made sure he used ice and anti-inflammatories when his shoulder acted up and offered a daily massage to any of "the boys" and Taryn. She loved her job and she loved that they'd moved to Fool's Gold. She had a new kitty waiting at home. Life was very, very good.

She returned her attention to Jack and waited. Because that was the kind of silence in the room. The one that said he had something to tell her.

"You seeing anyone?"

The question surprised her. "You mean like a man?"

He shrugged. "You never said you dated women, but sure. Either sex will do."

"I'm not dating right now. I haven't met anyone in town and besides, I'm too busy."

"But it would be a guy?"

Amusement danced in his dark eyes.

Jack was one of those men blessed by the gods. Tall, handsome, athletic, charming. He pretty much had it all. What very few people knew was that there were demons he carried around with him. He blamed himself for something that wasn't his fault. A trait

Larissa could relate to, because she did it to herself all the time.

"Yes, it would be a guy."

"Good to know." He continued to study her. "Your mother is worried about you."

Larissa slumped back in her seat. "Tell me she didn't talk to you. Tell me!"

"She talked to me."

"Crap. I knew it. She stopped by, didn't she? I knew there was something going on." Her mother was nothing if not determined. "Let me guess. She wanted to know if I was seeing anyone. I hope you told her you didn't know. Or did you tell her I was? Because that would seriously help."

"She didn't ask me if you were seeing anyone."

"Oh." She straightened. "What did she ask?"

"She wants me to fire you so you'll move back to Los Angeles, fall in love, get married and give her grandchildren."

Larissa felt heat flare on her cheeks. Humiliation made it hard to think, let alone come up with something reasonably intelligent to say.

"She already has two married daughters," she muttered. "Why can't she leave me alone?"

"She loves you."

"She has a funny way of showing it. Are you going to fire me?"

Jack raised both brows this time.

She drew in a breath. "I'll take that as a no. I'm sorry. I'll do my best to keep her away from here. The good news is Muriel is due in three months and the new baby will be a distraction." In the meantime Larissa would figure out a way to convince her mother that she'd moved to Borneo.

"Anything else?" she asked.

"Yeah, there is. Your mother said you're never going to settle down and get married because you're secretly in love with me."

JACK HADN'T KNOWN how Larissa was going to react, but he'd guessed it would be a show. She didn't disappoint. Her face went from red to white and back to red. Her mouth opened and closed. With her jaw tightly clenched, she muttered something like "I'm going to kill her," but he couldn't be sure.

Nancy Owens's words had hit him like a linebacker. Larissa in love with him? Impossible. For one thing, she knew him better than anyone except Taryn and to know him was to understand he was all flash and no substance. For another, he needed her. Love meant a relationship and having a relationship meant she would eventually leave. No. There was no way Larissa could be in love with him.

But he'd been unable to shake the words and had realized he had to get the truth from the only person who actually knew.

Larissa drew in a breath. "I don't love you. We're friends. I like working for you, and the charity work is terrific, and I know you have my back, but I'm not in love with you."

Relief eased the tension in Jack's always aching right shoulder. He kept his expression neutral.

"You sure?" he asked.

"Yes. Positive."

He shook his head. "I don't know. I'm pretty hot. I could understand you having a thing for me. You've seen me naked. Now that I think about it, your reaction is inevitable." He sighed. "You love me. Admit it."

Larissa's mouth twitched. "Jack, you're not all that."

"But I am. Remember that fan who had my face tattooed on her breast? And the one who begged me to father her child? And the woman in Pittsburgh who wanted me to lick her—"

Larissa rested her arms on the desk and dropped her head to her arms. "Stop. You have to stop."

"Stronger women than you have been unable to resist my charms."

"In your dreams."

"No. Apparently in yours."

She looked at him then, her blue eyes wide, her mouth smiling. "I give."

"In the end, they all do."

The smile faded. "I'm sorry about my mother. She shouldn't have said that. I swear I am not, nor will I ever be, in love with you. I love my job and you're a big part of that. But we're friends, right? That's better. Besides, you have terrible taste in your 'let's end this now' gifts."

"Which is why I let you buy them." He hesitated a second. "We're good?"

"The best." Her smile returned.

The last of his worry faded. This was the Larissa he knew. All funny and earnest. Hair pulled back in a ponytail and not a speck of makeup on her face. She wore yoga pants and T-shirts and always had some cause to discuss with him. She believed the world was worth saving and he didn't mind if she used his money to try. They made a good team. He didn't want to have to do without her and having her love him… Well, that would have changed everything.

Jo's Bar was the kind of place you'd only find in a quirky small town. From the outside, it looked perfectly normal, but the second you stepped inside, you knew that this was a bar unlike any other.

For one thing, it was well lit. There were no dark shadows, no questionable stains on the floor. The colors were girl-friendly mauve and yellow, the windows were uncovered and the big TVs were always tuned to the Style Network or *Project Runway*.

Larissa walked inside. She saw the countdown sign that pointed out the number of days until the new season of *Dallas Cowboy Cheerleaders: Making the Team* started and grinned. Yup, life was different here and she liked it.

She glanced around and saw her friends in a booth by the windows. They looked up and waved her over.

When she'd first decided to leave Los Angeles for Fool's Gold, she'd been nervous about starting over. What if she didn't fit in? What if she couldn't make friends? But those fears had been groundless, she thought as she waved back and crossed to the big table.

"I saved you a seat," Isabel said, patting the empty space beside her. "You're just in time to join the debate about whether we're going to order nachos for

the table and have margaritas and pretend we don't
have to get back to work or if we're going to be good
and order regular lunches and drink iced tea."

Larissa settled in the chair. She glanced at Taryn
and grinned. "My vote depends on my boss. If she's
drinking, I'm all in."

Because right now, a drink sounded great.

What had her mother been thinking? The same
question had circled in her brain for much of the
morning. Talk about humiliating and inappropriate.
As soon as she'd calmed down and could talk about
it rationally, she was going to have a very long chat
with her mother.

She was lucky that Jack had handled the situation
with his usual easy charm, but jeez. What if he'd
thought her mother was telling the truth? She didn't
want to think about it.

Love Jack? She had flaws but being an idiot wasn't
one of them. Besides, they were a great team. She
would never mess with that.

"You okay?" Taryn asked quietly.

"Yeah. Great."

Because faking it was much easier than telling
the truth.

Taryn, ever stylish in a designer suit that probably
cost more than half a year's rent on Larissa's apartment, tossed her menu onto the table. "What the hell.
Let's be wild."

Dellina, a local party planner and Sam's fiancée,
tossed her menu down, as well. "I don't have any cli-
ent meetings this afternoon."

Isabel laughed. "I have a store to run. I'd better

be careful or I'll accidentally put the new merchandise on sale."

"I love being bad," Taryn announced. "I just love it."

"You've always been bad," Dellina told her. "You're the type. I can tell about these things."

Larissa leaned back in the booth and prepared to listen. She enjoyed being around these women. They were smart, successful and yet so very different. Taryn was one of the partners at Score. While all four partners were equal owners, the three guys would admit that Taryn was just a little more equal than the rest of them. She was good at keeping her "boys" in line.

Larissa had always admired her. Taryn dressed in beautiful clothes, walked around in five-inch heels and had a handbag collection that belonged in a museum. Better than that, Taryn was a good friend.

Dellina handled events of all kinds in town. Birthday parties, weddings. A couple of months ago she'd planned and managed a big weekend event for Score's biggest clients. She was also recently engaged to Sam.

Isabel owned Paper Moon. On one side, a clothing store, on the other, wedding gowns. All three women were professionally dressed in suits or dresses. Larissa glanced down at her yoga pants. Maybe in her next life she would inherit the fashion gene, she thought wistfully. Until then, she was going to dress for comfort and practicality.

Jo, the owner of the bar, came over and took their order. Taryn ordered nachos for the table and a pitcher of margaritas. Jo raised her eyebrows.

"Not planning to work this afternoon?" she asked.

"We're going to see how it goes," Taryn told her.

"I've heard that before."

"She doesn't think we're behaving responsibly," Dellina murmured when Jo had left.

"Then my work here is done," Taryn said. "So what's new with everyone?"

"I'm busy with fall clothes." Isabel smiled. "You have to come in and see what's new. There are some beautiful things." She turned to Taryn. "There's a suede jacket you'll love."

"I'll come see it when we're done here."

Dellina shook her head. "No way I'm stopping by," she told her friend. "You tempt me with gorgeous clothes."

Isabel laughed. "That's the point."

"I'm saving my pennies."

"For a wedding?" Larissa asked, her gaze settling on Dellina's shiny new engagement ring.

"No. I'm going to be moving into an office. Sam's house is great and he's mentioned that I can set up my office there, but I think it's time I joined the real world and had an actual office." She wrinkled her nose. "I'm kind of getting to the point where I need to hire an assistant. That means more space."

"Wow! Good for you." Isabel leaned over and hugged her friend. "That's a big step. Congratulations."

"Yes, congratulations," Larissa said, pleased her friend was doing so well.

"You're a tycoon," Taryn teased. "Impressive."

"I'm no tycoon, but I'm doing well. So what's going on with everyone else?"

Taryn mentioned a new account Score had just signed, then all eyes turned to Larissa. She froze, painfully aware that her life wasn't like theirs. She didn't own her own business. In fact, there was a sameness to her days that was kind of sad. The newest thing in her life was her mother's talk with Jack and there was no way she was mentioning that.

"I adopted a cat," she said instead. "A lady died. She was ninety-three. Her kids couldn't take in her cat, so I did. Her name is Dyna. She's a Ragdoll cat. Really beautiful."

She pulled out her phone and showed them a couple of pictures.

Dellina's eyes widened when she saw the photograph. "She's stunning." Her mouth twitched. "Taryn, if she were human, she'd give you a run for your money in the fashion department."

"I'm more impressed you committed to an animal," Taryn told Larissa.

Isabel frowned. "I don't get it. Larissa is always jumping into causes. That cat rescue last month was fantastic."

Larissa squirmed in her seat. "Taryn means that I tend to give in big gestures. Saving forty cats, not adopting one."

Jo appeared with a very large pitcher of margaritas and four glasses. She poured and said the nachos would be out shortly.

Isabel raised her glass. "To the women I adore. Thank you for getting drunk with me. One day very soon Ford and I are going to be getting pregnant and then I'll be on a drinking hiatus."

"Anytime," Larissa said. She was going to add something else when Taryn slapped her hands down on the table.

"Okay," her friend said. "Here goes. I'm getting married."

Larissa looked at both Isabel and Dellina. They seemed equally confused by the statement.

"You're engaged," Larissa pointed out gently. "You have a really big ring. We all noticed."

"Yes, but I've decided on a wedding. Angel and I are going to have a real wedding."

Larissa nodded slowly. "That will be nice."

"I'm happy to help you plan it," Dellina added, sounding equally cautious.

"I have some gorgeous dresses I want you to come see," Isabel told her. "Designer stuff that will make you look like a sexy fairy princess. Or a slutty one, depending on what you want."

Taryn squeezed her eyes shut, then opened them. "Really? You think it's okay?"

Then Larissa got it. Taryn and Angel weren't young kids. They'd both been married before. Taryn wanted the fabulous dress and traditional service, but she wasn't sure she deserved it. Because everybody had their weak spots. Some were just better at hiding them than others.

She reached across the table and touched her friend's hand. "You should have the biggest wedding ever. In a dress so beautiful, it will make us cry."

Taryn's mouth quivered. She squeezed Larissa's

fingers then shook off the emotion and reached for her margarita. "Thanks."

Dellina reached for her bag and pulled out an appointment book. "I'll call you in a couple of days and we'll talk."

Isabel turned to Larissa. "I nearly forgot. Your mom was in yesterday. She bought a dress and a handbag. She's my new favorite person. Did you two have a nice visit?"

Larissa grabbed her margarita and took a big gulp.

"Uh-oh," Taryn murmured. "That's not good. I thought the visit went fine. That's what you said this morning."

If only, Larissa thought. "That was before I found out what my mom did."

Her three friends stared at her. "And that would be?" Isabel prodded.

These women loved her, Larissa reminded herself. They wouldn't laugh and point. Or if they did, it would be when she wasn't in the room, which was almost the same thing.

"My mom went to see Jack. She asked him to fire me so I'd move back to L.A. and get married and give her grandchildren."

Dellina frowned. "Okay, that's not great, but it's not horrible, either."

"There's more," Larissa admitted. "She said the reason I had to leave Fool's Gold was that I was secretly in love with Jack."

She paused, waiting for the hysterical laughter. Or any laughter. Instead, the three women exchanged a look.

Larissa felt herself start to blush. "I'm not in love with Jack," she insisted. "I'm not. I work for him. He's great. But there's nothing between us."

"If you say so," Isabel said knowingly.

"If Felicia were with us, she would say that the boss-secretary romance is a classic archetype," Dellina said.

"I'm not his secretary."

"Close enough," Taryn told her, then picked up her drink. "If you say you're not in love with him, then I believe you."

Just then, Jo appeared with the nachos and the subject got dropped. Larissa reached for a chip, but found that she wasn't the least bit hungry all of a sudden.

This was all her mother's fault, she thought grimly. She'd opened a can of worms. Larissa was going to have to find every last one of them and put them back where they belonged.

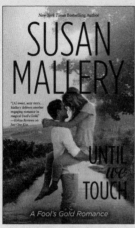